"Well-paced . . . vibrant . . . an enjoyable original twist on the mysterious legacy story . . . Wings writes straight-forward, intelligent prose." —*Publishers Weekly*

"Wings' most successful novel . . . an intriguing psychological thriller." —*Lambda Book Report*

"A chillingly lush tale of twisted love and vengeance . . . a multilayered thriller of lesbian passion, repression, and deception . . . The psychological tension she creates kept me up late at night."
—Barbara Wilson, author of *Trouble in Transylvania*

"Wings' best book yet . . . a riveting tale written with great skill . . . There's a wonderful sensuality about the book, particularly in the relationship between the narrator and Ilona, who just by herself is worth the price of admission."
—Michael Nava, author of *The Hidden Law*

"Wings has a saucy, witty way with dialogue and description."
—*Elle*

"Immensely readable, tightly plotted . . . *Divine Victim*'s final pages crackle in a multilayered, breathtaking conclusion."
—*Bay Area Reporter*

"A suspenseful page turner, this gothic mixes horror, religious oppression, and eroticism in a well-paced plot . . . an atmospheric and readable novel." —*Library Journal*

MARY WINGS is the author of two previous novels, *She Came Too Late* and *She Came in a Flash* (Plume), which have been translated into Dutch, German, Japanese, and Spanish. With historian Eric Garber, she co-wrote and produced *Greta Garbo, A Woman of Affairs*, which has been shown at lesbian and gay film festivals in London, San Francisco, Los Angeles, Melbourne, Turin, Amsterdam, and Chicago. Wings was awarded the Best Fiction prize in 1987 by London's *City Limits* magazine. Born in Chicago and raised in the Baha'i faith, she now lives in San Francisco with her two cats, Sylvester and Sylvia.

Also by Mary Wings:

She Came Too Late (1986)
She Came in a Flash (1988)

Mary Wings

DIVINE VICTIM

A PLUME BOOK

PLUME
Published by the Penguin Group
Penguin Books USA Inc., 375 Hudson Street, New York, New York 10014, U.S.A.
Penguin Books Ltd, 27 Wrights Lane, London W8 5TZ, England
Penguin Books Australia Ltd, Ringwood, Victoria, Australia
Penguin Books Canada Ltd, 10 Alcorn Avenue,
Toronto, Ontario, Canada M4V 3B2
Penguin Books (N.Z.) Ltd, 182–190 Wairau Road, Auckland 10, New Zealand

Penguin Books Ltd, Registered Offices: Harmondsworth, Middlesex, England

Published by Plume, an imprint of Dutton Signet,
a division of Penguin Books USA Inc. Previously published in a Dutton edition.
Originally published in Great Britain by Women's Press Ltd.

First Plume Printing,
10 9 8 7 6 5 4 3 2 1

 REGISTERED TRADEMARK—MARCA REGISTRADA

The Library of Congress has cataloged the hardcover edition as follows:
Wings, Mary.
Divine victim / Mary Wings.
p.   cm.
ISBN 0-525-93626-2 (hc.)
ISBN 0-452-27210-6 (pbk.)
I. Title.
PS3573.I53213D58   1992
813'.54—dc20   92–38876
                                                CIP

Printed in the United States of America

For Suzanne Bennett
who makes much possible

Acknowledgments

First of all I would like to thank Eric Garber for his warm encouragement and steadfast friendship. Also a ready group of readers have been most helpful, specifically Melinda Cuthbert, Jan Johnson, Danielle Fitzpatrick, Erica Marcus, Elissa Perry and Jane Tierney. Sherry McVickar was ALWAYS there. Roz Pendlebury MADE me do it. Barry Lazarus and Teresa Swanick supplied valuable information and Bill Walker drew a portrait of Montana that was personal and vivid. Thanks to Kathy Gale for her understanding of the gothic. Very special thanks to my literary agents, Jane Gregory and Lisanne Radice, who got me started writing again.

Most of all, thanks to Terry Baum who gladly sacrificed her time for *Divine Victim*. In helping me shape the plot and characters in the first stages she also made the process a whole lot of fun.

I had a little Sorrow
    Born of a little Sin,
I found a room all damp with gloom
    And shut us all within;
And, "Little Sorrow, weep," said I,
"And Little Sin, pray God to die,
And I upon the floor will lie
    And think how bad I've been!"

—from "The Penitent" by Edna St. Vincent Millay

Prologue

Fingers spread and grasped a petit point flower, dark magenta, stiff with blood. Her white lace skirt, the brownish stains as big as handprints, blew behind her as she raced down the stairs and into the night.

Don't drop it! she told herself as she flew up the drive, her feet quick, registering every stone, her arms clinging to their cumbersome load. Her mind was sharp and clear with the terror of being caught. Her fingers tightened on the objects wrapped in the cloth. Her feet fairly flew over the gravel and for a moment she felt she might levitate, leave that way.

She kept up the pace, until she saw the adjacent farmland, but she didn't stop to look back, not yet. She gripped the sharp edges tighter under the black cloth and kept on going. Finally, she reached the edge of the property and came upon fields.

Those familiar fields, which she had seen so often from her high window, were former friends. But tonight the fig trees, marching along in straight disinterested rows, hardly provided camouflage. Even the moon was working its spotlight on her, picking her out between the branches as she fled, following her with its cold and unrelenting light. She ran faster, a frightened white figure, splattered with blood, over the quilted earth.

She kept on, racing against time, against discovery, thoughts of various horrible fates making her feet run faster, faster. She stumbled on clods of earth, glancing backward now from time to time.

Surely they would find her, come after her! She knew they would. And the punishment would be dreadful—not as yet devised by human minds. Because her crime was so horrible it zoomed off any moral scale into a black hole of evil. What she had done, what *she* had done, went against every moral precept of her universe. It was inconceivable.

She hadn't even thought of it herself. Who could have thought of such a thing? But they would never believe who had given her the instructions.

And now it didn't matter. It was done, irrevocable, and the only thing to do was to get out.

Sensing the moon as an enemy, she stopped and unwrapped the objects and put them carefully on the dirt. Then she unfolded the black cloak in which they had been wrapped and threw it over her dress. Invisible now, she resumed her burden and glided quickly under the shadows of the trees.

1

It was the final freezing night of driving and I was nervous. We were getting closer. There wouldn't be any more truckstops or cheap hotels. Interstate 90 had taken us through forgotten railroad towns, forgotten just like the railroads themselves. But now, for hours, there had been nothing but black. Our headlights were two shimmering cones along the icy road. A sudden slip would mean a trip to the ditch and an entrance to the sleepy world just beyond freezing. I reached over and touched Marya for reassurance.

Somehow the last leg of our trip—through Big Timber, Greycliff, and past Park City—made us both feel disconnected from the landscape, from the larger world, from each other.

Guiding the car carefully along the icy gray path, in an unhospitable, howling darkness, we laughed too hard, and I clutched Marya uncertainly whenever the car slipped on the road, finally leaving my hand in her pocket for warmth and contact.

We were on our way to the estate of Marya's late great-aunt Rebecca, who'd died some weeks before. Marya had received the telegram only three days ago. I remembered seeing the little yellow envelope slide underneath the front door of her San Francisco apartment.

"Rebecca Cascia, who we believe to be your aunt, was deceased two months ago. She has named you as sole heir," it read. "Vandalization of the deceased's property has necessitated the hiring of a security service. As this is costly to the estate we request that you please contact Ryan and Rutledge, Attorneys at Law, immediately."

"Your aunt's died," I said, reading over her shoulder and rubbing her back comfortingly. "I'm sorry."

Marya shrugged. "I hardly knew her, only met her once, in fact. Kind of an eccentric, very religious, with a big spooky scar on her face. Oh well, guess I have to call these lawyers." She sighed. "It may mean a quick trip to Montana." She looked at me. "Wouldn't care to come with me, would you? There's a lot of nice glacier-climbing out there. And the election's still nine months away. Those local politicians can do without my marketing for a bit and my partner can look after the mail order business."

Marya was a serious rock climber. The fact that she was engaged in a hobby which carried the risk of serious, even fatal, injury had initially made her seem adventurous and attractive to me. But she was being slightly dismissive, I thought, about her Aunt Rebecca's death. Marya called the lawyers for details.

"She was lying in a reclining chair when they found her. Her death had probably been fairly painless. A massive heart attack, probably only lasting seconds." Marya sighed. An undisturbed linen napkin was found tucked into the collar of Rebecca's blouse. She went too quickly, never had time to remove it or to reach her collar buttons and unfasten them at the neck. The length of time that passed before discovery meant that her body was in advanced rigor mortis.

Rebecca Cascia had been buried in Laz-E-Boy recliner shape, I thought. Nobody seemed very interested, certainly not Marya. I remembered her cheerfully stashing the rock-climbing equipment in the back of the car: 165 ft. perlon nylon rope, harnesses hung with D-shaped carabiners like huge keychains, and a lethal-looking ice-pick.

I'd left my new home, San Francisco, with reluctance. It was hard to go, even for a week, from the light, the hills and the powerful and colorful lesbian and gay scene there.

But the news had come just at the six-week semester break. Pacific University had been closed and I had just finished grading a fistful of exam papers. "Theories of Research" wasn't a class I'd chosen to teach. It was one I had been assigned.

Marya and I were fresh off the honeymoon express and it made sense to make the trip together: I didn't want to break the rosy bubble we'd created. Soon we would be arriving at, of all places, a small town outside Billings, Montana and in the dead of winter.

It was our first trip, Marya's and mine, outside the Bay Area. It would be nothing like being on holiday in Siena with my recent ex-lover, Ilona. The rhythm of work and recreation with Marya had kept my past at bay. The truth was, I was still healing from the horrendous break-up with Ilona in Italy.

I packed the woolen sweaters Ilona had knitted for me, the fisherman's cables, the mohair, the diamond patterned vest, and filled Marya's new car with antifreeze. I wondered why I had kept those sweaters. They were proof, warm, tangible, high-quality homemade, multi-stranded proof that Ilona had loved me.

I had agreed to go with Marya without asking for more details. Marya wasn't very forthcoming about her background, her family, and I didn't seem to need more. But then Marya, even though we were in love, and often in bed, hadn't asked me many questions about my personal history either. We all make mistakes.

I looked over at my new lover. With her dark curly hair and strong jawline, she looked nothing like Ilona. I shivered. Marya was wearing one of Ilona's sweaters. I shouldn't have lent her that woolen turtleneck. It was too soon, I thought.

"This sure is a warm sweater, sweetheart!" she said. She

used little terms of endearments more frequently than I did, although we both congratulated ourselves often on how well suited we were for each other.

The billboard above the road read "Danroy Chemical Company." A big paper sunflower coated with frost. "Serving all your fertilizer and pesticide needs for thirty years."

"I hope *we* last thirty years," Marya grinned, glancing away from the whitened highway as the sunflower zoomed past us. But my smile had faded.

That's what Ilona had said too. Odd . . . Thirty years, Ilona had said. Who knows what kind of shape I would have been in after thirty years with her?

"When I talked to the lawyer yesterday I asked her if there was a funeral or anything. But apparently she was a real recluse," Marya explained.

"Nobody cried, nobody claimed her estate, and all her sins forgiven." I was looking at a sign that announced "Billings, Montana."

I had certainly traveled a long way, I thought, arriving at places I'd never imagined I would ever want to go. But sins go anywhere, quick and light, easy to pack. I wondered if they were baggage that got tucked into the grave.

2

Now, in Billings, Montana, the past was as far away as I could keep it. I looked around; a 7-Eleven convenience store beckoned from a distance.

"Let's stop there, Marya, please."

"Of course, sweetheart. We can make sure our directions are correct."

We strode into the brightly lit interior, refrigerators with glass doors offering soda pop and beer, cholesterol snacks clipped together and a large display of colorful candies, their boxes promising novelty shapes.

"Nerd Family," I read from one box. "Nuclear family members in correct gender shapes, modeled from sugar, with artificial colorings and flavorings."

"Thought you were going to watch your weight," Marya murmured, sidling up to me and running her hand over my buttocks. "But don't bother for me." She leaned over and kissed me, and we heard an explosion of giggles from behind the rack.

Two young boys stood there, gawking at us—the real-life version of the nerd family. About fifteen years old, they knew enough to put their fingers up to their mouths and stick their tongues out, a cunnilingus impression that was startling for boys so young, especially in a backwater area such as Billings.

"Let's get out of here," I said. *"Fuckin' dykes,"* their words followed us as we walked back to the car park. We got on to the road quickly and I pored over the map, nervous now, unsettled by the boys' hostility and feeling that we'd somehow entered enemy territory.

At last we neared Rebecca's house. The neighborhood was hardly comforting. Wind whistled over empty miles, sliced by barbed wire and blasting bits of ice and snow against an occasional dwelling. We were miles away from anywhere, but then there was a lot of nowhere in Montana. A few other buildings dotted a distant horizon, backed up by the Beartooth Mountains. High snowdrifts lined each side of the road, a white-walled gallery with only the night sky above.

Hollowed out of one of the snowy walls, I saw it first; the country mailbox which marked the spot, just as the lawyers had said. We stopped the car, skidding slightly, and peered down a corridor of ice. Far away, the dark shape of a building beckoned.

"Last night I dreamt I went to Manderley again. It seemed to me I stood by the iron gate leading to the drive, and for a while I could not enter, for the way was barred to me," I quoted.

"Stop! It's creeping me out!" Marya laughed, but she was clutching me, and there was nothing funny about the long icy tunnel we were about to enter. I could feel Marya's strong hand gripping my arm through the thick parka material.

"Do you remember this road?" I asked, as we skidded up the drive, our car swaying like a boat, swerving from side to side, held fast on course by the towering snowbanks.

"Yeah, I remember it," Marya said, and then coughed as if to dilute the association.

"Do you remember Rebecca?" I spoke in a deep voice, making light of our fear.

"I just met her once. With my mom. Only saw her for half an hour," she murmured.

Suddenly the banks seemed to give way and the large, dark shape of the house loomed up in front of us. Within the field of white its solid shadow was a dark blot, pierced only by blank windows, and covered crookedly with shingles like a skin that was scabbing over. I cut the engine.

Bang! A screen door, unfastened, with iron curlicues and ripped mesh, demanded our attention.

"I only met her once and now I've inherited the contents of her life." Marya stared at the banging screen door. Like a tattered false eyelash, it winked at us and dared us to come closer.

Marya was clutching my arm so hard she was cutting off the blood supply to my fingers.

I looked at her. "I guess we'd better move."

We pushed the car doors against icy gusts which tried to keep them closed. Outside, trees crackled with ice. Nobody had bothered to shovel the path to Rebecca's house.

"Gee! I thought it was much bigger," Marya said. I looked up at the big old house. It didn't make me feel hopeful. Was Marya somehow disappointed in her legacy? Perhaps holding out hope for an unexpected windfall?

"What the hell! It'll be easier to pack up," she remarked suddenly. I shivered, not sharing her optimistic temperament.

The old gothic horror house had a skin of asbestos shingles, warped and graying. The bay windows were stripped of their former Victorian ornaments. A stone wall extended on either side of the house and claimed a piece of land for the dwelling, holding it close.

Marya took a look at my face. "Maybe you'll get interested in rock climbing," she suggested hopefully, but I was still looking at the house. How my travels had taken me from the sublime to the ridiculous! I thought.

"Okay, let's get it over with," I said, grabbing the flashlight from the glove compartment. I put a tentative foot outside the car and it sank into the snow. Hard clumps of ice invaded my socks. We crunched our way toward the protesting door.

I put the key to the front door lock as Marya held the

flapping screen behind me. But the lock was so cold I couldn't even get the key in. I put my mouth over it, blowing hot breaths into the cylinder.

"When you've finished tongueing the lock!" Marya put her hand over my parka'd breast, but I was worried about my lips freezing to the worn, plated metal. I pulled away, leaning into Marya's arms, and pushed the key in. It turned and the door swung open.

We were silent as we stepped inside. The interior was darker than the night outside and cold as a coffin. I played the flashlight quickly around the baseboards, looking for a heater.

In a dark room to our right stood a large gas appliance, its ceramic spine elements shaping a toothy grin. I hoped that the gas hadn't been shut off.

"Do you have a match?" I asked Marya, who stood shivering behind me. She passed one silently. It sparked and reflected in her dark eyes, making the down on her top lip gleam. Black curls rimmed her oval face.

"Still visiting Aunt Rebecca?" I teased.

"Yes."

"Let's warm this fucking place up!" I realized, suddenly, that the house belonged to her.

I bent down and opened the gas spigot; a reassuring hiss came out and when I struck a match warm blue flames played on the ceramic elements. We drew closer and rubbed our hands near the glow. The house extended, beyond our gaze, into gloomy darkness.

"You know," I said, after the worst of the chill had left us, "if the gas is on, the electricity might be too."

"You mean we don't have to stand here in the dark?" Marya gave me a quick kiss on the lips.

I played the flashlight over the wall, found a switch and flipped it on. Marya and I stood still in amazement. We weren't alone.

We were standing in a devotional Disneyland. Statues of the Virgin Mary covered the place—poised on armoires, inside glass china cabinets, crouched in wall niches. Divine, maternal, serene, she stepped on serpents' tails, balanced herself on crescent moons and floated on lavender clouds. Attended by Saints Martha, Rita, Theresa, Catherine and Clare, Our Lady and her friends were cloned many times over. And above them all stretched a sprayed plaster celestial ceiling, dripping with stalactites and embedded with millions of particles of glitter. The whole place was decorated in Motel 6 charm with the Pope as set dresser.

"I guess we're safe in the company of saints," Marya mumbled.

"Yes, I guess we are." Suddenly Italy came flooding back. Its devotional objects were all around me, in cheap reproduction. Alla Americano, but the message was still the same. I shivered again.

"I remember the glitter ceiling." Marya pointed upward. I imagined her as a child, wondering at the sparkling stalactites made of sprayed plaster.

"Like bad Christmas ornaments," I muttered. What an amusement-park version of the glorious statuary I'd seen in Rome, Florence and Siena!

Marya was wandering around, her mind replaying the past as her eyes swept over the rooms. All the windows had been covered in plastic, a successful attempt to keep the wind, and air, out; and the place was well-insulated with plastic panels simulating wood. Cardboard strips had been tacked around the windows to hold the plastic in place. It puffed in and out, like shallow lungs that could barely keep the house alive.

I walked into the living room and found fake wood paneling, with prints depicting episodes in the life of the Virgin scattered across the walls: the Immaculate Conception, Annunciation, Nativity, Purification, Assumption. Rebecca's living room sparkled with glitter, and the cheap, gaudy prints of holy figures.

"The saints," I whispered. "The cult of saints."

"What?"

"In Medieval times the worship of saints was quite the thing. Almost the *only* thing. People at that time saw miracles everywhere, and before the Church instigated strict canonization proceedings, the cult of the saints came close to replacing the worship of Jesus Christ."

"Hmm. God, this is ugly wallpaper!" Marya remarked.

"Everything—the bodies of saints, their clothes, even the instruments of their torture—became relics, drawing crowds of worshippers, and every positive event in a town would be attributed to their intercession. Without the bureaucracy of the Church, Christianity might have developed into a kind of Hinduism, with a whole crowd of deities."

"Ugh! what's this?" Marya was pointing at a replica of Saint Lucy, who offered her plucked-out eyes to us on a plate. "That's gruesome," she said, her tone engaged, curious. "At first I thought they were Easter eggs."

"She was an early Christian martyr," I explained. "The Romans plucked them out."

"How come she's got an extra pair in her head then?"

"I don't know. Saints get issued two sets or something." I picked up the Lucy statue and examined it closely, turning it over. Hand-made, not molded, it consisted of low fire clay, and Lucy's delicate blind expression was painted in tiny individual brushstrokes.

"Great decor," Marya muttered, walking over to a bricked-up fireplace. The mantelpiece was coated with wax drippings, indicating a history of personal offerings to a Madonna positioned above the ledge.

"Let's light the candles," I said, striking a match which threw little flames of flickering light onto the portrait.

A cheap print of a Russian icon, Mary's face was flat, her head tilted at an angle only a chiropractor could appreciate. She offered her breast to a disproportionately large Jesus, who viewed her nipple suspiciously through slanting eyes.

"Ugh!" Marya muttered and I followed her gaze.

Still in repose, the Laze-E-Boy reclining chair Rebecca had died in was situated at right angles to the mantel, as if for easy Madonna viewing or an eternal view of the glitter ceiling. They must have put extra glitter into the plaster mix, I thought. Mylar chips, that was how they did it. Or was it mica in the old days?

I walked over and put my hand on the back of the recliner. It had rigor mortis too. I gave a shove. With a squeak and a squeal the footrest folded in and the chair popped into an upright position.

Despite the poor quality of all this stuff, I thought, the place suggested a faith so positive it went beyond the cheerful. There wasn't a hint of the solemnity I usually associated with the pious. And there was a nice proportion of small objects to the larger pieces. Little prints and icons never upstaged the more important moments of triumphant kitsch.

I went over to the statue of Saint Lucy again and contemplated the way her hands curved around her eyeball-laden saucer. "I think I've been away from museums too long," I said. "This stuff looks kind of good to me."

"Oh, you just miss Europe, honey." Marya held me close. "We'll go visit there some time."

"Yes, darling, of course," I replied. But would I really go with Marya? Would she want to troop around on excursions, wearing big puffy white tennis shoes to save her feet on the cobblestones? No. In my fantasies, Marya looked much better on the tennis court or on an American rockface.

She stopped talking and we stood silently looking around us. Vinyl floors marched crookedly across the entire house, their seams splitting at the uneven thresholds of doorways. In the kitchen, pine veneer cabinets winked their knotty eyes at the new inhabitants.

"So this must be the gourmet kitchen," Marya remarked, moving quickly away from me into the next room.

"Hey, looks like somebody's started ransacking the cupboards," I commented, opening a door and peering at the chaos inside.

"Yeah, lawyers said there'd been a break-in."

"Grave robbers could have scored better in the cemetery," I sighed. "But you don't seem too worried at how little there is here."

"Why should I be?" Marya said, ever cheerful. "Let's just clean it up and get back home."

Yes, I thought, why should she be disappointed? Marya was financially secure and on a middle-management track to success. Her dreams were realized in the pragmatic world of San Francisco local politics, while sport provided the outlet for her anxieties. It was a million miles away from my life as an art historian, an academic.

"We can go gourmet on an electric griddle," she decided, prying back a piece of laminated vinyl lining the wall behind the stove. The material had turned yellow and brown in spots from the heat.

"How I hate all this Catholic crap!" she said suddenly, spying a Saint Martha and the Dragon, framed above the stove. "Fried dragon!"

"It's just the stories of miracles, darling. It's just fables. They relate more to a way people *used* to think."

"I wouldn't compliment superstition with such a description," she grumbled.

"It's the remnants of medieval thought. Think what it was like in those times, for people who never went more than a mile or two from home in an entire lifetime. Their lives were governed by forces they couldn't understand, and so they had to imagine, that's all."

"So why is this nun poised above the stove?"

"She's just one of the baseball-card saints. She's a guardian angel, there to guide and protect you." I smiled at her, leaning over to rub my hand across the side of Marya left breast. After all, this wasn't Marya's field.

"Religious relics from Woolworth's! I suppose they must be worth something, to some collector, somewhere." Her hand was running through my hair at precisely the same speed as I was stroking her breast.

"The reading of the will is tomorrow, Marya. You go to that, while I pack up this junk. See if you want any of it, then we'll get in the car and be out of here in a few days."

"That's why I love you. You always keep things so simple," Marya looked at me admiringly. She kept things simple too. We were two people who knew how to get on with life, I told myself.

That's why we got on together. With Marya there were no complicated, tragic twilight roadblocks, days of drama taking weeks to haul away.

"I wonder if there's any hot water." I stood up and walked over to a narrow door. I peered down the stairs where spiders had taken over a small cellar. A water heater burbled away in a corner next to metal shelving, loaded with cobwebbed canisters. A root cellar that would be no fun to clean out.

"You must be cold, darling. Your feet are never warm enough." Marya moved toward me. "Take off your socks and let me rub them," she offered.

"I've got a better idea," I said. I went to the kitchen tap and felt the cold water become lukewarm, then hot. "Bet there's a great old clawfoot bathtub upstairs."

"I'd love to get in it with you and fuck your lights out," Marya purred.

I wasn't feeling excited, but that wasn't the reason why we both suddenly fell silent. Marya was staring at a photograph which lay on the metal kitchen table. I knew who it would be, but I wasn't prepared for the setting. It was Rebecca, our ghostly concierge. In Siena.

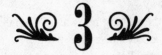

I t wasn't the sight of Rebecca that made me sit down, it was the setting. A sudden feeling of nausea hit me as I recognized the background. Medieval buildings complete with hammer beam roofs, pendant posts and collar braces lined a narrow, twisting street, and in the middle of that particular street, a niche—a famous niche where so many tourists stopped to have their picture taken. In that niche the Virgin pointed to her sacred heart, lit with flames and pierced with thorns.

A simple photograph. In the foreground of the picture a dated American tourist clutched an old Kodak Brownie. That tourist was Rebecca. I myself had stood in that very spot, and my image too had been captured along with this Madonna of the Sacred Heart. That photo still existed somewhere. It recorded the moment when I had completely and utterly lost all respect for myself.

I ran to the sink and turned on the tap.

"What's wrong?" Marya asked, startled. She leaned over my bending form, putting a concerned hand on my back.

"Nothing. Don't touch me." I took several deep breaths,

splashed some water on my face and stood up. I looked at Marya's concerned, frightened expression.

I must make an effort to forget the past, I told myself. If coincidence had brought me here with Marya to face this photograph, then perhaps I could get over the events that had led to that unfortunate collapse last summer. The collapse that had begun as I stood in front of this very Virgin.

I would force myself to look at the photograph. I picked up the image with a trembling hand.

"Please," I said, "stay holding me." With Marya's arms tightly wrapped around me I forced myself to look at it.

I squinted at the face, avoiding the background. Rebecca was a bleak image on tattered paper—a woman in a plaid pleated skirt, one hand clutching an oblong handbag, the other, it seemed, adjusting her bra strap.

"That's her all right." Marya let go of me and reached for the photo. She brought it close to her face and we peered at the figure together.

Rebecca loomed large in the picture, the chapel looked squat. Funny how the unpleasant woman could overwhelm that perfect piece of artistry.

I tried not to make the worst stereotypic assumptions, but Rebecca seemed every spinster cliché in the book: an exact replica of the Old Maid card. I blinked away from her suspicious gaze. Her hair was pulled back tight enough to give her an automatic facelift. The jagged scar was pulled back, but even without my glasses I could make out the gash pointing at her ear. I wondered again how she'd got that scar.

A pair of cotton-gloved hands clutched her handbag. Germs everywhere, and hold on to your money. The felt-covered bag would be full of rosaries. I wondered about the next few days. I wondered what it would be like packing up the symptoms of Rebecca's personal piety.

"Get me my glasses, would you, honey?" I asked as I stood squinting at the photo.

Marya returned quickly and I centered the half-moon lenses in front of my eyes and brought the photograph toward me. The images came into sharper focus. And then I realized the woman wasn't as pinched and pained as I'd thought. Indeed there was something wild and triumphant in her gaze. There was no disappointment in her expression and her lips formed a self-satisfied look that would have made the Mona Lisa seem a spoilsport. She was enjoying herself immensely, posing in front of the statue of the Virgin. That same statue, that same horrible spot.

"She looks interesting," I said. "See that mad little glint? I can really picture her in this crazy goddess glitter palace." The photo was awakening an enthusiasm for the place in me and for the woman. It was a welcome enthusiasm. Rebecca was forcing me to visit that terrifying shrine, but she made an almost comforting guide. Maybe that was why I'd come to Montana.

Who had taken Rebecca's picture there? I knew who had taken mine. My expression wouldn't have been anything like hers. I took a breath and repressed the memory. Looking closer, I realized that Rebecca wasn't adjusting her bra strap after all. She was pointing behind her, to the blessed Virgin, as she looked directly into the lens. She was looking at me.

I whipped off the lenses and her features diminished rapidly into blurry approximations. I leaned against the wall and threw the photo on the table.

"Yeah, it's not that interesting," Marya murmured. "You're still looking queasy. Let's have some tea."

"I'm sorry, I don't know what came over me," I lied.

"Don't apologize. After all, Rebecca's *my* unpleasant relation." Marya was teasing, tentative. I realized once again how new we were with each other.

It was good to make noise, open cupboard doors, bang around the cabinets finding a charred enamel pan with which to make tea. I even found a box of Red Rose teabags which didn't look more than a decade old. It was good to be alive, to be thinking of immediate concerns.

There was a switch above the sink. Surely Rebecca wouldn't have a garbage disposal? I thought. But when I flipped it, a scene lit up in front of my face. The black glass of the window over the sink was erased as magenta and purple patio lights illuminated the walled enclosure behind the house.

"Hey, look at that!" I said, and something in my voice made Marya come to my side. Big snowy hulks were standing in the garden.

"I wasn't allowed to play in the garden," Marya smiled. "I had to stay indoors. I remember sulking."

"Maybe those are dwarf fruit trees."

"Maybe it's a crop of crucifixes." Marya turned off the light. "This place really gives me the creeps."

I found chipped white teacups in the cupboard and plopped teabags in them.

"What did your mother do when you were here with Rebecca and she wouldn't let you go outside?"

"Oh, she stuck up for me. Even when I sulked, she promised me a cartoon matinee. I'd been in the car all day, so naturally I wanted to get out and play."

"I like women who like their mothers," I said, remembering Ilona again and wishing I hadn't. Ilona had hated her mother.

4

Tuesday morning was gray and bitter. We woke at six, listening to the wind and the pulsating plastic on the downstairs windows. The upstairs had storm windows, which Rebecca had probably never taken off. The house was so well insulated it was completely sealed against fresh air.

I had turned off the heater the night before, but warm stuffy air filled the house all night. Our bodies were slightly moist with sweat under Rebecca's blankets. I had a headache. Dehydrated, my mouth was dry, sour.

I got up, pulling my bathrobe around me, and looked out of the window at my first Montana morning. The wind had died down and outside a white snowy blanket extended to the very feet of the distant Beartooth Mountains. Big fluffy cumulus clouds floated overhead, like ships with billowing sails. I felt strangely immune to the bright sweep of blue and white outside.

"Isn't it lovely, darling?" Marya breathed by my side.

"Yes," I replied, lying to her, and even my body lied as she started touching me. I pulled away.

"The reading of the will's today, isn't it?"

"Yes," she said. "I'd better go alone."

I didn't say anything. It was painful and awkward. If Marya and I were married heterosexuals, we'd be newlyweds. We'd probably go together to the lawyers, or at least I'd be introduced. As it was, I had no part in the day's events.

"I'm sorry, darling," she said. "It's just better that I go alone. It would be inappropriate—"

"Sure. I'll go and make tea." I went downstairs.

"I'll bring back some cardboard boxes," Marya said, coming into the kitchen minutes later. "Tomorrow I can help you with some of this stuff. Let's just take it to the dump and the Salvation Army."

"Nothing personal of Aunt Rebecca's you might want?" I asked. "Maybe I'll find some retro clothing. A cloche with feathers? A perfectly tailored business suit you'd love to wear to the lawyers?"

Marya came over and kissed me. "Not in this dump!" She laughed. "Support hose and granny shoes, more likely." She shrugged her shoulders and looked around the room. "I don't need the iconography either. I just need you."

But after Marya left I wasn't in the mood for anything except bad thoughts. The sooner I started packing, the sooner I could leave. I stood up. But get back to what? My career conflict? Would I perish if I didn't publish? Surely not. But even my students weren't inspiring me these days, and all the subject matter seemed dry and dead. I was glad to have the six week semester break ahead of me.

I sat down again and looked at the teabag floating in the cup. My future was locked up like those tea leaves in their flow-through bag. Maybe my career wasn't at a dead end. Maybe it was worse than that. Maybe *I* was at a dead end. I put my head down on the table and cried.

After a while I quieted down, walked to the window and watched the clouds drift back and forth across the sky.

I blew my nose and looked about, wishing I could find a vacuum cleaner.

I spent the morning in the kitchen and the afternoon sifting through tarnished, dented silver plate in the dining room cupboards. I stuffed Rebecca's picture in an empty drawer without looking at it again. Everything was worthless. It was all so ordinary. A lifetime devoid of anything except devotion. My fantasies about Rebecca's expression in the photo were just that. Fantasies.

The living room was nearly finished and I was glad. Packing up Rebecca was time-consuming, sad and, finally, freaky. I wasn't looking forward to her bedroom.

My eyes swept around the kitchen. Everything got so dusty so fast. I noticed once more the narrow door leading to the cellar. I opened it cautiously. There was only a normal musty smell. I had probably been feeling over-sensitive last night, the Sienese Madonna in the photograph had made me paranoid. To prove I was no longer afraid, I would go down into the cellar.

I found myself looking down a steep wooden stairway. Grabbing the flashlight from the kitchen table, I descended into Rebecca's dungeon.

5

The flashlight pierced veils of spiderwebs. Weak daylight filtered through a small high window covered with yellowed newspaper. The fading tones of sunset shone dimly through old advertisements, a hermit's version of a stained glass window. In the corner, a water heater wheezed and hissed and icy drafts glided around. Cobwebs billowed like curtains in front of metal shelving.

I walked past the deep shelves, waving at some webbing with my torch to see what lay beneath. The blue steel of a hacksaw blade glinted, and the rip saw teeth of a circular saw. Sharpened chisels, laid out like obedient bodies, occupied the front row of the top shelf, and behind them a bevy of pointed tools and an ice-axe, just like Marya's and just as sharp.

Behind the tools corroded canisters, metal armature, vinyl adhesives, plaster bonding agents, chicken wire, fixatives, caulking, and glues stood testimony to Rebecca's care for her saintly statues. The latter stood assembled behind the hardware section, waiting to be taken apart or mended. When Marya returned from Billings I would suggest we keep the tools, a surprise heritage from Aunt Rebecca.

I walked toward the window, moving past the old water heater. Light filtered through a farming equipment supplement from the *Billings Banner*. "Danroy Chemical" read the headline, heralding the discovery of chemical pesticides.

I scratched away a corner of the newspaper. Through the cracked window pane I could see the side of the stone wall, the long driveway and, at the end of it, a car peeking out of those six-foot snowdrifts. It wasn't Marya's car.

It was cold outside and the car's motor was idling, rocking the big boat of a vehicle gently behind the drift.

Eventually the engine revved, and the invisible driver put the car into gear and sailed off. I put the corner of the newspaper back up. Our sightseer was probably just curious about strangers in this lonely house.

I tried to imagine Rebecca, with freezing fingers, applying the paper to the window with flour-and-water paste. The water heater let out a sigh of escaping steam. I found a box of rat poison, next to a Saint Lucy whose arm was broken off at the elbow; no hand, no plate, no eyeballs.

"What were you up to?" I asked the cupboards, wedged between cheap statuary with their mouldy old bottles of bleach, oil, lard and tar. The contents of the cellar intrigued me, teased me about Rebecca's purpose in life.

"Ouch!" My toe stubbed something and a prickle of pain traveled up my leg. I leaned over and saw a tiny figurine on a chain trapped in the split concrete and dirt of the cellar floor. Reaching for the chain, I pulled the thing toward my face.

A heavy cast iron figure swung from my grasp. Madonna Milagrosa. The little figure was about three inches long, perched on a cloud, two rays extending from either hand.

As I brought it toward me the Madonna figure snagged my cheek and I jumped. It had pierced my skin.

Carefully, I swung the icon higher into the air, its pendulum action lessening as I brought it near my eyes, where I could see it more clearly in the pale light that filtered through the window.

"Jesus Christ!" I said out loud. Carefully welded onto the back of this icon were small nails and tacks, still sharp, with slightly hooked ends. An invitation into the cult of suffering.

6

I dropped the tiny Madonna on the floor as I felt my stomach turn.

I looked at the implement at my feet and remembered that, for religious women, the devil could be an everyday internal temptation. The devil, it was thought, inhabited women, while for men the devil was outside. A challenge to be met. Although men used self-inflicted punishment as a road to perfection, women had to start by beating the devil out of themselves.

I had a sudden vision of Rebecca down in the dingy room, rhythmically swishing the lethal little Madonna at her back, its vicious, hooked nails piercing and tearing her skin. Unaccountably, for a moment, the thought of Marya's ice-axe flashed into my mind.

"Hey, Rebecca! Anything that gets you through the night!" I called out, my voice splitting the silence. "Okay, so what else is down here? Anything of value? Why didn't you just stick to statues?"

I started up the stairs, letting my eyes rove over the shelves of tools, cobwebs, canisters, chipped plaster—and something shiny and red in the corner.

The glint of copper caught my eye. There, shoved between a leaking can of Bon Ami and a tin of matches, a copper cube glimmered.

"Hope this isn't some handy dandy homemade thumbscrew, Rebecca," I said, but I couldn't have been more wrong.

I thrust my hands through spidery webbing and past ancient cleaning compounds toward the small object. Finally my fingers found its edges and I pulled it into the weak light, blowing dust off its surfaces as I did so.

It was a copper filigree box, elaborate with insects so real they could have crawled off and bitten my hands, and flowers with pearl-studded petals that seemed to curl in a heavy summer sun. It was so different from anything I had yet found in this house. It was so lively, so fecund. So Italian. What was it doing here?

I cradled the little jeweled box in my hand. I felt it was mine, not only because I'd found it, but because it had no place here among the clutter of despair. Just as I had no place in Montana. I belonged to Italy.

I ran my fingers over the coppery surface. I remembered the photograph of Rebecca and the Sienese Madonna behind her. Even if I never recovered from Ilona, I thought, I must not recoil from things Italian. From Siena.

I must make room for thinking about that country, that city. Italy. Siena. Holding the box in my hand I was propelled over longitudes and latitudes.

I remembered those glittering reliquary boxes, holding the gruesome delights of sainthood. A chip of bone, a scrap of cloth, sacred relics of the saints. Italy. That campsite where the end had begun with Ilona.

How happy I had been when we got to Tuscany! The dark green umbrella forms of cedars of Lebanon were sharply delineated on the horizon of hills. I saw things there that I had seen only in paintings. I hadn't known, hadn't really understood that the paintings I had studied had depicted something real—an actual place that still existed. And the architecture! Buildings that existed in the collective unconscious. In my unconscious. It was like waking up and walking around in a dream.

But the camping had been a nightmare. I had tried to express my excitement about Italy to Ilona, but that was wrong. This was the culmination of Ilona's teaching. This was hers to give *me*. My reverie irritated her, took something from her. It was something she couldn't participate in, and she usually participated so thoroughly in my thoughts. But the beauty of that place was so strong, it was mine alone.

And now I was holding a replica of that beauty in my hands. I moved it up and down, testing its weight. Something rattled around inside. It was heavy. Too heavy for plated metal.

Solid copper? Cast or hand-forged? Copper was later—this had no feel of Nouveau, Liberté or Jeugenstil. It couldn't be Germanic, anyway—not with the grace and vitality of its ornamentation. It wouldn't be copper. I drew in a breath. Gold, I thought. Gold could be red.

It wasn't possible, not here in Rebecca's house of homely horror. The stuffiness, the unrelenting ordinariness of everything was forcing me to see beauty and value where none could be. But I looked down at the box and knew that my judgment was correct. Italian churches had been sacked by US GIs as surely as they'd been sacked by the Lutherans in 1527. It wasn't impossible.

A sound above. Was Marya home? Or was it a cat? The room was getting darker, the light nearly faded away from the window. I looked around for the stairs.

A high-pitched whine broke the dusky silence of the cellar—it came from the water heater. Suddenly I heard, or saw, steam starting to leak out of the old appliance. Should I turn it off? Was there a gas spigot somewhere? The small stream of steam thickened—became a cloud. I didn't budge. I was rooted to the ground, watching it.

Swelling and shaking like a huge cauldron it began to rock on its spindly legs. I had to move. I looked around for the stairs but couldn't see anything beyond the glow of the demonic appliance. Steam seemed to be filling the room, wrapping around me as I turned. The water heater was in front of me, behind me. Where was Marya? I said a quick Hail Mary as I caught my breath and made a stab at the darkness.

I ran, my hands in front of me, only to be scalded by the boiling hot metal of the water heater. Turning, my scorched palms in front of me, I plunged again into the darkness.

I felt the edge of something metal and suddenly I saw the tall shelves in front of me, twisting in their frames. Then my head was battered as objects toppled onto me—torsos of plastic saints buckling in the heat, cans pounding me with their metal edges and leaking their contents into my hair.

I felt something sharp at the crown of my head and then a sickening cool feeling came over my skin—a liquid becoming vapor. I was coated with kerosene and trapped in a dark hole with an exploding water heater not too far away.

The pilot light began to burn brighter, and now I could just make out the stairs. Clambering over tubs, tools, cans and the wreckage of metal shelving, I made my way toward safety.

The water heater was rattling violently as I heaved myself up the stairs. I slipped and scraped my shin harshly against the concrete. The steps seemed too steep, too long. I thought I would never reach the top. Then, finally, I burst through the door into the kitchen.

I ran out of the house and thrust my hands into the snow, scooping up handfuls and rubbing it into my hair.

My scalp was burning with chunks of frozen ice, as I plunged my arms, still coated with kerosene, again and again into a deep snowbank. My hands were pulsating and trembling violently. The ice was searing the burns.

Standing there, on the frozen ground, in February, somewhere in the hinterlands of Billings, Montana, I baptized myself into safety.

Eventually I stopped scooping and rubbing the snow across my skin. I waited for the sound of the water heater exploding. It never came. The icy air brought me back to reality, and after a while I ventured back onto the porch. I waited some more. I was catching a fierce chill, but I didn't care. I looked for head-lights but there was only darkness stretched out over the white plains.

Finally I went into the house, down the hallway and into the kitchen. I paused by the door to the cellar.

I heard no sound. I waited, but the water heater was silent. Dead. I opened the door. Tomorrow I'd call the plumber and have it replaced.

Then I went upstairs to strip off my frozen, clinging clothes and dry my hair. I looked at my palms. Small watery blisters were swelling, riding up and down my lifeline. They were full of blood.

7

I filled the long, thin, clawfoot bathtub with hot water and got in. The water heater was apparently doing its job.

I picked up a bar of Ivory soap and just as quickly put it down. My palms were raw and burnt, oozing clear liquid. I rested them on the cool, cast iron edge of the tub. My body looked big and pink, magnified under the aqua water. My mind drifted away from my pain.

I missed the little university town in Germany where I'd studied. The traveling, the pawing through original legal documents in archives of cool, dusty libraries. How I loved the sounds and smells of foreign cities after emerging from the tomb-like museums with their secretive vaults.

It was in such a cathedral in Ghent, Belgium, that I first saw her. I remembered that my feet were cold and damp as I walked into the vast cavern of the main building.

Engulfed in the huge space, the tourists looked like tiny figurines, their ears cupped with earphones. They listened to explanations of the architecture in four different languages as they strolled around, craning their necks back and squinting up into the soaring gothic arches.

I saw a sign before a passageway; it indicated a chapel containing a famed *Annunciation* painted by one of the Lippi brothers. I walked into the dark passage and saw the flicker of a far-away candle at the end. As I progressed down the tunnel, the light became clearer, whiter, and then I saw the painting. It seemed like a window into another world.

Casting my eyes down as I entered the tiny chapel, I approached the rail and looked at the painting. Close up it dazzled my eyes. Within a golden frame two saints stood guard on either side of the main figures. They were telling their story in gestures.

Mary has been reading a book in front of her miniature pillared castle. The Archangel Gabriel has floated down from above, interrupting her. He glows, his wings glorious with color. Mary is dressed in embossed gold.

It was probably worth a half million dollars and here it was, hanging over an altar with just a few candles under it. No security system, just the distancing rail. There must be electric eyes somewhere.

"I hope so, Mary," I said. The Virgin looked frightened. She pulled back from the Archangel Gabriel's news, knowing what was coming.

I became conscious of someone standing behind me but, thinking it rude to turn around, kept looking straight ahead. I could feel a gaze running up and down my back and I grew hot. It was hard to concentrate on the painting.

"Do you like it?" A voice spoke in German. I jumped, and turned to see a woman standing behind me. She had a heart-shaped, pale face, with light red hair, freckles on her forehead and little wrinkles at the corners of her eyes. She stood with her weight on one leg, a finger crooked in the belt of a dark green motorcycle jacket. The pull tabs of zippers flickered in the candlelight over black Levis and motorcycle boots made to tolerate thousands of miles of wear. She was coming closer.

The arm of her jacket rubbed against my parka. The dark

leather was stiff. I felt like a colorful balloon next to her, my white tennis shoes, inappropriate for the rain, made squishy sounds as I moved my weight from foot to foot.

Her face seemed to glow out of the darkness of the chapel, out of her dark, animal hide. I looked back into the painting.

"You do like it?" she asked in an accented German. What *was* that accent? "These blues are supposed to be the most brilliant of the fourteenth century. The warmth and thickness of these whites and yellows are incomparable . . ." But her German was too fast; she was losing me.

"Yes," I said quickly, in English.

"You are American?" she said, reverting to English. She seemed somewhat amused. She let a tiny smile escape.

"Yes. This is a lovely city. I've waited so long—"

"Yes, you Americans do wait so long, so very long."

"It's not my first trip—" I protested, but she was sighing, and looking me up and down. I blushed and hated myself for it. She was right. I had waited a long time to see the history I had so carefully studied. I caught her eyes lingering at my hips.

"If you want to look at a naked woman, there's a painting of Eve right behind you," I said.

"I'm sorry. I don't mean to interrupt your, how do you say, your viewing pleasure." Her sharp s's suddenly clicked into place. She was Scandinavian.

"Thank you. I don't watch television," I said in German, wanting to establish my cosmopolitan credentials even as I defended myself.

"I guess I'm being rude," she replied in English, her lips turning with a slight smile.

"Yes, you are."

"It's just that I saw you standing here and I watched you. Even behind your back I could feel that you were involved. In the story, in the artistry. I didn't think you were a tourist. Then, when I heard your accent I thought, no. I didn't want to have my fantasy spoiled. But now I have made a silly assumption and interrupted your enjoyment."

"There's time to turn it around."

"You see," she went on, "I am particularly attached to the Madonna. As story. As living symbol. Perhaps I can fill you in on a few details about this painting," she smiled authoritatively.

"Please."

"You can see here, even so early," she pointed at the Angel Gabriel and Mary, "how the Italians saw the body as sensuality, as an example of truth defined by its ability to invoke the ideals of beauty. And of pleasure."

I nodded. Sensuality. Truth. Pleasure. Her voice was a pleasure. The painting became more animated with her words. I could smell her leather jacket. It must have been new.

"In addition Mary is seated here in the Basilica. That's where you'd really expect to find the altar. That means she is functioning as the altar herself, in an iconographic sense."

I gazed at Mary and then back at the living woman's face, pale with the bright pink cheeks cold gives to such creatures. Pointed chin and pale, pale eyebrows and eyelashes. When she smiled, the lines moved up at the corners of her eyes and made her face look almost rugged. Swedish, her accent was definitely Swedish.

"But that's enough of my lecturing," she said. "Goodbye, be seeing you!" And then she was moving past me, fading down the long, dark tunnel.

"Wait!" I cried. But by the time I had registered her movement, the tunnel was dark and empty. I ran down it and into the huge center of the cathedral. Was that her, the black figure just disappearing behind one of the large carved altars? Or there, that figure stepping out into the drizzle?

I ran out of the entrance but saw no one. A drip from a gargoyle tapped me on the shoulder. It was time to return to my overheated rooms in the little university town just across the border.

That evening on the train I heard her voice in the wind and rain. And I never stopped hearing it. Every night as I went to sleep I thought about her startling appearance in the chapel and her deep appreciation of the miraculous painting above the altar.

* * *

Some weeks later I heard about the fabulous lecturer who'd just been hired and was arriving late in the semester. I recognized the name immediately. Ilona Jorgensen had made waves which had reached the parched patriarchal shores of academic historians years ago.

Her first lecture drew a huge crowd. Anticipating her intellectual antics I pressed into the stuffy lecture hall. Her theories were the stuff of current controversy and she had already made a name for herself as a new kind of art historian, and as an intellectual entertainer. I stood in the back and strained my eyes through the darkened room. The lights dimmed further and then colors streaked through the air, an image shot through the darkness onto the screen in front of us. A Virgin seated beneath a canopy.

"*You can see, in these works, even in these early works, how the Italians saw the body as sensuality.*" That voice! Not the words but the tones entered my head. The Virgin seemed to swim on the silver screen in front of me, the hall darkened and I gripped the armrests of my chair. I gasped as the Virgin grew huge, expanding beyond the screen, her moon face rising above me. She seemed to wink as she offered me a lily. I pinched myself hard and she shrank.

"*An example of truth defined by its ability to invoke the ideals of beauty,*" continued the voice. In the dark lecture hall I could make out a black figure, a shadow behind the lectern. In a fantasy spotlight, I imagined I saw that red hair, that pale face, that slow smile. Ilona Jorgensen was the woman I had met in the chapel in Ghent.

We had visited the Madonna, together, alone in a stone chamber. I had stood before the altar of high aesthetic theory with the loftiest practitioner of them all, Ilona Jorgensen.

"Throw away your preconceptions of medieval history. The times were more matriarchal than anyone thought." Her skinny hands wouldn't rest long at her sides. "It was the rise of mercantile capitalism which put women in a place of subjugation as property. You must learn to look with their eyes, and then learn to look through your own."

I sat fascinated in the darkness, watching her animated, shouting shadow, cut out of the projected painting. The saturated colors on the screen showed a monumental Madonna with Ilona in front of her, the silhouette subverting the image. And then the screen went off, the house lights came up and revealed the professor. Ilona in black velvet ski pants, tight as a drum, a soft chambray shirt draped over her torso. Her boots had cuffs, rolled down. I could see they were lined with red kid.

For weeks I followed that striding shadow, marveling at her perceptions and her wardrobe. She wasn't a fashion victim. She was a fashion victor. And her mind! Ilona made me aware of myself, introduced me to myself. Ilona, a striding, gesticulating figure on a stage. Ilona, on a perpetual roll.

She gave us a new way of seeing which would empower the female viewer. Not that she used the word "empower." It was just power. New and awesome power. I took notes furiously trying to keep up with her.

"How can we look at Leda and the Swan? How can we experience this female looking at us from the canvas? She is us and she is looking at us. Forget the male mediator—find your own original experience and take it from there."

But I wasn't prepared for the original experience Ilona Jorgensen was to offer me.

I never joined the line that formed in front of her, students wanting guidance, information, attention. I didn't have to wait in line. Ilona noticed me in a local cafe and remembered me from Ghent. We graduated from coffee to gin. She asked me about my dissertation but didn't seem very interested when I explained the topic. A bit too specific, a bit too limiting she said, but she was smiling.

She was taking a break from a rigorous research period. The politics at the university in Utrecht made her sick. She was happy to be here. And that wasn't all.

"I'm so glad it was you in the chapel," she said.

"Me?" The gin was just keeping my hands from trembling.

"Yes. The quality of your gaze is special. You see from many perspectives. You see yourself seeing," she smiled.

"I'm so glad I'm in your class."

"I am too," she smiled. And then she asked me back to her apartment.

Her apartment! Did she mean sleeping together? Was I ready for anonymous sex? But this wouldn't be anonymous sex, I thought. This would be sex with Ilona Jorgensen.

She hailed a cab and it pulled up to a narrow brownstone building. I climbed the steep staircase in front of her, anxious to be at the top as I felt her eyes upon my hips, my buttocks, swaying with each wobbly step I took. Finally we were on the landing and she opened the door, fumbling with her key. She was drunk too.

Ilona's apartment was sparsely furnished, but piles of books ran in columns up the walls. It was bare of paintings, posters or bric à brac. Her mind must supply the imagery, I thought.

Except for a photograph lying casually on the floor. It was a picture of a woman, a pleasant middle-aged face beaming at the camera lens. Wasn't that Geraldine Pompton, the famous feminist poet? I thought, and leaned forward, squinting. I had heard she had had a nervous breakdown, had been hospitalized.

"Would you like to go to bed?" Ilona asked and there was nothing colloquial or coquettish about it. She grabbed my hand and pulled me through the living room. We stepped over the big art books piled everywhere, a floor littered with thousands of dollars of full-color reproductions. Her foot caught the photograph I thought was Geraldine Pompton and she kicked it into the corner as she opened the door to her bedroom.

I barely had time to look around. Ilona had turned on the brightest of electric bulbs and there was a bare field of white walls, white bedspread and very white Ilona.

She took off her clothes quickly and faced me, almost defiantly. I stood looking at her. Somehow I felt more naked in all my cotton swaddling than she in her beautiful perfect flesh. Long arms, tiny pink breasts, legs which stood slightly apart, claiming the ground they stood on. I couldn't move. I didn't breathe. I swallowed.

But then Ilona started kissing me. And what full, warm lips she had! A long string of gin-flavored kisses, each one longer and deeper. I sank into the luxury of her soft silken lips. This was coming home, I thought, as she undressed me.

Ilona was working her way wetly down my collarbone. I watched all that red hair like flames on my skin. Her searing tongue found its way into my cleavage, until it was impossible to stay standing. I peered over her shoulder at my hands as I laid them on her white, white back. This was making love. This was Ilona Jorgensen.

I fell back onto the bed. I moaned as I hit the bedspread. I wasn't quite ready for this. I felt tears on my eyelids as she made her way between my legs, her red hair falling softly over my thighs.

I closed my eyes and saw auburn fields and a tear ran down my cheek.

I let her, I let her. I let Ilona touch me where she wanted, without knowing how I'd suddenly become so passive, except that my breathing was making me faint. She was working her fingers along the slick grooves in between my legs. Higher, higher, I was thinking.

Ilona went higher and then she was high enough. I cried out and felt her lips, smiling. I cried again and thought for one minute that she might be laughing. But it was just the rushing in my ears, the long tunnel I was flying into with wings refracted into colors.

And then I flew out of myself. I was gone. I wasn't there any more. There was just my soul, some kind of glove, wrapped around Ilona Jorgensen's fist which pumped at an endless universe beyond my mind.

8

Only now do I wonder why her light had chosen to rest on me. Perhaps it was because I was an American, perhaps it was the quality of my adoration. My naïveté made her feel tender. She was so relaxed and happy when we were together. Or perhaps it was the possibility of going to America. I thought of Geraldine Pompton, her face still turned to the floor in its picture frame, smiling at the floor-boards. The thought worried me for a moment.

Yes, Ilona was on the rebound. But everyone, I told myself, is on the rebound from something.

I hadn't realized the complicated combination of a student/lecturer love affair. It seemed easy to imagine the basic situation. Her guidance and instruction. My acceptance and enthusiasm. I became busy, my time filled with Ilona, my calendar adjusting to fit any free time she might have in her busy life.

I joined forces with her, deriding other academics who so jealously guarded their own inferior thought forms; their unconscious assumptions revealing banal unconscious prejudices, leading them to erroneous conclusions. These were the forces who opposed life, who opposed Ilona.

I could feel my own depth of inquiry expanding under her proximity, even as my fingers flew over the typewriter keys.

Ilona suggested a certain historical figure as a basis for research. Wilhelmina of Breught. Archaeologists were busy in a nearby province with the ruins of a convent of which she had been the abbess.

I went to my advisor, who was reluctant, but finally agreed to let me change the topic of my dissertation. She said she thought the topic was too narrow, too confining. I worried that she thought I wasn't capable.

Ilona let me in on some obscure documents, a primary influence on Wilhelmina's thinking. And so it was that Wilhelmina, an ecumenical writer of the Middle Ages, came to absorb my attention entirely, along with Ilona Jorgensen.

My intellect was expanding, but I felt a growing anxiety as I accompanied Ilona in her intellectual and social life.

"Sweetheart," she would chide me, remarking on something I'd said to a local artist at a reception, "you don't compliment someone on their *taste*." And then she would smile indulgently at my gaffe. I stood corrected.

My clothes were wrong, my hands flew about when I spoke, my voice, she said, sounded like braying. But I was speaking German, a language that belonged to someone else, I said. But that didn't matter. Braying was braying.

"If you don't understand someone don't say, 'What?' say 'Sorry'," she'd remind me, along with other tips on grammar or idiomatic usage.

She took me to the market, where colorful cheap trousers and sweaters could be bought to replace my old garments which I suddenly realized were very American and intrinsically unattractive.

And so I changed. These things seemed obvious, and I was grateful. I also learned to ignore the sometimes unpleasant stares she garnered. I forgot that she had been asked to leave a certain committee.

Then the unbelievable happened. Ilona's contract would not be renewed. Ilona was hot, but a bit too hot to handle. The termination increased her estimation in my eyes, and I felt angry for her, with a righteous feminist feeling.

After giving Ilona my dissertation and waiting three days for her to read it, she finally told me how wonderful it was. I knew then for the first time that I wasn't just a researcher or a writer who could make a logical argument. I realized that I, too, could be a theorist, a medievalist.

Ilona had said she'd be late for the reception honoring the graduate students. I was not just graduating but graduating with honors and attention.

I made my way through the narrow streets toward the cafe where the graduate reception was being held, feeling relaxed. My German was now fluent, colloquial and finally even witty. Such a cocktail party held no fears for me. And Ilona, the creator of my transformation, would be there.

As I reached the cafe I began to feel nervous. A van from a radio station was parked outside. But nobody, not even Ilona, could have prepared me for what was to come.

Friends thrust flowers at me as I walked through the door, and a freckle-faced, skinny young journalist sidled up to me with pencil and paper. It seemed Wilhelmina's remains had just been discovered at the archaeological dig only fifty miles away. A few phone calls from journalists had located my advisor and she had told them about my thesis and the reception. I could see her now, in the corner, looking unhappy. Was she irritated at my success, having warned me off the ambitious project? I didn't want to think about that for long.

I looked down into the journalist's freckled face as I carefully told her, "All the credit must go to my mentor and teacher, Ilona Jorgensen." Glancing up at the happy faces around me, I smiled and wobbled away on the spikes of my heels.

Then came the courting of a few minor bureaucrats from the University and a stag from an art-book publishing house. The flowers were making my nose run and I had gulped down a few drinks too quickly.

Where was Ilona? I'd seen her in the corner not too long ago. I took another drink. Ilona, come to me, I thought, ignoring the continuing questions and congratulations of the group which gathered around me, holding me tightly in their center. I pushed my way through them, jostling the arm of the Anthropological Studies Chair. Some pink drops of Campari splashed across her silk waistband. Where was Ilona? I didn't even mumble a "sorry." I couldn't find the formal or colloquial phrases that would have socially saved such a mistake.

I scanned the room, looking at all the people talking and guzzling their drinks. I needed Ilona to make it real for me. And I needed to reposition myself in our relationship. Teacher and student, lovers. I also needed to pee and headed for the door marked "Dames" in the back corner of the bar, suppressing a wave of panic. I wanted Ilona, and I needed her at that moment to tell me who I was.

I pushed open the door, squinted at the brightly lit tiled interior, turned the corner and looked into the stall. I'd found Ilona.

She was standing in front of the toilet, her back to me, lifting up the skirt of the freckle-faced journalist and working her hands between the woman's legs.

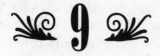

9

The bathwater was cooling, and my skin was getting wrinkled. Where was Marya? Why was she so late after the reading of the will?

I got out of the tub, dried myself and put on clean cotton underclothes and a thick jogging suit. Pulling a wool sweater over my head, I went downstairs. Returning to the cellar door I pressed my ear against it. Apart from the steady hiss of the pilot light, I couldn't hear a peep from the water heater. The water in the upstairs sink was normally hot.

I ran a sponge over the formica counter; it seemed to get dirty so quickly in Rebecca's house. But when I looked closer at the surface, I saw that it wasn't really dirt. Little flecks of metal were caught in the cellulose surface of the sponge.

Then I heard someone coming up the walk. I ran to the door. It was Marya. She saw my face through the window and brightened up. Hurrying, she slid on the ice but made the step and flew into the door. There she almost tripped over her climbing equipment, the rope, ice pick and pitons I'd put inside the front door.

She drew her foot out of the snaked nylon coil and lunged at me, laughing.

Hugging me hard enough to crack a rib, Marya pirouetted into the living room. She hardly looked around the emptying dining room, or the kitchen where I'd put the piles of junk.

I'd arranged all the replicas of saints in tight rows on the dining room table. Somehow beautiful in this austere household, their plaster surfaces and happy flesh tones made me feel safer. Marya laughed. She laughed loudly as she looked at them. I could see her teeth.

"Can you bottle it and sell it?" I asked, watching her glowing face.

"Fuzzy, you won't believe this!" Marya danced back and took my arms, squeezed them and looked straight into my eyes. Then her gaze shifted to the right of my face. I turned and saw the crowd of saints I'd arranged so carefully on the table. She let go of me and walked toward them. Standing in front of the table, she stared at the group. Mostly Virgin Marys, there was also Saint Jerome, patron saint of lost items, and Lucy with the eyeballs.

"I got them from all over the house," I explained. "I just couldn't pile them on top of each other like a scene from the holocaust—"

Marya stretched out her arm and suddenly swept the whole crowd of figures off the table. They crashed into a pile of colorful tinsel shards on the floor. Lucy's palm leaf broke in two and her hand came off completely. Saint Jerome rolled all the way into the living room and came to rest at the foot of the recliner. I looked at Marya, who was walking around in circles, whooping, laughing hysterically, eyes glowing.

"I'm rich!" she said, shrugging her shoulders and grinning. "I'm fucking rich!"

"That's no reason to break all those saints."

"Sweetheart, I'm *rich*! In one stroke, my life has been completely changed." She came over, kissing me, and talking. "You're looking at a rich woman. Fuck direct mail! No more shrink wrap, inserting, sealing, labeling, metering! I can do whatever I want! Five million dollars after taxes! Rebecca was rich! And now, so am I!"

"You're rich," I repeated. I knew we were having a stupid conversation but somehow everything had changed in one sentence. "But how is it possible? Where did she get it?"

"Rebecca was a miser, but instead of keeping her money under the mattress—"

"But what money?"

"She must've taken her paltry savings and kept it all in mineral rights; probably bought them for a song—"

"What kind of minerals?"

"Who *cares*!" Marya came toward me, put her hands across my back and drew me to her. I hugged her back. "All those money stresses!" she nuzzled my neck. "We could go great places together. Italy!"

"Italy?" I glanced at the leftover saints on the table.

"We could have some exciting trips—after a while." She bit her lower lip.

"What do you mean, after a while? How long is it going to take to close the estate?"

"It's not that."

"So what is it?"

"I have to live here," she said, looking away. She stared at a particularly clumsy angel in a cheap print of the Annunciation. "In Montana. For a year. To collect the money. In this house."

"You're not serious!" I laughed. The map of Italy rolled up like an old sock in my mind. A horsehair blanket rolled out. Was I ready to lie on it?

"She who contests the will gets one dollar," Marya grimaced, walking toward me. "I've been talking to that damn lawyer for hours."

"Is he good?"

"He's a homophobic closet queen is what he is. Completely unconscious. But he knows a conditional bequest when he sees one. And I think he's getting the job done."

"There must be a way to get out of it. Her sanity?"

Marya sighed and looked pityingly at me.

"Marya, what about your job? The community?"

"That's what I've got a business partner for, darling!"

"You wouldn't really live here, would you? Rather than San Francisco?"

"For five million dollars I'd live in Beirut!"

"But what about the election? Renquist Falkenburg is counting on you in his campaign for Supervisor. You were to be his campaign manager!"

"Yes, well, there'll be other elections, other campaigns. And all I have to do is stay here and collect! There's great peaks to climb in Montana, you know," Marya hoisted a coil of rope over her arm and swung the ice-pick over her shoulder. The tip glinted evily behind her back. "I could become a rich and famous explorer!"

"What about your friends?"

"They won't go away, sweetheart. I can sublet the apartment—"

"Do you want to sublet me?"

Marya walked toward me slowly. I turned away. I'd seen her red nail polish through the reinforced stocking toes. The contrast with her climbing equipment was ludicrous. This kind of thing might have turned me on in the city, but in Montana it seemed sad.

She put down the rope and ice-axe. Everything was so different all of a sudden. It was the wrong season for those sorts of shoes.

I let Marya hug me from behind. We didn't say anything. Rebecca rich. Marya rich. A lot of Catholic kitsch the harbinger of fabulous wealth.

I wondered how much five million dollars really was. Rich and a resident of Billings, Montana. What could you do with money in Billings? Buy extra Miracle Whip? New chains for the car? Reinsulate the attic?

"So, Saint Theresa of the Tundra was saving for a rainy day," I remarked, looking at a poor reproduction of Mary leaving Egypt. The donkey was out of proportion. It looked like a big Bedlington Terrier.

A few fragments of saints glimmered at the foot of the table.

"I don't want to sublet you, darling. I want to live with you. Here in Montana."

I shuddered. "Marya, are you out of your mind? I wouldn't live in Montana," I said. "Academic jobs in the San Francisco area are hardly plentiful. I know Ph.D's who are washing dishes."

"They are not," Marya said. "They're driving buses. Listen, you wrote that incredible dissertation, got it published—"

"Well, I haven't had anything published lately."

"You haven't written anything lately."

"That's why."

"Then why not take a break from teaching?"

"I don't want to live in Montana," I said finally, softly.

"Think about it. Take a sabbatical. Say it's for health reasons."

"I don't like lying."

"Yes, but you've lied before. You could do it again, for me. For us."

Marya started kissing me, her sharp tongue darting in and out of my mouth. "I don't want this to change anything," she was saying.

"No, don't change anything," I mumbled, kissing her back. But I knew there wasn't a hope in hell that nothing would change. And just for a moment, that really turned me on.

Marya laid me down on the sofa and I didn't protest. What kind of minerals? I was thinking. Was that the secret of Rebecca's satisfied look?

I let Marya unzip my jeans, but lifted my head to peer over her shoulder for a second at my scalded palms.

"What is it?" she said, following my gaze to where my hand lay face up on the upholstered sofa. My palms were mapped with broken blisters. "What happened?" she breathed, frightened. I felt the hooks of her bra strap in the middle of her back. I felt her soft breasts behind the stiff lace against my chest. I grasped her with my forearms.

"Actually, there's no pain," I reassured her, "no pain at all.

Just a plumbing bill which you can well afford." And I described the water heater's near explosion. I let my forearms drop to her side, finding her waistline curve. "It was probably just that some sort of pressure built up in the pipe, because the gas jets hadn't been used for so long. And I found a little antique box. Italian. Before the water heater blew up, or almost did, it seems to be fine now. I just had a bath—" Marya was kissing me again.

"Bath?" she asked, unbuttoning my blouse. For a moment I felt resistant. The thought of the antique box had drawn me back to Ilona, to Ilona's face, Ilona's fingers.

Marya's curls fell across my chest as she sucked.

"Not so hard, Marya," I said.

Mineral rights, I was thinking. I wondered how much five million dollars really was. And then I wondered if she'd give any of it to me. What would Ilona have done?

Don't think about Ilona, I told myself, but Marya's fingers felt tentative, clumsy. Ilona had been such a good lover, I'd been reluctant to instruct Marya in the personal mechanisms of my orgasm. I didn't want things to become rote.

I moved her hand up, until her fingertips found the spot and I could forget the blisters on my palms and the painful ebbing of my talent ever since Italy.

This woman had to take me, heal me from the sick memories and sin that had followed me over continents to this vast American plain. But she was going too fast.

Her two-and-a-half-million-dollar hand was inside me, pumping, and her thumb, her hundred-thousand dollar digital, was outside, rubbing hard and insistently.

"Ouch!"

"What's wrong, sweetheart?" Marya leaned back and fixed me with a puzzled look, drawing her hand from between my legs.

"I'm—I'm just awfully tired. That accident with the water heater—I think I need to go to bed."

"Okay," Marya looked disappointed. I buttoned my shirt.

We mounted the stairs and took off our clothes, slipping

under the cold bedcovers without touching. As the sheets warmed our separated bodies Marya sighed again.

"It isn't someone else, is it?" she asked quietly, in the darkness.

"What?"

"That student in your class? The one who keeps leaving long whiney messages on your answering machine," Marya said almost harshly. I wondered at the bitterness that sometimes surfaced in Marya, the stony, brittle look that now crossed her face. I tried to tell myself that Marya was just hurt and disoriented with the life-changing events which had befallen her.

Marya's voice echoed in the pitch black chamber.

"Don't lie to me," she said. "Just don't ever lie to me."

It was a while before we both fell asleep.

10

Sometime in the early morning, Marya and I did make love. More asleep than awake, our primal unconscious selves knew what was good for us and didn't let inheritances, careers, jealousy and competitiveness intrude. We opened to each other like flowers and then fell back into sleep.

Several hours later, I awoke. The surface of my body, curving along Marya's back, was sweating slightly. I remembered my hands and looked at them. My palms were nearly healed. Now there's an immune system! I thought to myself. I rubbed my itchy eyes. My second day in Montana and I wasn't feeling well. I got out of bed and put my feet on the floor, draping a terry cloth robe loosely over my shoulders.

The floor was so dirty. Too dirty. I looked around in amazement.

I peered up at the ceiling and then glanced down at my feet. A thin golden film covered the floor, turning the blanket a sparkling yellow and dusting into our hair. I held my breath against the accidental beauty.

Marya was still asleep. I stood for a moment looking at her.

A few flakes of glitter landed on her cheek, a perfect garnish to her sleeping figure.

I suppressed an urge to wake her, wanting to be alone. And I wanted to go into the cellar and repossess that little box in the basement.

I slipped on my shoes, now gilded leather, and went into the hallway. The linoleum was covered with minute metal particles. Billows of golden dust rose as I ran downstairs. The recliner, the pine rococo dining room set, the plastic paintings—all had been touched by a menacing Midas. And the flakes were still falling. I took a few in with every breath; I could feel them in my mouth, small and sharp, piercing the surface of my tongue.

I got up on a chair and looked closely at the ceiling. Why were the gilt flakes falling? Could some atmospheric condition or chemical in the air have dissolved the glue that held the glitter in place? Or were there chemical properties in the plaster that had reacted with the glitter, rejecting it all at once, like the ginko tree that sheds its leaves all on one day during the year? Perhaps it had been the weeks of cold, followed by the sudden overheated condition of the house?

I walked to the door of the cellar. The house was quiet. A train whistled in the distance. A cat meowed plaintively. I opened the cellar door. The water heater was burbling gently.

I put my feet carefully on the worn treads of the stairs, my dressing gown billowing in a cool draft. The cellar was quiet. A few more stairs and I could make out the twisted wreckage of shelves, the overturned square can of kerosene. There was no spilled fuel. The water heater barely made a sound, doing its work quietly, efficiently.

Then I saw the copper box.

Scuttling quickly down the last of the stairs, I picked up the kerosene and all other containers of flammables and carried them up to the landing.

Then I scooped up the little Italian copper box and stroked it. I would find a soft piece of flannel and start polishing the box. I wondered just how much it could shine.

I brushed off the dust and examined the object more closely.

A life force seemed to pulsate from its lightly wrought surface. I peered closer, holding my breath.

Quattrocento. Could it be an original? Impossible. About as impossible as Rebecca having all that money. I looked at the box and blinked hard. An hallucination made whole.

What did it contain? A chip of bone from the shoulder of Saint Anthony? Or the intact finger of some saintly nun? A beetle's wing? A dandelion with miniature pearls? I couldn't find a latch to open it.

What vitality the little object had! Stamens, ejecting from cherry blossoms, held little irregular seed pearls. I brushed away a dust mote and found a butterfly with cloisonné wings flying into a corner. A collector's item. No, more than a collector's item, I was sure of it. It was museum quality. My hands started trembling and I coughed. This was surely the source of Rebecca's smile.

A cold gust howled over the prairie, rattling the house, and a swoop of wind made its way into the cellar. It picked up my dressing gown, sending the light material up around my waist and encasing me in a sudden frost. And then all became quiet again.

I peered behind the water heater to the vicious little Virgin Mary pendant reaching out from the dust. Against my better judgment I went toward the buried figurine. I squatted down, transferring the golden box to one hand, and peered around the floor at another object buried there. Cords crept out from under a chip of concrete, a fissure in the floor. I reached out a tentative finger and ran my fingers along one. Yes, each cord had a knot.

I dug down into the crack, my fingers finding a hollow. Inside was a heap of decomposed leather, once the handle of a whip.

Well, nobody had used *that* in a long time. I had been wrong again about Rebecca. These objects hadn't been lying in readiness. Rebecca had buried them here.

"Who were you, old lady?" I asked the slimy stone walls

and the water heater in front of me. It was eerily quiet. Too quiet.

And then I saw it. The shadow. Hovering behind me was the silhouette of a woman, coming closer, with the shadow of an axe held high above her head.

11

"That's not funny!" I snapped.

"I'm being Judith Anderson playing Mrs. Danvers!" Marya laughed.

"Judith Anderson was a better actress. Don't go sneaking up on me that way, please!"

"Now, darling—you're just letting your imagination run away with you."

"Imagination? You think *I'm* imaginative? Look at this weird stuff—this whip, all these tools—and then you sneak up behind me with an ice-axe!"

"Yeah, and it's a great ice-axe. I can use it on McAlteer Peak when I make my first climb the day after tomorrow. Honey, come on, where's your sense of humor? Let's go upstairs and I'll make you breakfast."

I stood up and followed Marya, cradling the golden reliquary carefully in one hand and hoisting my dressing gown with the other. "Yeah, upstairs! I suppose you've noticed that there's been a glitter storm."

"Or the fairies have come." Marya turned at the top of the stairs and gave me a quick peck on the cheek. "Hurry up, I've got to get started on my day."

"Marya, there's something really weird going on here. I'd be the last to talk about bad vibes, but—"

"So the ceiling doesn't have any glitter left?" Marya said. "Probably all the steam from the water heater evaporated the glue. It's still pretty warm in here." She put some water on the stove for tea. "How strange," she shrugged. "This place really is a hell-hole. And stuffy. But who cares? Next stop the Ritz!"

I brushed some glitter off the little box and blew it at her. "How can you be so uninterested? Maybe there's some new chemical properties yet to be discovered in plaster, or maybe— maybe the house is haunted!"

"Yeah. By bad design."

"But don't you think it's spooky—the water heater, the glitter?" I cradled the box closer to me.

"Odd but true. Is that that Italian box you found yesterday in the cellar?" she went on, looking at the antique resting so simply on our kitchen table.

"Yes." Couldn't she see its golden glow?

"You can have it if you like," she said easily. "For risking your life in the line of duty." She wandered upstairs.

How quickly Marya had bestowed this valuable on me, I thought. To buy me off? To swathe a path of privilege before her? Was that what was going to happen now? And she wanted me to stay for a year in Montana. Give up my job. Just like that. I made tea and fumed while she changed for her visit to the lawyers.

I'd always been attracted by Marya's ability to do deals, further Falkenberg's political career and still run her mail order business with supreme efficiency. She spoke a kind of super-edited corporate speak I found wondrously controlled when I first heard her in action.

But now I felt that the politics of accomplishment paled next to the richness of art, art history, or just history. I realized that

I'd been hiding these treacherous thoughts from myself. I didn't want to fall out of love with Marya. Or was I just jealous of her fortune? Falling out of love to dull the pain?

I picked up the antique box and was reaching for my reading glasses when I heard Marya's footsteps on the stairs and looked up to see her. My girlfriend in a pencil stripe business suit, a skirt with pleats as sharp as knives. Corporate drag for hard-hitting girls.

"Do you really need to dress for success? I mean, the money's already yours, so why the power suit?" I smiled, but my tone, meant to be joking, missed the mark.

"It's how I feel comfortable," Marya said, adjusting a bra strap underneath the blouse. "Besides, I'd rather not have the probate pals getting off on my uncontrolled cleavage. Would you? Listen, I'm *sorry* about the Danvers joke and yeah, the kitchen does look pretty weird with all this glitter. Okay?" She stared at me defensively, then looked down at the copper box and stopped.

I looked down at it too. It seemed to be always in my hands.

"You know, I don't really want the box," I said testily.

"Hey!" she threw up her hands. "I thought you wanted it. I wanted to make you happy. And I've really got to go now. I'm late."

"With your bank account you could buy me off forever, so don't get started." I glared at her. "This isn't a situation I recognize."

"You aren't a person I recognize," she tightened her mouth. "Look, I *have* to do this," she said stiffly.

I looked at the millions of flecks which had insinuated themselves into floor cracks, under table legs, into our tea and over all the fragments of saints littering the dining room floor.

"I've got a lot of phone calls to make. To my partner. To Falkenberg. I'll make them at the lawyers," she said coldly.

"Fuck the fucking will! You're dancing to a dead woman's tune. You could get out of it if you wanted to, Marya. I've seen you bend CEO's of stainless steel to do your bidding."

"This is different. It's an iron-clad conditional bequest."

"I think you're feeling guilty," I said. "About having a lot of free money. Rebecca's money. You don't know where it came from and you don't even care why she gave it to you."

"I hardly even knew she existed!" Marya exploded, her voice resonating painfully between my ears. "How can I feel guilty?"

"Maybe it's unconscious."

"I haven't got time for this." Marya put on her overcoat.

"How can you leave me with this mess?" I said.

"I don't have any choice," she replied through clenched teeth, turning on a sling-backed heel. "Don't forget to have that water heater replaced!" she called from the hallway.

"Fuck you!" I said, but only after the door had closed. Her stocking seams needed straightening. I heard the car door slam. She was angry and I'd been unfair, but I didn't care. She was lying when she said she had no choice. Of course she had a choice! But I'd been lying too, I thought as I took a flannel rag out from under the kitchen sink and put on my glasses. I *did* want the little quattrocento box. I started rubbing it in small circular strokes. I looked at the rag, which was quickly getting dirty, taking off all the tarnish from the precious metal. It wasn't copper at all. I polished it faster. It was gold.

12

Golden Italy! I could smell the Italian campsite—ripe portable toilets, bleach in buckets, pieces of food left in the sink in the washing house. I could still hear the yowling of stray cats.

Ilona and I hadn't had much money when we took that trip to Italy. Her CV was still making the rounds of Euro universities and we were both short on cash. A camping vacation was all we could afford and we needed a break.

Her affair with the journalist had been short lived. Limited, in fact, to that bathroom where I'd found them. A few days, a few scenes later, Ilona and I were back together again. She'd asked me to forgive her and I had. I'd seen how much she needed me—my American optimism, my good humor. And I needed her European ideas, and that long red hair glimmering on the pillow beside me every morning.

The Italian trip seemed perfect: Ilona would show me Italy for the first time, as she'd showed me so many things for the first time. And I would supply her with my rapt attention and appreciation. I was a flattering mirror which she seemed to need.

But the campsite brought out tensions between us. Some two

hundred people were on vacation here, and as one big unrelated group we struggled and sweated to have a good time together in what was essentially a big carpark just outside Siena.

On those bright Italian mornings the heat of the sun was intense, and Ilona and I would wake sweating in our tent.

I remembered how insistent she was that the laundry be done every day. Any exception to this brought caustic comments about my personal hygiene.

"I don't suppose you learned anything from that mother of yours," she'd say from her campstool as I collected my toilet bag. I'd look up startled. Her pale face was freckling in the sun but her legs, carefully annointed, were deepening dark with tan. Her sandaled foot tapped impatiently in the dust. "A silver spoon in your mouth and only a silver pen in your hands. She sure didn't teach you anything useful."

"You didn't think so when we first got together," I reminded her, hoping she would remember her earlier gratitude, how she'd shuddered under my touch.

Ilona expected me to laugh about my bad housekeeping, and usually, for the sake of peace, I did. But I remembered how she let the milk boil, spill over the edges of pans, collect on the stove until it became hard and flaky, or soft, breeding new forms of cellular life, usually green. Ilona always accused me of her own transgressions.

Except once when the transgression was so clearly mine. It was the first day I saw that damned cat.

I remember that particular hot morning: the air itself was sweating. The children in the campsite had woken up early. They took cold showers, their voices echoing in the concrete chambers as we struggled to sleep on.

Later Ilona took a long time herself in the showers. I went to get her, and found her squeezing a pimple. She stopped as soon as she saw me, and flicked her hair back. Whipping a streak of red behind her shoulder, she started rubbing sun block into her face.

"You're looking tired," she said after a moment. I stood behind her, looking over her shoulder into the mirror.

"Do you think so? Actually, I think I'm getting a fairly nice tan," I said. My eyes looked clear. I had simply been feeling good being in Italy. My features reflected my pleasure with the discoveries around me.

"Stop leaning over my shoulder," Ilona muttered. "You're blocking my light." I drew back, sighed, and wandered back to the tent. I should have known then that she was in a terrible mood.

Ilona returned, threw her toilet bag into the tent and flopped into the lawn chair. Flicking offending strands of hair back over her shoulder a few times she looked around, avoiding my eyes. Leaning over our cookstove she started assembling the coffee-maker, measuring coffee out into the basket.

"Let's get the laundry done so we can go into town and do something fun," I said. "There's a big market with household things and cheap lacy underwear—"

"Fine. If you *have* to get started so early, *you* can do the laundry and leave me with my coffee—"

"It won't take me a minute."

"You're interrupting me. You know I can't bear that." She stirred her coffee, narrowing her eyes. "Do the laundry. Keep yourself busy."

Ilona tossed the coffee measuring spoon into the grass. After a moment of digging in the tent she emerged with a pillowcase containing our laundry.

"We don't need to do everything today," I protested, looking at the socks, T-shirts and long bermuda shorts. I could already feel them slipping away from me, to be replaced by suds and saturated cottons.

"Then just do the whites," Ilona said. "Or don't do anything. Do what you want. Just please let me get back to my coffee and *La Repubblica.*" She held the Italian newspaper up in front of her nose.

I fished among the soiled garments, pulling out the smaller, whiter things, tore open a box of detergent and spilled the grains into two buckets. Then I stuffed the clothes into them and set off for the washhouse. This vacation wasn't turning out the way I wanted. It was turning out the way Ilona wanted.

Well, we both needed a rest, I thought. Ilona's class load had been heavy and her lectureship hadn't been renewed. As for me, I had little to feel bad about. My dissertation had become a publishing deal and my editor said it might be released quickly, for the summer season. They were anxious to capitalize on the recent discovery of Wilhelmina's remains. Maybe it was published already.

I owed everything to Ilona for this trend in my interest, I thought forgivingly, filling the buckets and letting the water splash over the soiled socks.

At first I hadn't been too excited by this trip to Italy. I was missing my mail at home, the surprise success of my enterprise, the advance check against royalties. Maybe reviews were already piling up in my mailbox, inquiries from other scholars, interview requests from the intelligentsia. But Ilona had booked this trip immediately after the academic year ended.

I looked down at the overflowing buckets at my feet and began to scrub the gray feet of our socks and the double cotton crotches of our panties. The sooner I got them hanging to dry on a string in front of the tent, the sooner we could get on with Italy. I didn't want one more precious Italian day spent on daily duties. It would suddenly be siesta and everything would be closed.

"Batti il gatto!" Glancing up, I saw a boy throwing stones into a bush. He took careful aim, his little sister looking on. I walked over and he stopped, stuck his lower lip out, and stood his ground fiercely by the bush. Under the scrubby foliage a thin cat lay like a chewed-up rag. It was trying to catch its breath, its tiny ribcage barely covered with fur, flies swarming around its eyes and the fur around its tail wet and stringy with fecal matter.

"Leave it alone!" I said to the boy. "Let it die. *Cosa fai lì?"* He grimaced at me and strode away, already an Italian man.

I looked at the horrible animal. Its breath had a gravelly, rasping sound. I spotted a polystyrene plate in the garbage nearby and went back to the washhouse tap to offer it water. But the cat wasn't interested. It was dying.

I didn't want to touch it. It was lying on a ground covering of dry pine needles under the shade of a bush. Except for small Italian boys, it wasn't a bad funeral bower.

I returned to the laundry, wondering how quickly I could finish with the sock feet and dirty necklines of T-shirts, when I noticed something odd about one of the buckets. The suds foaming over the lip were a deep magenta. The water inside was pink.

Oh, no! I raced toward the bucket. Was it too late? I thrust my hands through pastel suds into maroon water, pulling out socks, underpants, an expensive bra. Everything was a sickening fuchsia hue. Eventually my hands found a small sweatshirt—cut-off sleeves, high waist, furry and flannelly—something that was undeniably red and had polluted a lot of good underwear. I was really in for it now.

I threw it out of the bucket onto the grass and poured the pink clothes into the sink, filling it quickly with cold water. But the color was indelible. The clothes would be permanently various hues of red. Pink panties, salmon T-shirts, cerise socks.

I turned and looked across the campsite, past all the people and over the bonnets of parked cars. I could see Ilona in the distance drinking her coffee and flicking her hair like a cat flicks its tail just before it pounces. The buckets bumped against my legs as I tiptoed over the sharp stones, tripping over tent ropes strung with the laundry of others.

The dust was sticking to my legs and settling on the clean clothes in the buckets as I approached Ilona. She was still fidgeting with her hair and taking small sips of her morning brew.

Not wanting to disturb her, I started attaching the clothesline to the tent.

"*What* is going on here?" I looked up and saw her peering into the bucket of pink clothes and then forcing her face into mine.

"What the hell's happened?" she demanded.

"Sorry—that red sweatshirt of mine got mixed in and I guess it—" but Ilona had gripped my wrist and was turning it, wringing and burning the skin. "What the hell are we going to do now?" she demanded, her spittle hitting my face. I was too frightened to brush it from my cheek.

"Ilona, it's just the laundry—it's just clothes—" I explained.

"Just *clothes* she says! Well, let me tell you, if you think clothes are expendable, something you just put on a credit card and walk away with, then you don't know anything about the value of anything."

I turned my back on her and ducked quickly inside the tent. I didn't want to air our dirty laundry in public.

Ilona burst into the tent, a pink mottled bra waving in front of her.

"This is a fucking fifty dollar Bali!" she yelled, the bra taut between her two hands as she leaned forward. I fell back onto the pillow. The bra came closer.

"We can't all be born with a silver spoon in our mouths," she yelled, stretching the bra in front of my face, fixing me with a look of fury. She lowered it toward my throat as I stared into her eyes.

"Ilona," I gasped, and then I felt it on my skin. I could feel the elastic give to the end as it became tighter across my windpipe. Ilona's hands were twisting it around my neck.

"Ilona!" I cried, but I was choking and her name stuck in my throat. Suddenly she stopped and looked at me, leaning back. She let go. The bra retracted with a snap that split the air. She stared blankly at my face.

Then she scrambled out of the tent. I heard her running through the dust.

I waited a few minutes, looking at the pink socks scattered around the inside of the tent and rubbing my hands over my sore neck. My fingers were shaking and I started to cry.

After a while, I picked up the laundry and left the tent. I found Ilona leaning against our old Peugeot, arms folded, her reddish hair a glowing curtain around her glowering face.

"Ilona," I took a deep breath. It was desperately unfair, but I knew I had to apologize, or there would be no peace. "I'm sorry, darling. Please—I didn't mean it wasn't important. What's important is us, our vacation, this time we've been having together. Please let's not spoil it—"

"*I'm* spoiling it, aren't I?" she asked plaintively, slowly my heart went out to her. "I'm making you miserable—"

"No, you're not," I lied. "It's just the heat, the crowded conditions. It's making us both a bit crazy."

We sat there in silence listening to the campsite noises—children yelling, flies buzzing, cars speeding by on the road next to the carpark.

"Please, come back to the tent," I said quietly. Then, thinking quickly about the laundry, I said, "No, let's just get into the car. Here, I've got the keys. We'll go into town and find a terrace cafe with the best cappuccino. I'll buy you *Le Monde*. I'll buy you an *Arbitaire*," I said.

But I didn't offer to buy new socks, a new bra. I didn't want to think about the pink underwear. I just wanted us out of that campsite, away from the scene of the crime. "We could go to that library you mentioned."

"The best library's closed for the summer."

"Maybe we could just do some ordinary sightseeing."

"Sightseeing's a bourgeois concept, tourism a capitalist invention." Ilona laughed impatiently. Suddenly I was glad to hear her sarcastic, light-hearted criticism. "You Americans just want to *consume* Europe."

"I'm not in *Europe*, I'm in Italy," I would say when Ilona made such remarks, but this time I kept silent. It was easier to give in to her, especially since she was coming round.

"All right, there *are* some things I could show you, I guess." Ilona smiled suddenly. I opened up the car door for her, got in and started the engine myself. While the car was idling I ran back to the tent, hid the pink laundry from sight, collected our bags and ran back to the car. What would we talk about? I wondered, remembering that Ilona had promised to show me something special in the town, but when I got in the car and asked her about it, she wouldn't tell me.

"Later," she said. "I'll save that sight for later."

Later was a better time for everything. After parking Ilona

on a picturesque terrace with a bowl of coffee for a few hours she became affectionate again, teasing and full of kind little remarks on my architectural commentary.

We found a secondhand store full of old dresses. Ilona bought a blowsy chiffon frock with poppies and chose a lilac seersucker dress for me. We teased each other about being girls, but as she tightened her belt and pirouetted in front of the mirror, her hair the color of those blazing poppies, she looked perfect.

Wearing our prizes, we retired to another terrace under the shade of a wisteria to sip Campari and view the valley beyond. Our equilibrium was back.

I had no regrets about that summer in Siena. I had learned something from Ilona. A lot of genuinely crazy people never get locked up. They make their way in the world, and make other people crazy along the way. Madness, unlike headaches, has a certain contagious quality. And craziness is compelling. Ilona was like nobody I'd ever met before. Nobody as brutal, but nobody as brilliant either.

13

That afternoon Marya came home angry. My mood hadn't improved much either. I'd done nothing but agonize, picking the scab off the painful past and watching it bleed.

The golden box was shining. I'd been polishing it for hours now, and its surface glowed with a new life even as a darker past took me over. My efforts at finding a way to open it had been stymied. I heard something move inside every time I turned it over—something lightweight and soft.

My eyes followed Marya with a guilty sadness. She went upstairs, changed into jeans and came down carrying a file and high tech engineering boots in her hands.

"I'm sorry," I said.

She sighed. "Let's just forget about it." She took a topographical wilderness map out of her pocket and unfolded it on the table. "I'm going to the McAlteer ice field tomorrow."

I stared at the colorful map, its swirling concentric circles signifying higher and higher altitudes. It made me dizzy just looking at it. Marya started filing her footfangs. As she worked away at the metal point the tips started to twinkle.

"Carbide tipped crampons," Marya muttered, holding the deadly spiked soles up to the light. "There's nothing like the feel of sinking these babies into the sheer face of an ice wall and crawling up it." She moved the file rhythmically back and forth across the teeth. "One foot at a time, balancing, pushing and then wham! Smack that ice pick into the wall and pull myself up."

"Isn't it dangerous?"

"I'll log in at the Ranger's office. I always do that when I'm free-climbing. And I'll take an avalanche beacon with me, but I know that stuff's pretty solid up there."

"Snow can melt."

"Yep. Glaciers are constantly moving. That's what makes it a challenge. But that's why I'm taking the beacon. It runs on a frequency that changes during an avalanche." She finished with one of the shoes and picked up the other one. "And I know my limits. That's what half the sport's about.

"It's the most awesome feeling, being a tiny person clinging to this enormous wall of ice. And then, when you reach the top, the view! To see those mountain peaks, to be totally alone, nobody else to rely on, to have got there with the power of your own arms and legs. It sounds hokey but you really feel at one with nature. Wonder what the view will be like from the top of McAlteer peak?" Marya took a silver flask from the dresser and stuck it in her waistband. Single malt scotch. It would be her communion at the top of the peak.

Marya got up at six. I watched her put on her long underwear. The muscles of her legs were well defined—long, confident bulges clearly visible through the knitted material. Then she pulled on the fluffy polyester jacket that would hold most of her body heat while she pulled herself up the face of the mountain, and a pair of bright blue Gortex pants. The matching parka was waiting downstairs.

"I'll stay," I said to her. A pale winter sunlight made its way through the clouds, the first sun I'd seen in Montana. Marya looked so young. The early light made her features seem small, childlike, and her dark hair framed her face like a polished mahogany frame. "I'll stay with you at least through my semester break. I'll consider applying for a sabbatical."

"You will? Oh, darling! I'm so happy!" Marya hugged me hard.

"There will be conditions."

I watched her willing face, her bright blue Gortex pants shining like the tail of a mermaid child, or a woman who could make her way up a frozen wall of rock.

"I'll need a computer."

"Yes, money's no problem," she said quickly.

"Something simple. With a standard Hayes-compatible modem, 2400 baud rate. And a subscription to fifteen state-of-the-art information retrieval services."

"I really appreciate this," she said. "I know it's a sacrifice. I know it's rearranging your life."

"Maybe it's just a good idea to stay." I reached out a hand to touch her cheek. The blisters on my palms were healing nicely.

"I'll do anything I can to make it bearable."

"I don't want to make it bearable, Marya. I want to make it creative. Sweetheart, there are databases that could link me with a world of libraries. And maybe I can get a piece of work started and finished here. With occasional field trips to get material."

"Fine. I'll fund anything."

"Friends?"

"Yes, friends. Let's fly friends up for the weekend. What the hell!"

I explained the rest of my conditions. Trips back to the Bay Area. Research jaunts.

And other things I wouldn't mention to Marya.

"It's yours," Marya smiled. "Now I'd better get going. Don't want to be up there when the sun goes down!" She gave me another kiss. It was wonderful making her so happy. Almost as happy as seeing the view from the top of a big ice wall. I needed to think about the future, not the past.

Montana with Marya and my own computer network! I

wouldn't be isolated. I would roam the databases, harvest millions of units of information. I wouldn't be alone. I'd be online.

Besides, I knew just the project. It was downstairs on the kitchen table, containing holy hair or a bit of blessed bone.

It wouldn't be easy to get the background, but there had to be a story behind the little box and how it got here. Works of artistic merit or historical significance often weren't insured or catalogued, and didn't get reported as missing when they were stolen. There was a wealth of treasure scattered about in unexpected places. Why not here? And why not in my possession?

The whole subject of ownership of antiquities and religious objects was legally hazy. The endless looting after World War II, the constant clandestine marketing of objects to collectors who fancied such items for their own personal reasons, the massive forgeries that had taken place since the Crusades to satisfy a greedy public. These elements would make my hunt delectably difficult and I could lose myself in what I did best. Research. Even Ilona had been amazed at my ability to accumulate data.

I heard Marya downstairs gathering up the last of her equipment. The front door slammed and then the car engine turned over and softened to an idle. I wouldn't mind being left alone for a day. Except for the briefest of glances I hadn't examined Rebecca's room yet.

And, to be truthful, I was also staying *because* of Rebecca. I wanted to know everything about her. When had she ever left this house? When had anyone come to visit? How had a Quattrocento antique gotten here anyway? I had a funny feeling about Rebecca and her house. And why I was here. Perhaps Marya was destined for my future, but Rebecca was the one who would release me from my past.

14

That morning when I went downstairs the house was somehow different. The saintly figures looked inviting, pleased that I had decided to keep them company. I knew their stories and smiled at their happy faces.

I picked up the Saint Lucy which had so attracted my interest on that first night. I tapped a spoon against it. Glazed porcelain, but not from a mold. And this Lucy even had biceps.

There was more to Rebecca than met the eye. I'd just seen her bedroom briefly. A metal cupboard, tightly stretched bedcovers over a thin metal frame. Today I would make that my project.

I heard a noise outside on the road. I hadn't expected any visitors. Company wouldn't come to call on the survivors of a cranky religious hermit, I thought. But I was wrong.

A car door slammed, splitting the nippy morning air. It was a heavy car door and it made an announcing noise, the way official car doors do.

A willowy female figure emerged from a vehicle emblazoned with a county seal. Somewhere she would be carrying a replica of that seal, on a business card or even a badge, and I wouldn't mind asking her for it either.

Slowly the woman made her way up the snowy path. She was thin, wearing a navy blue wool cape which flapped in the wind and nipped at her elbows. A small cloche tried to dominate her angular face and failed. Large skinny feet in galoshes spread the slush on the sidewalk and she scowled. Her expression was vaguely familiar and discomforting.

She hesitated when she saw me behind the glass window of the front door, almost slipping on the walk as she broke her stride. Then she looked at her feet and concentrated more carefully as she made her way to the door.

She had dark, sunken eyes and a curving nose protruding between angular cheekbones. Wisps of black hair escaped from a short veil underneath her hat.

I realized with a shock that she was probably Marya's age; the dated clothing and pinched expression just made her look years older. I opened the door.

"I didn't know if anyone would be here," she said, explaining her surprise. "As there was no car in the driveway, I thought I'd just leave a note or something—"

"I work at home," I said simply.

"Glad to meet you." She plunged her hand into a breast pocket of her cape and came out with a thick wallet. From between stacks of credit cards and an archive of family photos she came up with a business card. I didn't have time to read anything but "Sweetwater County" before she snapped it closed.

"Helen Danroy, county nurse." Her voice was gruff and spoke of too much cigarette smoke. "Mind if I come in?" She didn't wait for an answer, but with a fast smile and fancy footwork she was inside. She stood on one foot and then the other, taking off her galoshes which left little puddles of gray water on the floor. She was busy looking around, her neck twisting around in the collar of the cape. I helped her off with it and saw a London designer label on the inside.

Underneath, a well-tailored gray wool suit gave her an air of importance. This was no uniform—the box jacket was hand-stitched all around the collar and the lapels. Her hands sparkled with antique rings.

"How're you taking to God's Country?" she asked, her eyes deep and dark as they traveled quickly over the rooms, taking in the cheap Annunciation print, the Stations of the Cross, the mantelpiece with its puddles of wax, frozen in some earlier moment of devotion, and Mary with her truncated neck above the waxy offerings.

"Like it? Oh, great. Just fine," I said. I didn't like the way she was looking around, assessing the estate.

The kitchen! The little box glimmered on the table there. I didn't want the curious nurse to see it.

"Please, have a seat," I guided her firmly to the Laz-E-Boy recliner and practically pushed her into it. It reclined too quickly, forcing her almost flat on her back, from which position she stared at the glitterless stalactite ceiling, her feet waving in the air.

"I'll go and make tea," I said, moving quickly into the kitchen. I snatched up one of Rebecca's thin old dishtowels and wrapped the golden box in it, secreting it in a cupboard over the stove. Then I took the kettle and filled it with water.

The county nurse was busy trying to get the chair upright again. I let her struggle. She was probably dripping sweat inside that wool suit. I fussed with the cups and saucers in the kitchen until I heard a screech of metal on metal that meant she'd managed to spring herself out. By the time I'd returned she was wandering around the room, fingering some of the books I'd put out.

"I never liked recliners," she said, flipping the pages of an old text, snapping the paper. *"Religious Gothic Art of the Thirteenth Century, Butler's Revised, Updated and Concise Lives of the Saints,"* she read out aloud. *"Nouveaux Mélanges D'Archeologie et D'Histoire."* I was shocked by the accuracy of her French accent.

She fingered the tissue over a frontispiece. I caught her staring at a lascivious Venus, and her black eyes seemed to glitter.

"Yes, the most comfortable chair in the house. But perhaps

a bit dangerous for drinking tea. How about the dining room?"
I held my hand out and the woman strode over to the table.

We each pulled back a hardback chair and sat in it. I poured
the steaming liquid into chipped cups with silver rims.

"So you're Miss Cascia's niece?" She stared at me with her
dark eyes over the rim of the teacup. "Mind if I smoke?" But she
didn't wait for an answer to either question. She reached inside
her skirt pocket and pulled out a soft pack of Marlboros encased
in a simple black leather box. The woman went to a lot of trouble
not to carry a purse.

She cupped the cigarette as if she were in a strong wind, lit
it with a pink lighter and leaned back on the first puff as though
she owned the place.

"May I ask how you knew Rebecca?" I said.

"Miss Cascia had the kind of health problems that so many
elderly have in this county," the nurse began in a deep sing-song
voice, blowing a smoke ring.

"Miss Cascia was especially solitary," I confirmed.

"Of course that exacerbated many of her conditions," she
went on, as though she was reading out of a textbook. Her words
rode my way on a stream of smoke.

"What kind of conditions?"

"Oh, usual things, you know. Heart condition. Blood pressure."

"I didn't know she was under a doctor's care—"

"Not directly. She could have used some help around this
place, though." Helen Danroy's dark eyes had Egyptian kohl
eyeliner applied to the inside rim of the lower lid as well as the
upper, like two black holes in her face.

"Yes, no one seemed to know if the poor old woman was
dead or alive," I said.

"No one seemed to care." Danroy's voice rose but she
stopped her words with another puff. "God bless her soul, I
guess maybe she liked it that way."

"Yes, a hermit by choice. All this religious junk seems weird
and a little crazy, to me," I half laughed, half coughed on her
smoke.

"A good soul, a kind soul," Helen corrected me.

"How often were you here?" I asked.

"Not often enough," she sat up straight again, as if reminded of her mission. "Fortunately a health care system, not entirely stripped of funds, managed to send someone out here once a week to check up on her." She looked up at me with her dark, strong eyes. She sounded like an odd mix of Boston and Billings. I found it hard to escape from her gaze.

Then she leaned back and, with some trouble, crossed her legs. Although thin, her legs were strong, and she clutched her teaspoon like a pipe wrench. These country women were tough. Even her voice was sinewy, I thought, as I wondered what other skills she had besides nursing.

I smiled and leaned back, more relaxed. Now I thought I knew what I was dealing with. Prairie nurse and survival model. I smiled to myself, but the nurse noticed and it took her off guard. Ranch women, women of the American West have always had their own businesses and ranches, whether inherited from fathers, mothers or husbands. There has always been a population of strong, highly capable females under that big sky, equipped with skills considered as masculine in the big city. I thought I saw that heritage in Helen's face and body language.

She moved her gaze from my sudden smile and I saw her look at the plaster shards, the shattered remnants of saints stuck under the cupboards where I hadn't been able to reach them and sweep them up. I wondered what she was thinking as she looked at the dusty bits of colorful plaster. She was a county nurse, after all. An accident in the home? Domestic violence?

"Everything okay around here?" she asked, breaking the silence, her skinny foot making circles in the air.

"Sure. Fine. So, tell me something about Rebecca Cascia."

"There's not much to tell. Tell me about yourself. Always interested in how outsiders find Billings."

"It's beautiful country."

"You home much during the day?"

"Yes. May I ask what the purpose of this visit is, Miss—?"

I caught her glance and her ring at the same moment, "Ms. Danroy."

She grimaced and uncrossed her legs and leaned forward, stubbing out her cigarette in the ashtray. Her hands engulfed the little teacup and then she began the speech she'd apparently come to make.

"You must understand that the Public Health Department has gone out of its way to find relatives of our senior citizens who desperately need care."

"Apparently the lawyers had trouble even locating the heir to the estate," I concurred.

"You know, having all these kinds of service supplied by the state is something we rather frown on here. We like to pitch in to help neighbors and family out in these parts."

Cut the violins, Ms. Danroy, I thought, and get on with it.

"Ms. Danroy," I took a breath, "I don't mean to be rude but I'm sure you don't want to spend any more precious taxpayers' money taking the time to interview an out-of-state relation. Now, please, if you have any business here, come to the point."

"I just wanted to see the place again. I wanted to see who had—well, who her relation was."

So it was personal. "How close were you to Miss Cascia?" I asked. It was the right question. She hesitated, sighed and looked around for a moment.

"You don't know anything about her last months? The last years?" Her voice trembled.

I shook my head.

"I came here every week," her quiet tones sounded almost pious. "Why, I washed those sores on her feet. You know old folks—they just don't heal." She shook her head and clucked and took in several deep sighs. She looked at a chip on Rebecca's teacup. She was waiting for a response.

"I see."

"No, you don't see."

Oh, God! I thought. Is she going to tell me something really spooky about the wounds on Rebecca's feet that wouldn't heal?

"It's difficult when you lose a client, and then relatives, who should have been on the scene for months, even years—" her voice caught in her throat. "When you're the one giving all that kind of personal attention and strangers only show up to collect the goods later on." She didn't look at me. The goods! So that's what it was about.

"Listen, it took the lawyers two months to find the heir." I sounded defensive, even to myself. Was I now feeling guilty about Marya's money?

"Well, Miss Cascia needed care, and I provided it. I rubbed ointment into her shoulders, I did her dishes," the nurse continued.

She had a point there. I watched her well-manicured hands play with the teacup. No cuticles and no nailpolish either. But how could she possibly know about the inheritance?

"And did her laundry," she finished. I looked over at her hands, nervously fingering the teacup. Reaching into the black leather case, she pulled out another cigarette and lit it.

"Perhaps a small personal memento . . ." she said, looking up at me and blowing smoke straight in my eyes.

I was immediately ashamed of myself. So that was what it had been about.

"Of course, I'm so sorry," I said, thankful that she wasn't asking for money. I probably would have insulted her anyway by mentioning a figure—someone with such perfectly mani-cured hands. "We all appreciate your work." I tried for graceful, rounded tones. "Please, would you like to choose something? I'm afraid there isn't too much left." I thought about all the scattered shards of saints, the sickly reproductions of Mary. The nurse just sat there, waiting.

"How about in her bedroom?" she said.

"I haven't really gone through her things up there," I objected.

"All the more reason to take a look now," she went on. "Perhaps there's some special item which would remind me of Miss Cascia. Something I'm sure she would have liked me to have." She smiled.

"Well, then, let's go upstairs, shall we?" I sighed.

The nurse rose, hesitated and stretched for a moment. I noticed her belt hung loosely from her hips. Her forearms were hairless—unusual for such a dark woman. She must have them waxed, I decided.

She let me go first, but at the landing I stopped and made her walk in front of me. At the top of the house she stood for a moment, perhaps remembering her former, unpleasant nursing duties.

"To the left," I said, and watched as she placed a hand on the doorknob leading to Rebecca's room.

I took a breath as she pulled the door open, expecting some warning—a shower of glitter, an exploding water heater. But instead a welcoming atmosphere seemed to draw us in.

The plank floor was painted a cream color and a bed with a white woven bedspread seemed to shine in the sunlight. A painted cigar box and a silent selection of saints stood on the nightstand, and a metal cupboard stood against one wall with a hexagonal hatbox on top of it.

"Would you like one of these, uh, figurines?" I asked, but Ms. Danroy was making her way to the metal cupboard, which served as a wardrobe.

"Wait, I haven't looked in there—" I said as I watched her open the doors. A few dark garments hung inside but Helen Danroy was examining a large cardboard box at the bottom.

"She always said she wanted me to have those rosaries," she explained. "She *told* me I could have them. They must be in here somewhere," she went on, her hand moving inside the box, feeling in the corners.

"Yes, well, I'll certainly let you know—" I said, leaning over and putting the lid back on the box, nearly catching her hand in it.

"Just a lot of old clothes," she said, pulling on the door to raise herself. "You're very kind," she stood up hastily, her ankles twisting, and she stumbled. Grabbing one of the flimsy metal doors to steady herself, the whole cupboard tilted, ready to rain all its contents on our heads. I looked up, relieved to see that no heavy plaster saints were roosting on the top.

Only a hexagonal hatbox, feather-light, shifted and slid toward us as the cupboard righted itself. But the box continued to fall, to fly as if in slow motion. It soared across the room, its lid coming off and releasing from within a tumble of golden red and yellow strands. Human hair, a lot of it, long and slightly curly, just like Ilona's.

15

"Are you feeling all right?" asked the nurse, and I wondered if her cape downstairs held smelling salts. She seemed surprised by the hair as well. She was leaning over the bed, running her hands along the perfumed curls. She turned around to me and stretched out a bony hand.

"Yeah, I'm fine," I said, refusing her help. "No, I'm all right really. It's just *hair* after all." I stood up straight.

"Why the hell did she have all this hair?" I said aloud to no one in particular, grabbing the curls from underneath the nurse's fingers, stuffing the long tendrils quickly back into the box and catching strands on my nails.

"Old ladies save funny things," she said.

I worked quickly, worried that the sweet smell would linger on my hands. The nurse was staring at me, those dark deep eyes looking surprised.

"So, do you want anything here?" I tried for a normal tone, extracting a long pale hair from a ragged cuticle on my finger. "I'm afraid the legacy is rather limited," I sounded hysterical even to myself. "Mostly just a lot of weird religious junk." I pushed the lid back on the box with such force that the lower portion crumpled.

"You sure you're okay?" she asked, but her concern was false. She held the painted cigar box in her hands and was looking inside it.

"I haven't looked in there either, Ms. Danroy—"

"Well, no rosaries in here." She frowned and snapped the lid shut and walked with me to the door and toward the stairs.

"You're okay now?" she asked again at the top of the landing. "You sure you're okay?"

"Yes, yes. I'll let you know if I find any rosaries."

"Okay," she smiled and we started walking downstairs. "It's a pity we didn't know you were around when she was so sick," she started up again. I sighed. How to get rid of her? "Now, if we had known that you were her heir—" she continued as we reached the bottom of the stairs.

"But I'm not."

"You're not?" Her thin dark brows knotted.

"I never said I was."

"Well, then—"

"The heir, Marya Gibbons, is away for the day."

"So what are you—"

"I'm her companion," I said, and watched that settle in. "I'm her good friend." The nurse raised her eyebrows. "Her lover," I finished.

I looked for signs of recognition, but her face was closed for business.

Well, I thought, Marya wasn't coming out to anybody but she didn't say that I couldn't Besides, this woman looked a bit dykey. I could do my own missionary work here on the prairie. I picked a long red hair off my sweater.

"Do you plan to stay, now that Miss Cascia has gone?" she asked. Was she being neighborly, I wondered, or interested?

"We like it here," I lied. "It will do for a while."

"I wouldn't think Billings would be your kind of place," she looked at me intently.

"Nobody's sent out the welcome wagon, but we haven't met any vigilantes either."

"Surely this kind of quiet life doesn't seem much fun? I mean, the big cities—wouldn't that be more suited to you?" she said drily.

To people like you, was what she meant, I thought. "The solitude is useful for my work." I was getting irritated.

"And what *is* your work exactly?" Her sudden disapproving tone made me realize I'd made a mistake. Her look wasn't dykey at all. It was something else. Something unpleasant.

"I'm a historian."

"A historian, really?" Her tone went up as her eyes went up and down. I was apparently full of surprises. "What kind of history would you be interested in?"

"Courtesans of the Renaissance," I said, remembering a paper I'd written with Ilona's help. Those Northern Italian women with the long pale hair posing as Venus, Mary and Leda. The nurse was staring at me, as if I was something she'd never imagined before. A big-city-educated queer.

"Do you mean whores? What's so special about that?"

"It's erotic, Ms. Danroy. That's what it is. A real turn-on. But it's also a lot of work, so if you don't mind—" I finished, fetching her cape from the living room and opening it up so she could slip her arms inside. She nearly yanked it out of my hands instead.

The bell rang. We both walked to the door. The shape that loomed in the window was large and male.

"Plumber," the lined old face said. That's what the red pickup truck parked at the end of the walk said too. He took out a card from his wallet and I squinted at it. It confirmed that he was a plumber. A lot of locals were testing my eyesight today.

"Come in," I looked over at the nurse and back at him. His skin was ruddy from the elements.

"Hot in here," he remarked, shrugging off his jacket and draping it across the dining room chair. "Only been in here a few times myself. That Miss Cascia always tried to do everything herself."

"Yes, very sprightly," confirmed the nurse, perhaps more relaxed now that a man was in the room.

"No, that's not what I mean," he corrected her. "I mean she fixed up this place all by herself." We all looked at the crooked flooring, the mismatched vinyl.

"You mean she did all this—renovation work—by herself?" I asked.

"Yep, floors and everything."

"Even the paneling?" I looked over at the eight-foot-long panels of wood-print formica underneath the Madonna prints. The nails along the edges hadn't been countersunk. They made a silver studded line at all the edges, where insulation showed through.

"Yes, that too," he confirmed. "With that Parkinson's, it got pretty hard for her to handle a Skil saw, but she never stopped tryin'."

"She had Parkinson's disease?" I turned to the nurse.

"Yes," the nurse confirmed, head bobbing up and down. "I'd better be going." She bent over and started to pull on her galoshes.

"I'll see you to your car," I offered, hoping to hurry her out. "You wait here," I commanded the eager plumber. But with a few quick steps the nurse was out of the door. She didn't need an escort.

"Goodbye, Ms. Danroy!" I called and she turned round once to wave as she ploughed through the slush to her car, off to another elderly patient, hopefully still warm.

"Lead me to your plumbing problem, lady—there isn't an overflow valve I can't fix in thirty seconds."

"It's not that," I said. "It's the water heater, down in the cellar." I pointed toward the kitchen. "It practically blew up on me the other day."

"What happened?" he asked.

"I was down in the cellar and it just about exploded. Seems to be okay now. The water's pretty damn hot though."

"I'll check the cellar," he said and disappeared below.

I stood there in the hallway, surveying the house. So Rebecca had tarred and feathered the place all by herself. And saved a box of very old, very red, hair.

Parkinson's. The nurse hadn't mentioned that, but then I had misread her entirely. I was already so desperate for company that I was turning the most ordinary, boring heterosexuals into potential friends and allies, I thought. Then I realized what Helen Danroy reminded me of. The Salvation Army. How depressing.

I heard a noise. The plumber was behind me.

"You missed your calling," I said. "You could have been a cat burglar."

"I know. My mother said I was the quietest kid of the bunch. I was a bookworm. Don't know what went wrong, though. Just became a plumber, I guess."

He eyed the front door. "Just going out to check the gas meter," he said, opening the door and taking a deep breath.

"Hey, it's really warm outside." I stepped onto the front porch and looked around. Icicles were melting with a steady drip from the gutters and snow was falling in big clumps from the trees.

"Chinook. That wind," said the plumber, bobbing his head at clouds bearing down from the north.

"But it must be sixty degrees!" I protested.

"Yep, that's the way it happens. Comes down from Canada and before you know it, in twenty minutes it can go up twenty degrees." He turned toward me and waved his pipe wrench at the sky.

I left him to his work, went back to the kitchen and opened the cellar door. I thought about what a clean-up job it would be. Should I offer the nurse Rebecca's tacky Madonna on a chain? I realized I didn't even have her number.

The plumber came back in, shaking his head and holding out his big red hand toward me. I squinted at what lay there. On his palm were little metal filings.

"Good thing you've got all this holy company," he said, waving a hand at all the Virgin Marys on the wall. "I don't hold truck with this kind of stuff, but you've got a guardian angel floating around here somewhere." He looked at the filings in his hand and pushed them closer to my face. The metal came into focus as I peered at them.

"Someone's been messing with the pressure on your gas meter, little lady," he explained. "I'll bet you can make tea straight out of the tap. Why, you've got so much gas pressure going in there I'm surprised this place hasn't shot straight through the clouds, just like something out of Cape Canaveral."

16

I sat there in the aftermath of his pronouncement, after paying him, after thanking him and after listening for a while to how lucky I was not to be scourged alive by the appliance. I was patient with the plumber. It was his way of making his work important. His work *was* important. The amenities of modern life are important and deadly. He didn't want me to forget it.

"By the way, looks like you've got a little leak upstairs in the bathroom," he said, hesitating, swaying in front of me. "Want me to take a look?"

"Okay. Go on." I went and stood by a window for a while. I felt some sunlight through the plastic and a little fresh air. A headache was coming on and I thought about a nap. The plumber was still upstairs. I didn't want him to reinvent the toilet so I mounted the stairs, wondering what he was fixing.

He was standing in the doorway of our room. I crept up behind him. His hand was moving inside our dresser drawer.

Marya's bra was slung across the bedpost. Panties probably littered one side of the bed or the other. Or both, I thought.

"Do you mind?" I asked.

"Oh, sorry! Thought maybe some of the pipes from the bathroom ran through this room. If they run outside, you know, there's always the danger of freezing—"

"Well, if they were in my chest of drawers they wouldn't freeze, would they?"

"No. I guess not, heh! heh!" He kept his eyes fixed on my face. "I'm goin', I'm goin'," he said, turning and sauntering down the stairs. He took his time putting away his tools, and I waited at the front door till he had gone. Halfway down the path, he stopped. "Just keep your curtains closed at night!" he remarked. I slammed the door and wished I had a pipe wrench, too.

New locks for the house. After all, maybe he kept keys from former jobs. And he had worked for Rebecca. But Rebecca had done a lot of the work on the house herself.

Could she smell an evil plumber the way Saint Catherine the Astonishing did? Catherine levitated when she smelled sin, but that was in the thirteenth century.

I was glad it was a sunny day. The locals were too much for me. I went into the kitchen and walked to the sunlit window, where light streamed in over the sink. Bright rays filled the nurse's teacup. Now, *there* was an odd character, I thought.

I was so absorbed in the memory of my recent visitors that I hadn't realized I'd been staring out of the window. The window that offered a view of the enclosed garden. White lumpy shapes, probably bushes that had been hidden under the snow.

But now the white blanket had vanished. The warm Chinook winds had melted all the snow off what was Rebecca's great accomplishment. I gripped the edge of the sink and stared. This was the garden where Marya had been forbidden to play the day she'd visited her Aunt Rebecca. And now I knew why Rebecca had kept her out.

"Oh, my God!" I gasped, running to the kitchen door, drawn by the sight that had been waiting under the drifting snow. I pushed at the rusty hinges until the door gave way and opened. I stepped into the sunlight and the slush, into the scene that Rebecca had created.

There, all around me, were lifesize statues—an entire colony of women in stone. These were no white Florentine ideals—they were stately figures, poured out of cement and covered with colorful pieces of glass, shells, semiprecious stones, a rainbow of minerals and mother-of-pearl, even car chrome. Porcelain faces looked about joyously, smiling at each other and at the wild costuming they'd been assigned.

A massive figure of a woman in a flowing gown of green pearlized malachite headed the flock. "Saint Hildegarde" was spelled out in bright coral mosaic along the diagonal fold of her gown. She held a book under her arm and a sort of pipe wrench in the other hand. Hildegarde was a medieval plumber and published author, circa 1179. "A half-forgotten memory of a primitive state which we have lost since Eden . . ." read the inscription at her feet. "A bridge of holiness between this world and the world of beauty."

An ancient aesthete. Oh, Rebecca—that was how she'd spent her time here. I suddenly saw hers as a life of joyful creativity. What celebration there was in this work! Her happiness had formed Hildegarde's features, shaping those cheeks and giving her those iridescent feldspar eyes.

I hurried over to the next figure. Saint Teresa Couderc had opened a hostel for women pilgrims. She was leaning on a miniature mountaintop which supported her strong, sturdy frame. She must have been hardy. The hostel was at four thousand feet. I stood close to her and saw that her eyes were not just blue; they were real lapis lazuli.

Teresa stood, as the others did, on a raised pedestal on an irregularly shaped plateau. Next to her, Saint Clare of Assisi held the *ostensorium*—the monstrance containing the Holy Sacrament. She held the serpentine vessel boldly in front of her. This was how she had saved her sister nuns from the Saracens. She thrust the object forward into space, her muscled bare arms extending out from her habit.

I ran my fingers over the cold stone. The mark of the chisel was on her brow and mouth; Clare's face was quartz granite, bold with resolution, fury and force.

Next, Saint Bridget, an aristocratic rôle model for female

academics. In her Order, men were subject to the abbess in all temporal matters and each religious could have as many books for study as he or she pleased. A few hibernating rose bushes tangled in the tapestry of her clothes—a kind of brocade composed of jade and coral, shot with an occasional vein of silver.

I jumped. A woman was working in the garden. Among the withered tomato vines a thin figure was hunched over, as if tending the dead plants. So lifelike was she in her twisted stooping that I hesitated before approaching her. Lying at her feet were beautiful tapestries and sculpted baskets holding all manner of sewing notions—pincushions made of porcelain, real silver needles and buttons of lapis spilled out onto a miraculous marble fabric, dotted with garnet and festooned with flowering agate, their density carved into the softness of velvet.

"Oh, shit!" I gasped. The woman who was busy at work had something horribly wrong with her face. The sculptor had gone to a lot of trouble to inlay red granite to depict a skin disease. "Saint Rose of Lima," I read. I shuddered as the wind grew cooler. This would be Rebecca's role model—a woman with a disfigured face.

Another odd sight. A whole cluster of tiny, forbidding nuns, pointing their finger at a larger figure, laid out, arms extended, her body entombed in an anthracite habit, her face pushed into the dirt. "Saint Teresa of Avila," I read. She was being tried by miniature Nuns of Incarnation.

"I will not have you converse with men but with angels" was written across her back. Not a bad idea. Her hands had been decorated with thousands of tiny wings, abalone shell, which sparkled with the remnants of snow caught in the miniscule feathers.

At the end of the garden, her back against the wall, sat a throned figure. Her massive face spoke of great authority. Out of her right hand emerged tiny loaves of bread, while with her left hand she stroked the sweating brows of fevered supplicants. She was smiling. It was impossible to believe that such a delicate expression could be hewn in stone. Under her feet lay a pile of books, and furious, tiny scribes who gazed up at her, not daring to rest their pens as long rolls of paper flowed out upon the ground where crocuses and tulips would rise in the spring.

I sat down on the stone bench, handcarved out of a hardwood treetrunk, and ran my fingers over the seashell armrests. The figures in front of me, these large, bold women, standing on concrete floes holding the symbols of their accomplishments, were almost like a family. Rebecca hadn't lived alone after all.

It was at that moment that I realized Rebecca had hardly any male saints in her house. Best of all, there were no crosses, no crucifixes of bleeding Jesuses anywhere on the property.

I started laughing and the big stone women didn't seem to mind. They just went about their business—gardening, baking, dictating, plumbing, and defending, the snow melting off them by the minute.

As I stood there surrounded by Rebecca's complete gallery I realized what the conditional bequest had meant. No one would want to make this mark on the world and have it remain undiscovered. Or unpreserved. And who better to leave it to than the only living female unmarried relative, who had wanted so badly to go out into the garden in the first place. Marya.

"Oh, my God!" I cried, a thought suddenly striking me. I looked at the mountains in the distance. Who would have thought that snow would melt so fast? Was Marya stuck somewhere halfway up the face of the mountain, her ice-axe giving way as she dangled a thousand feet above a snowdrift? I'd forgotten about her, the excitement of discovery erasing my concern. What was the name of that peak? Why hadn't Marya given me the number of the Ranger Station?

"Hey what's this?" came a voice from the back door. I breathed a sigh of relief. It was Marya herself. Safely shimmering in her blue gortex suit, she joined the bejeweled statuary.

"Marya, thank God you're home! I was so worried—"

"Hell. I was off there when that warm wind came up. But I'll tell you I'm glad I started early. It was gorgeous at the top—" Marya stopped as she glanced about her. "What's all this?"

"It's beautiful, don't you see? This is what Rebecca did with her life. It's wholly original, it's *retablo*—the art of making personal shrines. Your aunt was incredible! This goes beyond anything I've ever seen. What a talent! How did she afford to make all this stuff? Look at this—lapis, coral, opal!"

"Hmm." Marya stretched her arms up and then bent down and touched her toes.

"What did you find out about her bank accounts anyway?" I asked.

"She made one large withdrawal in 1926, right before the crash," Marya said, walking over to Saint Teresa where she lay face down in the dirt. "Lucky for her, I guess. Ten thousand dollars."

"Must have been a fortune back then."

"Yes, must've been. This is really weird!" Marya squinted at Teresa's abalone-inlaid hands.

"Was that how she got into mineral rights?"

"I suppose so," she said. "It's not clear, actually. The properties she holds rights on weren't transferred into her name until after the War. Title search doesn't reveal any properties she bought before 1946, so it's unclear how she acquired those rights. She must have paid cash. Or perhaps she invested the ten thousand dollars in something and then turned it over some twenty years later and we just can't find the record." Marya took the silver flask from her waistband and raised it. She tilted her head back and the bright metal flashed in the sun. I saw for a moment the golden glimmer of single malt scotch between her lips.

"And Italy?" I asked, thinking of the little box stowed away in the cupboard.

"Who knows? A fluke?" she replied. "Who cares?"

"I care. And you should care too."

"Don't tell me what to do, you hag of hagiography!" She laughed, leaning against Saint Bridget, who started to sink into the wet ground under her weight. "Come here and kiss me instead." I did as she said. Our lips were cold and fumes rode on Marya's breath.

Afterwards she gave Bridget a good shove and the statue wobbled uncertainly in the soil. She took another gulp of scotch.

"Blasphemy or bust!" she cried, and with a final push, Saint Bridget fell, one shoulder and one hip embedded in the earth.

"Why the hell did you do that?"

"It feels like spring. Listen, there's two sides to the Nun's Story. Most of the really holy nuns were a bunch of anorexics. Their biggest pride was to live on the Eucharist. For years! Nothing was more holy than eating a cracker a day and drifting off comatose into some ecstacy. It was pathological. Sick. Anorexia nervosa."

"Anorexia miriblis was different," I argued. "Just because the same behavior occurs at different times in history, in different places doesn't mean it has the same psychological explanation."

"Sure, have it your way. Hey, what about a little mortification on a daily basis? Sleep on the ground? Better yet, how about foregoing pillows and using an iron grate! That's what Saint Clare did. Those women didn't need to get married to get beaten up. The Holy Church would just convince them to do it to themselves!"

"Yeah, I know, but the artistry that came out of those feelings—"

"And the misery!" Marya rolled her eyes at the sky. "Marvelous! And there's no racial integrity. All the Italian saints had blonde hair and blue eyes. Ever see a Semitic Mary! It's just a racial supremacist death cult!"

"There's black Madonnas up and down the Mediterranean. But that's not the point here. Don't you see? Look around you, Marya! This is the legacy that was meant for you. I think this is the reason for the conditional bequest."

"Hmm. I guess you have something there." Marya closed her eyes and took another swig of scotch. When she opened them again she seemed more thoughtful. "Yeah, I remember how the old lady said goodbye to me that one afternoon I met her. Mom and I sitting in the parlor and I kept wanting to jump up and play with all the dolls. The Virgins. I'd never seen little statues before."

" 'Let her touch them,' Aunt Rebecca had said. She had a really deep voice. It made her seem creepier, that voice coming from a face totally destroyed by her scar. Then she took one of the Virgin Marys down from the mantelpiece and let me play with it. I was disappointed. I couldn't take her clothes off."

"And then what?"

"You know how scary it is for a child when adults want a certain kind of attention from you and you don't know what they want but you know it's a really important moment for them? Rebecca pulled me close to her just as we left. I remember my face up against that scar. Her cheek felt warm, tight and hard." Marya took another quick drink from the silver bottle.

"Then I felt my mother's hands on my back. I knew it was okay what was happening. At the same time I felt as though I was outside all of us. I could see my mother, her hands on my back, and Rebecca squeezing me in my little blue overalls, still clutching a Mary doll. It's just sort of frozen there, like a picture of us. It's the only picture I've got."

"It's a wonderful picture."

"Thanks for helping me remember it."

"It's why Rebecca gave you this garden, you know."

"Yeah, well—nuns and saints. You can have 'em. If you like, you can be curator."

"You're on!" I smiled. Marya and I would have a happy division of labor. I could be culture and she could be sports. And more in that royal blue spandex gear she had on.

"Let's go upstairs," she said, putting a wet scotch-laced tongue into my mouth and running her hands possessively over my body.

"Here, give me a taste of that stuff," I said, grabbing her flask. I wasn't actually all that thirsty; Marya was beautiful, and desirable, but I knew I was drinking in self-defense.

Afterwards we lay warm together on our bed upstairs. It had jiggled and threatened to collapse with every plunge of my fingers inside Marya—a frantic love-making that hid my lack of concentration. My mind was still in the garden as she lay quietly in my arms.

"Sweet darling, I found something I'd forgotten in the glove compartment," she said. "Wait a second—it's just downstairs."

She jumped out of the narrow bed, threw a blanket around herself and ran downstairs, returning moments later with a weatherbeaten old guide to gay bars.

"You travel around with that thing?"

"Sure. Never know when I might need to crawl out of the closet on a business trip."

She paged through well-thumbed entries. I noticed a few ticks in ballpoint pen. Had Marya kept a record? Was Marya a big scorer, heartbreaker at night and corporate consultant by day?

"Actually, I bought this at a rummage sale," she said, leaving me to sad fantasies about its former owner. "Look, here's an entry for a bar right here in Billings, 'The Puss 'n Boots Lounge!' Let's go!"

"Don't you think it's just going to be depressing, pointing out how isolated we are here?"

"Maybe you're right. But I bet they have a softball team," she smiled, yawning, and I remembered her proclivity for team sports. I knew she could quickly insinuate herself with a lot of well-meaning locals. They would have great wholesome fun. Maybe she would want to settle in Billings permanently.

This, the mundane everydayness devoid of glamour, was the stuff of real life. Marya had drifted off into sleep.

I looked at her and knew that I still wouldn't trade her charms and her sweet, even temperament for all the brilliant lesbian psychos roaming the planet on important academic errands. Even if they were the ones, the only ones, who really knew how to make love.

I thought again of that week in Italy, that dreadful day. My birthday. Maybe my newfound decision to stay with Marya would make it okay to remember, just for a moment.

❧ 17 ❧

Summertime, everybody's holiday, the honeymoon Ilona and I should have had. But every day got worse.

I remembered that morning, the morning Ilona wanted to make love. We had been lying on the little camping mattress, looking outside. Somehow, behind the thin privacy of our nylon tent, with a motorcycle parked about a foot from our shoulders, Ilona had wanted to make love.

I remembered how hot it was, how our dripping sweat made fresh lines through the brown dust that covered our skin.

"Come on, dear—you wouldn't let a little sweat stop you, a little public exposure?" Ilona had chided me. "It's a human urge after all." My eyes swept the campsite—the chasing children, the fat men in camp stools looking langorously about them. I leaned over and unzipped the front flap of the tent. We crouched and went inside. Why did our lovemaking have to become a political act? I thought. But I said nothing.

I remembered how I started to make love to her. I wanted us to lie apart with just fingertips touching each other in cool stripes so that a breeze would play between our bodies.

"What's the matter? A little neurotic about sweat?" Ilona teased me, but I could tell she was angry.

"I'm a tribade at heart, dear," I murmured, slowly pulling her nipple till she gasped. She let me make love the way I had wanted. We lay a foot apart on the floor of the tent, her body seeming to betray pain and anger at every moan that escaped from her mouth. Then she came, with an ear-splitting scream that I was sure would alert the entire Latin campsite.

I was aroused, holding her there—not the full body contact she had wanted, but tender, caring. When it was my turn, I moved upward to offer my breast to her soft and sometimes skillful lips.

"You slut!" she murmured with a smile that wasn't friendly. "You expect me to twist your little knobbies, don't you?" I closed out the sound of her words, knowing that her derisive tone was meant to cause pain, just when I least was able to bear it. "That's right," she chided, "just like a television set. I could change your channels whenever I want."

I had cried there on the floor of that tent, trying to stop my tears as I heard Ilona's further words. "Oh, don't be so sensitive. Stop playing the victim, for Christ's sake!"

Those words. Did she really say them? Were they as cruel as I'd thought then? I shook my head, looking at Marya and trying to banish the past once again.

The truth was Ilona had tried to convince me I was crazy. And she'd gained a small, but firm foothold in my mind, where reality seemed to stretch and sway before me.

And it was that same foothold that I trod here in Montana.

I would stay with Marya, I thought, and we would continue to make love, and it would be fine. Not the best, but more than good enough. My headache had gone.

I went to sleep and dreamed about a softball team of nurses. Their idea of a softball was a rolled-up cat, a dead one. The pitcher was Nurse Danroy and the cat was coming straight at me, claws aiming at my eyes. I woke up screaming. As Marya comforted me, stroking my back, I remembered that we weren't in Sweetwater County after all.

18

"It's women's night, by the way," Marya had said as we got into the car.

That night we went to Billings' gay bar. Except, of course, it wasn't in Billings. The Puss'n Boots lounge was an unmarked cement hotspot right in the middle of a cold industrial zone. Even with a map it was hard to find. It seemed caught in a time warp, when gay bars were known only to two groups. The queers and the cops.

And it was the kind of place that made me feel like an old queer. As Marya and I pushed open the double doors and walked under the heads of a few dead deer, I saw the familiar scene.

"You must have made a mistake," I muttered as we held hands and looked around. Dozens of men huddling together, clutching their drinks, expectant eyes straining toward a stage where I knew just what we'd see. A Latino Shirley MacLaine with size twelve feet and a Caucasian Roberta Flack dished up for the delight of other men.

"Fucking hell!" Marya mumbled as I cast about for signs of females. Twenty years ago drag bars were my lair, too, since there were always more men than women and their drinks paid the rent. Besides, there had been no alternative then. We had forged peculiar friendships in those times, before the plague or politics came into the picture.

My eyes were watering from the smoke. I could hardly make out the light bulbs on the wagon wheels suspended from the ceiling. Dead animals hung everywhere—stuffed eagles, elks and even a little mountain lion. Only someone had strung Bambi's antlers with beads and stuck false eyelashes on Bullwinkle.

Marya kissed me on the mouth. Yes, I'd forgotten why we'd come. It was to have a public place for our relationship, even if we didn't meet a single kindred spirit.

"There's got to be a women's corner around here some-where," Marya said, tugging my arm and leading me through the crowd.

"This may be all Billings has to offer in the way of gay culture."

"Stop being so negative!"

"I'm sorry—it's just the first time I've been out of the house," I explained as Marya pulled me through crowds of men, their elbows invading our ribs as they ignored the path we made through them. A Carol Channing lookalike was doing a lip-synched rendition of "Hello Dolly" and the tenor catcalls made me glad the stage was far from view.

"I miss San Francisco. None of these drag queens have beards," I said.

"What's the problem—you only take queens as cultural com-mentary?" A dapper young waiter was in front of us, balancing a martini on a tray.

"Gee! Just when was I beginning to think I was invisible," I said.

"This is really unusual," his eyes glittered. "Two women— two women from out of town! Welcome to Puss'n Boots!"

"Where's the puss?" Marya muttered.

"I know it must seem to you like a dyke desert, but there's a *lot* going on here if you know where to look!"

"You speak in riddles, but tell me. I'm dying not to guess."

"The pool room. That's the main drag that's not drag, dear. It's women's night so we clear the boys from the billiards. It's just girl city in there tonight. You'll find every woman who is, was or wants to be."

"We're just interested in the 'is'."

"My, my—aren't we undemocratic? Let me tell you about life on the plain." He leaned forward conspiratorially, shifting his hand so his drink remained upright. "We don't have any time for political correctness in Montana. Save the identity debates for the big towns you kind of girls come from—San Francisco, LA, New York. All we've got is a drag show, a pool table and a liquor license. And homosexuality is still a crime here. Why, last year they lowered the penalty for bestiality to a misdemeanor! But the Montana Penal Code 45-5-505 states that a person convicted of deviate sexual behavior with a consenting human shall be imprisoned in the state prison or fined, not to exceed $50,000."

"Are you serious?" Marya asked.

"Serious? It gets worse. 1990 laws were amended to make the penal conditions imposed, and here I quote, '. . . left entirely up to the *imagination* of the judge.' So before you slam our club I'd advise you to be glad the Puss'n Boots is here to serve you beer and we're not serving time doing it."

"Amen," I said.

He was right. It was no use looking at this place from a viewpoint cultivated in large cities, in states where our civil rights were beginning to be protected.

"We may not be hip, but we're hospitable." He sailed off and took two more orders and two gooses on his cute little behind.

"Ready to hit the pool room?" I asked Marya.

"Nice of him to be our guide," she said. We walked through the thinning crowds toward a doorway where we saw pool tables and low cones of lighting illuminating the green felt.

We entered a recognizable scene. A history of lesbian culture spread out in front of me. I read my own past in young butches with D.A.'s, polished pool cues gliding expertly through their fingers. A femme stood stationed behind each one, offering her undying loyalty.

I had been one of those femmes once, crawling into bed with women who were afraid of nothing. Or acted like they were. Jesus, I thought. It still exists. But then, why wouldn't it?

Farther along the room, a few couples were locked in embraces, the demanding hand of a baby butch clutching the hip of her girlfriend, who responded by bringing her breasts closer to the button-down oxford shirt of her woman. Then their feet would slow to a crawl across the linoleum and lips meet as Patsy Cline crooned "I Fall to Pieces."

Behind the dancers, another decade was represented by the women sitting round a table, staring into the space they had created. These were throwbacks from the sixties and seventies—lesbians scratching out an existence in the local soil. Part-time tree planters, maybe even firefighters, they looked hardy, dirty and spaced out. Or maybe they were just travelers guided by the same book that had led us here.

The baby butches would make for more interesting visits to town, I decided as I looked toward Marya, but she had gone. She was leaning on a wall next to a pay phone, studying the bulletin board.

A bulletin board! What examples of lesbian lifestyle would be pinned into that cork? I wondered as I joined her.

All manner of roommates were sought—vegetarian, separatist, professional—and there were a few requests for ranch hands. Kittens, horses and sheep were offered, plus various one-way plane tickets. A colorful magic-markered notice announced the formation of a softball team.

"Hey, this is fantastic!" Marya said.

"You could buy a great catcher's mitt with your kind of money!" I smiled wanly.

"Oh, honey, I'm not going to be catcher. Shortstop, that's

where the action's at." Then, looking at me more closely, "Watch out, you might become a softball widow! Interested in the outfield?"

I was seized with a moment of unhappiness. My interests and tastes had become so specific, my point of view so developed, I despaired that Billings would ever offer me anything more than a voyeuristic sense of history, a distanced anthropological view of the people in it.

"Or first base is a good place to start out," Marya continued.

"I doubt it."

"Jeez! You're just so negative. Our first night out on the town—"

"Billings."

"Yes, Billings. That's where we're living, remember? Sometimes that chip on your shoulder is as big as a tree. Why don't you just get over yourself." Marya's voice was rising and a few ducktails flickered our way. "Maybe you could find someone to talk to. Maybe someone even smarter than you," she added. But before I could apologize, before I could fix what had gone wrong, I did see someone to talk to. Someone in the strangest drag of all.

Looking like a spy from a B movie, dark glasses shielding her eyes and the dark hood of her overcoat pulled up over her hair, her face, even in a shadow, was familiar.

I left Marya at the bulletin board with her softball future and went over to greet Helen Danroy, county nurse.

19

"Look what the cat dragged in!" I said, sitting down on a chair opposite the smiling nurse. I looked into the kohl-lined eyes through the smoky lenses of her glasses. I smelled the smoke coming from the cigarette clamped between her thin lips. Her hands were sweating; she looked supremely uncomfortable.

"No one had to drag me," she said, leaning back and crossing her legs, one booted foot making quick circles in the air. "It's women's night, right? And this is the only queer joint in town. It's the only place for a lesbo to be."

"What's with the get-up? Afraid you're going to see someone you know?"

"I came to see you. Just being that ol' welcome wagon you mentioned."

"Cut the country bumpkin act," I said, "or learn to hide your London labels."

"I don't see why you have to be so nasty," she said, but the twang was leaving her voice with every word, and her eyes were starting to dart nervously around the room.

"Because I don't like liars. Rebecca's house isn't even in

Sweetwater County. You didn't even know she had Parkinson's."

The nurse just looked at me, her eyes getting narrower, but she never blinked.

"You did her laundry and rubbed her feet? You didn't even know where her bedroom was. I had to lead you every step of the way. You did the dishes? That woman was busy remodeling her house until the day she died. Now do you want me to call the county and turn you in for impersonating an employee?"

"We all have something to hide," she winked at me. Her hand was trembling.

"You can hide if you want but I'm out of the closet, if that's what you mean," I said, my stomach turning at her insinuating tone.

"We have to be careful here, you know," Helen glanced at me, then down at the ashtray. She took another puff on her cigarette and then looked over at Marya. I followed her gaze to the bulletin board. Two locals were sizing Marya up as a team-mate and maybe something more. I was wondering about Helen Danroy myself. She was playing with her hood, pulling it farther over her face.

"Is there somewhere we can be alone? Let's go outside," Helen said. "I'll meet you in the carpark."

"Getting hot under the collar?"

"I want to talk to you."

"What about?"

"Topics of mutual interest."

"Okay, let's go outside. You won't be ashamed to be seen with me there."

Then the phony nurse rose, smoothing out her well-tailored tweed pants. The front pleats were stitched all the way down to her black city boots.

"Who's ashamed of who?" I asked, but she did a quick turn and disappeared. I glanced over at Marya, who had either forgotten about me or was freezing me out for a while. I decided it didn't matter. I'd make it up to her later. I left the pool room, following Helen Danroy through the male landscape out into the parking lot.

Outside, all was deserted between the cars. I looked over the bright metallic finish of several four-wheel jeeps and pickup trucks. Finally I saw her, leaning against the side of her own car.

I walked toward her and saw her stiffen as I came closer. Her hands were in her pockets but as I came into the narrow corridor between the two vehicles she slowly took them out. She was wearing brown leather insulated gloves.

"You can take off the dark glasses now," I reassured her. "Nobody will recognize you out here. The carpark is deserted." I clapped my arms against my sides to keep warm.

"Let's get in my car," she said.

"No, that's okay, I enjoy the outdoors," I said. The temperature would keep our conversation short. "I just want an explanation. I know you pretended to be a nurse. I want to know why."

"Miss Cascia was a sort of infamous hermit around these parts. I just wanted to see the house. I didn't know you'd let me in so I pretended to be her nurse. I was curious."

"You could have just asked."

"Okay, I'll tell you. But you have to keep it a secret. Can you do that?"

"Try me," I said. But I saw her eyelids drop suddenly and I knew she was changing her mind.

"How do I know I can trust you?"

"I could ask you the same thing. Listen, if you want something—from that house—you'd better ask for it. Because it won't do any good just hoping it's going to come your way."

"Maybe I'm not sure what I want," she began carefully. "Maybe I won't really know for a while, until I've done some investigating."

"Marya and I are going to be around for a year, so you can just keep your thinking cap on. But if you want anything, you'd better come clean and learn how to ask for it."

Her eyes looked me up and down. "What makes you think this town is so safe anyway?"

"You're not a very scary woman, Ms. Danroy. I've been out of the closet a long time and I don't scare easy. Don't bother to play welcome wagon or anything else." I turned and started walking away from her, through the corridors of cars.

"Hey!" she called, finally. "Come back!"

"Why?"

"Because I *do* want to welcome you to Billings!"

I stopped and let my curiosity get the better of me. After all, her search through Rebecca's things had netted her nothing. And if she suspected that there were valuables on the property I wanted to know the basis for her suspicions. It could mean further findings. For me.

I heard my feet crunch across the frozen gravel, back to where Helen was leaning sulkily against her car. She had gone to a lot of trouble to imitate a county nurse.

"Looks like your girlfriend is getting interested in some of those other gals back there," Helen said softly.

"What are you talking about?"

"That could leave you with a lot of free time."

"Yeah, as if I don't already have enough to do. Excuse me—"

"Bet you don't expect to find many extracurricular activities in Billings," Helen murmured and then a hand jutted out from her body and thrust itself under my coat.

"What are you doing?" I sputtered, grappling with her leather paw.

"Come on, don't you like—"

"No—what?" I grabbed her wrist as I felt her puffy gloves slide along my ribs.

"Aren't you worried about your girlfriend?" she said, breathing heavily, but she was hardly excited. She was agitated, and I could smell the nervous sweat emanating from inside her coat.

"You're going to listen to me," Helen yelled as we grappled and swayed in a strange dance that held no delight. The skinny woman was grabbing my neck and pulling my face down toward her.

I felt her breasts, big and flat, under her overcoat. The wool had absorbed a lot of cigarette smoke.

"Stop it! Get your hands off me or I'm going to give you a crotch kick that you'll have a hard time explaining to hubby,"

I growled, pushing her away hard. She tripped and grabbed a nearby car for balance.

I turned my back and walked briskly away. There couldn't be enough space, there couldn't be a mountain top high enough in Montana to separate myself from the pseudo nurse. She made me feel sullied.

"You might be surprised to know that I've spent a great deal of time outside Billings," she called to my back. "In fact," her voice went up a notch, "I'm on a sabbatical from Vassar College right now," she called. I laughed. Who was she kidding?

Then I thought about her fine woolen clothes, hand-stitching and custom-made boots and her perfect French accent. Great! Another academic psychopath. Were they just attracted to good researchers or what?

"I'm not in the market for a research assistant," I muttered. "Or anything else." I'd spoken softly, but she must have heard me.

"Oh no?" I heard her say as I reached the end of the carpark. I put my hand on the handle of the bar door and prepared to pull. Helen's voice carried clearly through the night air over the sheet metal hoods of the cars.

"Not even in," she paused and her voice lowered, "art history?"

I opened the door to the bar and walked in. Helen Danroy knew about Rebecca's money. And that wasn't all. She knew more than I did.

20

Marya was still at the bulletin board when I came in. She was riveted between the captain of Billings' softball team and their first base player who'd just moved out from Indianapolis. I could tell by the way she beamed at me I wasn't about to lose her to any locals. I came up and gave her a big kiss, just so they would get the idea.

"In insurance," the large, beaming woman explained, holding out her hand. I shook it, and feigned interest in their conversation. I barely managed some enthusiasm at the prospect of their end-of-season barbecue. Unlike me, Marya was fitting right in, like a missing piece of a puzzle.

Later we sat outside in the car for a moment.

"Marya, I'm sorry I'm difficult."

"It's all right, darling. I understand."

"Stop being so understanding. It's not all right. I don't want you to be so understanding," I said.

"All right!" she snapped. "I'm tired of your pretentious academic world, tired of feeling responsible for Billings, Montana. It's a place and you can decide to make a future for yourself here or not. That's not my decision." She reached forward and started the engine, leaving it idling as she leaned back and continued, "And if you think I'm going to sit back and watch you make it with some local in the carparking lot, you've got another think coming."

"Oh, she's just some hard-up closet case. She probably never met a really out lesbian before. I'm surprised she knew where this bar was. She was the county nurse I met the other day. The one that came to the house."

"So why did you go out to the carpark?"

"She said she wanted to talk to me in private. I thought maybe she didn't feel comfortable in the bar. I was just doing some country co-counseling."

"O.K." Marya slung her arm around my neck and brought my face close to hers. "I don't want to compete with any Mary Poppins of the Prairie." Then she thrust her hands into my jacket and pulled my face toward hers.

❧ 21 ❧

The next day found me alone in the house, with the saints inside and holy women outside. I was glad when Marya left to do more executrix errands, I needed to be on my own to walk around Rebecca's world. Now I would see its saintly population in a new light.

I walked outside and looked at the garden, at Saint Teresa tied down by a hundred little angry nuns and Saint Rose with her scarred face.

Rebecca's life had been joyful, and I felt that way too. I would have been content to wander dreamily around the house for days. I was learning to say hello to the different saints, wondering at what their selection told me about Rebecca. I felt I was just getting to know them when Federal Express arrived, reminding me I had no time to waste.

I wondered if research was the route to go in figuring out Rebecca's past. I thought about all the novel ways art thieves had of making off with valuables—through museum skylights, by-passing electronic eyes watching over priceless collections in private villas. This treasure, wrapped in Rebecca's well-worn dishtowel, suddenly had even more value.

I thought about where I would locate my office. I thought about Rebecca's room. Surely that was the appropriate place to unravel all the secrets. I felt it would make me closer to her.

I was all ready to go online. Marya had bought me several extension cords which I could run into my workroom. Electricity would permeate Rebecca's chamber; I looked forward to working there.

But first I went into the kitchen to ask her permission. I took her photograph out of the door and reached for my reading glasses. Yeah, she was definitely pointing at that Virgin Mary statue. Was that a clue? The Sienese Madonna. I put thoughts of Italy out of my mind.

I put the photo back, too. I went to the kitchen and opened up the high cupboard above the refrigerator. The little box was still there, wrapped in Rebecca's dishtowel.

I climbed the stairs with it, as if I were carrying the Holy Grail to my own altar, as Saint Clare had held the Host aloft against all enemies. I shook it once and heard the familiar soft, fluttery sound, like the beating of birds trapped inside a cage.

I breathed in the cold, clear air of Rebecca's unheated cell. Perfect for the computer. I looked up at the top of the cupboard. The hatbox of hair was still perched on the cabinet. Helen Danroy hadn't found anything inside, just some clothes and a dress box.

I decided to take it down and look at it again.

I reached up and pulled at the hexagonal box, until it slid off the cabinet and fell into my hands with a thump. I put it down on the bed.

The lid came off easily, despite the way I had crushed it back on the box. The yellow and red hair, loosely wound in long coppery waves, floated inside the box. I reached my hand in and felt something dry and crispy among the strands. I pulled the box into the light and saw tiny roses and violets. Fragrant flowers woven into the magnificent mane. The rosebuds still had a sweet scent, encapsulating the memory of a warm summer's day. I put the box out in the hallway, so that I could show Marya and then dispose of it.

I turned to the bed, a metal frame covered by a white linen cloth which hung two inches above the floor. Rebecca had made this bed so finally, so carefully on the morning of her death. And she had placed a Madonna, one with rays coming out of her hands, on the pillow.

I walked over to the windowsill, where I unwrapped the little box revealing its glowing leaves and petals to the austere chamber. I looked beyond it into the garden.

The statues were coated with clear ice. In cellophane raincoats they went about their holy business in the garden. I tried to imagine what they would look like in the spring. Rebecca had been a master in her own way. Maybe she was an idiot savant, but I didn't think so. I was convinced there was more to her story. A work of art that must have been divinely inspired and financed.

I looked forward to calling up the online court records and newspaper articles relating to stolen art. An art theft of some sixty-five years ago.

I went back downstairs to fetch the large plastic disk drive. I was sure it would fit easily inside the metal cupboard.

Removing the doors was simple. Small metal pins released the hinges and I carried them into the hall. Next I fetched the extension cords and took them into the bathroom, which had a three-prong socket. I draped the heavy orange cords over the sink and into the hall. Slowly I snaked them along the wall into Rebecca's room, where the metal cupboard stood exposed.

On the bottom shelf stood the sturdy cardboard box with its tin-reinforced corners. I drew it out and slowly undid a green cord wrapped around the middle. I took the lid off.

Black crinoline pushed its way out; starched and stiff it seemed to grow out of the box in a black bubble. Gathered at intervals of twelve inches, it was heavy, hardly festive. More black clothes waited to escape. Four calf-length black slips joined the parade.

Four pairs of heavy black stockings, a huge white flannel nightgown, a black umbrella, and a pair of thick-heeled granny shoes lay obediently beneath the top garments. Long white cotton drawers with two buttons at a back flap completed the collection. Everything was beyond plain—it was neutered.

I put the overflowing box out in the hallway along with the hair.

I went downstairs to bring up the keyboard and modem to the metal shelves now empty of the ghostly black garments. Pausing for a moment in the hall, I looked over the eerie black shapes lying on the carpet. These garments were dark shadows, something that had served to separate Rebecca from the rest of the world, like a funeral wreath.

Red hair that smelled like flowers, followed by neutered garments cut out of black cloth. I needed no more clues. Rebecca's soul hadn't originally been trained in the solitary garden and house. It had been trained in an institution, I was sure of it.

I tripped over an extension cord as I made my way into the room. I peered at the bed, then at the small night table on which the painted cigar box rested.

I opened it. No wonder Helen Danroy wasn't very interested. It contained a plastic cup, toothpaste and a soap dish with soap, explaining the absence of toilet articles in the bathroom. It indicated institutional hygiene habits maintained through life.

I opened up the drawer which I knew held only a Bible. I picked up the volume, taking off the rubber band which held the thing together.

The rubber band did more than hold it together. It held it shut. The Bible's cover was merely a lid. Rebecca had glued together the pages and cut out a hollow through the text to create a hiding place for some jewelry.

Inside, wound safely around a smaller Bible and a copy of the Holy Rule, was a set of beads. They were not rosary beads, there was no cross. Helen Danroy wouldn't be interested in this. I recognized the well-worn, humble little wooden spheres from an abbey museum. They were Perfection Beads. Examen Beads.

Nuns. The little abacus of guilt was worn around their necks.

Used to help nuns in their attempt toward a constant vigilance of every minor imperfection of character, the beads were worn daily. For every time she broke silence or broke a plate in clumsiness, a nun would slide a bead up behind her neck. At the end of the day this convenient way of tallying transgressions would help her and her Mother Superior to determine the amount of punishment needed to wipe the slate clean for another day.

In addition to the examen beads nuns had a small black book where the specifics of imperfection could be recorded. Rebecca was so thorough in her Catholic life, I felt sure it would exist somewhere—somewhere not far from the beads themselves.

I pulled out the table drawer completely and put it on the ground. The beads rattled around inside it where I had dropped them. I picked them up again and fingered them for a moment, wondering at all the guilt that could have been contained in the small wooden spheres.

I raised the drawer up and felt underneath it, between the raised runners. There, taped to the thin plywood, was a book—a volume small enough to fit inside the pocket of a nun's habit. I picked at the tape slowly, not wanting to damage the cover.

Finally it lay in my hand. I opened it to the inside cover. But another booklet fell out—a passport. I put on my reading glasses and looked at the date. There was the proof—a small picture of Rebecca, the usual triumphant expression with an almost demonic glint in her eye.

She'd been in Italy from December of 1930 to October of 1932. And then she'd returned and bought a house and a lot of mineral rights. Not many people came back from a vacation richer than when they'd left, I mused. Maybe the sin was recorded in her examen book.

The date 1927 sprang out at me in girlish handwriting. I prepared myself to read the testament to one woman's struggle with obedience and her strange fate.

22

"Move over, Mary, you aren't my girlfriend," I reminded the little figure on the pillow. I placed her carefully on the edge of the mattress and lay down, opening the little book and pulling it closer to my face, adjusting my glasses on the bridge of my nose.

"Domine non sum dignus," I read, "Lord I am not worthy", and wondered for the first time if I should have been reading this recording of transgressions. "Say but the word and my soul shall be healed," I replied to myself. The past could always shed valuable light on the present, I thought. And I was, after all, in Rebecca's house, residing with her niece.

"Jesus wants me to sacrifice in order to make reparation for all the pain. His heart has suffered because of my sins," I read. "I will make His load lighter by suffering." This was followed by a list.

4.21 Broke silence

4.21 Pride (Sister Mary Agnes)

4.21 Chocolate

4.21 Enjoyed singing
4.21 Depression
4.21 Broke silence

Clearly 4.21 hadn't been a good day for Rebecca, but who wouldn't have been depressed in a world where singing and chocolate were bad? Rebecca hadn't seen it the same way.

"4.21: Abstained from dinner. Took my morning meal kneeling," she wrote.

I continued leafing through the book, the mass accumulation of minor petty offenses, signs of humanity that Rebecca had punished herself for. "Physical humiliation" I read several times, and I could only guess what that was.

And then, in June, things seemed to change.

6.10 Broke silence
6.10 Pride
6.10 Particular friendship
6.11 Broke silence
6.11 Particular friendship
6.11 Pride
6.12 Particular friendship
6.12 Particular friendship
6.12 Self-stimulation

How exciting! The young Rebecca had formed an alliance of sorts, and, as I read on, the acknowledgment of the "particular friendship" didn't falter. For all of June, July and August, the "particular friendship" entries reappeared. Apparently, it was a sin she couldn't stop. Nor did she try very hard. The self-inflicted punishments abated just as the particular friendship notations increased. No longer on her knees for dinner, she was on her knees for something else, I thought with amusement.

I began to think about those nuns I'd seen in childhood and later in Italy. I put Italy out of my mind and instead imagined lifting a black serge habit over legs strong from scrubbing floors and working in the garden. I thought about the intellectual discipline that some orders demanded of their novices, and imagined hidden conversations on pillows in moonlit chambers. Stolen moments, to be written down, to be confessed, but to experience again and again.

And Rebecca had done it. I was sure, again and again. How would it be to hear a habit swishing furtively along a terrazzo floor, keys kept from clinking by strong fingers; to feel the same fingers stroke a pious face, to feel lips feverishly kiss a mouth that was otherwise reserved only for Christ? Surely He wouldn't mind, I thought, glancing over at the doll-like Virgin Mary and finding my own fingers moving along the inseam of my jeans. I closed my eyes. The bedframe squeaked and shifted on the floor.

Yes, it must have been good, good for Rebecca. It wasn't even like being unfaithful to Him, she would rationalize as she felt things she thought could only happen in dreams, forbidden dreams—the cool fingertips of a novice finding a breast hidden, perhaps for years, and ripe for this destiny. A woman's touch.

I unzipped my blue jeans and reached down into brown curly hair trapped behind white lace. I moved aside the elastic with a wet fingertip and slowly the bed began to rock with me as my mind roamed over decades, back to the sexual dramas realized by nuns in the confinement of cells. The bedframe squeaked.

"Ahhhhreeee!" Pain! Like tinfoil stuck between the teeth! Searing like a bolt of fire! Illuminating every cell! Nerves screeched raw with fire as the shock jangled and tore at my muscles, everything ready to explode, my eyes trying to leave their sockets. A roaring filled my ears as my body started shuddering, levitating off the bed.

It was a tremendous effort to think, to try to figure out the source of the shock that still continued to course through my body.

There, on the floor! The extension cord! The ends—they'd come apart! Prongs touching metal frame! Electrified! The entire bed! My foot, covered only by a damp sock, was in complete contact with the electrified frame and I was conducting 120 volts. I grabbed for the headboard to keep myself from lurching off the frame but I was unsuccessful. My jaw clamped, my torso arched into a convulsion and I lost my grip. I was thrown off the bed against the wall, landing with a full body thud on the floor as the air around me became brown and then there was no air at all. "I'm losing consciousness," I thought, and I did. I was being transported with my own supernatural passport. And then I awoke in Italy.

23

"This is *supposed* to be a vacation," I heard Ilona's voice outside the tent.

Inside, in the pale yellow glow of the nylon, I was frantically making notes, trying to remember all the stories, all the details Ilona had described that morning. It had been a lovely day. We'd gotten up early to visit a chapel in the countryside, a place no guidebook ever mentioned, no tourist ever found. Ilona knew that a particular reliquary existed there. An arm, a long silver arm, encasing the wristbone of Saint Ann.

"Hey, this is supposed to be a vacation!" I heard her repeat. She'd been unwilling to make the excursion, now she was in a bad mood and I didn't want her blaming me.

"Yes, dear—just let me finish this one thing." I dotted an "i", ended a sentence and clipped my notes together, filing them away in a cardboard portfolio.

I emerged from the tent and ran my hand up and down her legs. The tip of her nose was burning and her hair had gotten lighter, a sort of white-pink-yellow color, almost fluorescent, like the sun. Her carefully tended legs stretched out brown in front of me.

"You look so sweet and earnest and worried and sweaty," she said. I glanced around anxiously at the Latin families with their broods of aggressive children. I must have flinched when she hugged me, sliding her hands down my back and up the front of my blouse. "Still a little neurotic about sweat?" she asked.

"No, dear, it's just all these people around. I don't feel safe." I squirmed out of her grasp and tried for a hand on her arm instead.

"Come *on!*" she sniggered. "Why, there's two lesbians camped right over there."

"Those aren't lesbians," I protested.

"How do you know?"

"I just know," I replied stubbornly. Ilona saw lesbians everywhere, I thought. And I had to agree with these supposed sightings of the sisterhood or she'd say I was just prudish, uptight.

"Look!" she said, her attention suddenly diverted. A lurching, fur-covered skeleton hobbled toward us. "It's a sick kitten," she said. "Aww, poor thing."

The cat was coming closer. Please, I thought, don't come over here. Go away, kitty. Go away! But it was wobbling, making straight for Ilona.

"Look, it's sick," she crooned.

"Yes, I know," I mumbled. Ilona was already walking over toward the creature, picking up its diseased body and bringing it closer.

"Don't bring it over here!" I cried as she came over in front of the tent, holding the kitten before her.

"What's the matter? Creeped out by a little kittycat?" Ilona put it close to my face.

"Get it away from me!" I said, but I knew my reaction was only feeding her attachment to the horrible beast. I tried another tack.

"Ilona, I'm hungry. If we leave now, we can go and have lunch in the village," I heard myself whining.

Ilona ignored me, caught up in her careful ministrations to the sick animal.

"You could leave this sick kitten to die?" She shot me an angry glance as she tilted its head back and poured water into its tiny gullet. Most of the fluid ran out of its mouth and through its mangy fur, but it managed to swallow once. "It's thoroughly dehydrated!" she cried.

"Well, it'll be okay. I saw it the other day underneath the bushes over there. It's survived this long," I said.

"You just *left* it there, for children to throw stones at it?" she asked and I shuddered. Sometimes Ilona seemed to have eyes everywhere. How could she have guessed about the children and the stones? Of course she understood Italian, so she knew a lot more than I did about what was going on in the campsite, or anywhere else in Italy, for that matter.

"Listen, let's go into town. The cat will be okay for a few hours. You've watered it, now let it rest and we'll come right back."

"No," Ilona murmured, stroking its back. The little spine shuddered and something like a purr emerged from its throat. "I don't think I could do that."

The dusty campsite seemed to be getting hotter by the minute. I looked at Ilona and the kitten. Ilona's hair reflected so much light it was practically a halo around her head. They made the perfect pietà. There was something sick, I thought, in this tableau, in her attention to the kitten.

"Okay, I'll go to the supply store and get some lettuce and vegetables, then I'll heat up some spaghetti and we'll have a real Italian lunch."

"Good, that's very nice, dear," Ilona mumbled as she took a tissue and started wiping the mucus-lined orifices of the little animal, careful that her long hair didn't tangle with its fur.

I went to the little general store and even picked up an over-priced bottle of wine. I set up the campstove in a shadier spot on the side of the tent. There was some grass there and it was far away from Ilona's makeshift pet hospital. I could see her carefully stroking the animal, feeling its heart, occasionally trying to get some water down its throat.

During lunch Ilona entertained me with tales of the last of the Medici and their parties. Couples were hired to make love in the bushes, to give the guests a delightful surprise. Leonardo made lion robots and secret fountains were hidden in topiary trees.

"Tell me more," I pleaded, when she had me sufficiently intrigued.

"Oh, the kitten!" Ilona jumped up, leaving her plate of spaghetti and going over to where the sick animal was retching, its tiny spine arched, its tail pointing straight to the heavens. Eventually the fluid she had so carefully persuaded it to take spewed out of its mouth. Then the animal flopped over, exhausted, on the grass.

Ilona shook her head and returned. "Well, we can't leave it like this," she said. "And I'm not hungry. But it's siesta anyway. Do you mind doing the dishes? I think I'll take the kitten over there to that tree where it's really shady and cool."

"Okay," I agreed. I'd rather she dealt with the kitten. I wasn't in the mood to begin nursing the unfortunate creature. So it was with a sense of relief that I watched Ilona pick up a pile of journals and bound dissertations, wrap the kitten in one of our dish towels and set off to the far end of the campsite.

I busied myself with her leftover pasta, the skillet and pot that had held the boiling water. Everything was sticky with dried starch.

I amused myself thinking about all that Ilona had told me. The names, the dates she could rattle off so confidently rang in my ears. Ilona would always be a wonderful companion, I told myself. Endlessly intriguing.

24

Minutes or hours later, I was still lying face down on the floor in Rebecca's room. The extension cord had disengaged, the two ends safely separated, but that wasn't what worried me.

I felt the wood splinters of a rough hewn prairie floor on my lips, and I couldn't move my head. The continued force of the electrical shock kept the tip of my nose against the boards. I wondered if masturbation was indeed so loathsome to the Church.

Slowly I tried moving my fingertips and succeeded. This was just a shock reaction, I told myself. Soon the electricity would have coursed its way through my system and I would be able to move.

That was how Marya found me, stretched out on the floor.

"What the—" She stooped down quickly and drew me into her arms, and my extended limbs folded gratefully as I leaned into her chest. And then the spell was broken.

"I guess—I think I got an electric shock," I said. My throat was sore and my tongue felt tired. The roof of my mouth was raw, as if sandpaper had been rubbing it.

"This is no time to rewire the room, sweetheart!"

"I know, but I have to start my work," I explained, shivering. "I thought this was the best place."

"Christ, you're cold and clammy!" Marya pulled a blanket off the bed and wrapped it around me.

"Here, first aid for the shock. Let's get you bundled up and on the bed—"

"Downstairs," I pleaded. I wasn't ready for Rebecca's electrified rack again.

"Of course," Marya said, pulling me to my feet. "I don't know why you like this room anyway." She walked over to the Madonna, kicking her. The statue spun across the floor. "A lot of spooky superstition that never did anybody any good."

"Never did anybody any good," I repeated mindlessly, glad to have control over my voice again. My jaw felt as though it had been in a vise.

"Let's get out of here."

"Of course." She began to lift me.

"Take me away from this house, anywhere," I pleaded, getting shakily to my feet.

"Darling, it's only a year. You're taking this all too seriously. You can go back and forth to the Bay Area." Marya's hand accidentally swept the nightstand and we watched Saint Frances fall to the floor with a thud.

"This stuff just creates anxiety." She walked slowly around the room and I wondered what other conscious or unconscious destructive impulses she had. I realized I was sitting on the little black book—Rebecca's book of recorded sins. I picked it up and tucked it away in my jean pocket. Then the phone rang.

"Shit! I hope that's not Falkenberg. He's pissed off with me." Marya walked over and lifted the receiver.

"It's for you," she said. "Sounds like that woman you said would sublet your apartment."

"Hello?"

"Hello?"

"Hi, this is Helen Danroy."

"Yes?" A cold sweat had broken out on my forehead. I watched Marya go into the kitchen.

"Your girlfriend sounds suspicious. Having trouble?" She sounded as though she was smiling and I suddenly despised the insinuation in her voice. Helen Danroy was a creep.

"No, there's just a lot going on here."

"Like what?"

"Nothing that can't be fixed by hanging up on you."

"Listen, I just wanted to apologize for last night." I watched Marya open the freezer door. "I thought you'd like sex. I guess I was wrong," the would-be nurse laughed. "But if you're not interested in that, maybe I can offer to help you go through Miss Cascia's house. After all, you might need help. And you might find some things of interest to you."

"You mean, of interest to *you*," I said. "What do you know about Rebecca?"

"She was more than just a disturbed person. Perhaps I should talk to your friend Marya about this. After all, Rebecca was her relation. Perhaps she should know first."

"Go right ahead. Do you want to talk to her now?"

"No—wait. I mean, well, maybe we could work something out. I mean, after all, you aren't a blood relative of the deceased. You could be cut out of this altogether."

"Cut out of what?"

"I don't know exactly. Maybe we could find out together."

"I'm really busy now. I suggest you keep your fantasies to yourself. Because that's all they are—hyper-imaginative fantasies." I hung up the phone with a crash.

"Who was that, honey?" I heard Marya ask, coming in from the kitchen.

"Nobody, dear. Just wanted a newspaper subscription. Remember how we put the phone in my name?"

"Oh." I watched Marya return to the kitchen, slowly opening a can of soup.

I took Rebecca's little black book out of my pocket and flipped to the back page to look at something I had earlier thought to be an inky smudge. An old-fashioned stamp, in gothic letters, indicated the book's origin.

Sister Adorers of the Most Precious Blood, San Diego, California.

And underneath, a girlish optimistic script. The signature read "Sister Roberta Claire", and all the "i"s were dotted with little circles.

San Diego, I thought, almost smiling. How my destiny seemed to keep me rolling right along to places I'd never anticipated. I knew then that I would have to go there, to the Sister Adorers of the Most Precious Blood in San Diego, California.

"Honey," I called to Marya in the kitchen. "How would you feel about going to church tomorrow?"

"What the fuck are you talking about?" I heard her call back.

25

"I don't give a fuck about the Catholic Church and the weird trips or kooky crafts of some obscure relative of mine," Marya smiled indulgently. "But, for you, what the hell. I'll go to church just for the adventure." She sipped her tea. "God! I can't believe I said that."

Outside the wind wasn't quite as bitter. Perhaps it was a harbinger of spring, or maybe just a Chinook wind, but you'd have had to be a native to know. I stood for a moment on the top stair in front of the house. The sky was so big and endless in Montana.

My eyes roamed around the heavens, rested on the horizon and moved up to the gravel path on which our car rested. And then I saw something else. I grabbed the handrail, a cool, sick feeling emanating from my bowels. Someone had taken a sharp object and scraped through the blue paintwork on the car.

"Marya!" I called, but I didn't move. "Marya!" I heard her coming down the stairs. After a few moments she was by my side, looking where I looked and seeing what I saw.

Along the side of the car, in hastily, but deeply scratched

letters a foot high, someone had engraved the words QUEERS DIE.

I looked up at our bedroom window. The plumber was right—the curtains could be seen through at night. And cars could hide so easily behind the big snowdrift at the end of the drive.

"It's probably just those teenage kids down the road. I've seen them driving by, looking at the place any number of times. And they were in the 7-Eleven last time we were."

"Fucking hell! We can't even hold hands in the 7-Eleven."

"And they can't buy beer without an ID. They probably thought we were laughing at them. It's just teenage testosterone poisoning."

"It's nicer to live somewhere where gays have electoral power."

"You can get pounded just as easily in San Francisco as Montana. The only consolation in this situation is that people who do this kind of thing are cowards. They're not the kind of people who do bodily harm." She stroked my back. I looked around nervously. There wasn't anybody in sight down the long deserted road.

We took a can of green paint from Rebecca's stockpile in the cellar and painted out the letters. The scratches were deep, however, and the paint settled in the grooves. When the light hit it at an angle there were shadows. "QUEERS DIE" was still visibly etched into the side of the car.

I found a can of red and made diagonal stripes over it. The complimentary red vibrated over the field of green, making it impossible to focus long enough to read the hateful words.

"It's wonderful! Let's go!"

"Oh, fuck!" I felt in the inside pocket of my coat. "I don't have my wallet. Damn!"

"It's all right, sweetheart, I'll drive." We got in our defaced car, the death threat now patched and emblazoned with stripes, and headed into town.

"Where did you want to go?" she asked.

"Actually, I just wanted to run by the Catholic church." I

looked at my watch. "Saint Luke's. Mass should just be finishing now."

It seemed that all of Billings was coming or going to church that morning. Families rode five to a car. Daddy drove and Mom and Sis clutched prayerbooks as the boys squirmed in the back. The Catholic kids would go to Mass, and other Christian kids would be herded into Sunday schools.

Pulling up five blocks later I found Saint Luke's. We parked the car at the stairs and heard chanting inside. A metal rack just visible inside the lobby offered some leaflets. I bounded up the stairs and took one.

"Not over yet," Marya said as I ran back down again. We kept the engine idling and sat in silence. Suddenly the doors opened and people spilled out of the church. Bored kids released from inactivity raced down the stairs toward our car, while other vehicles pulled up behind us.

"Hey, look!" Marya suddenly cried. "Isn't that the weird nurse coming out?"

Helen Danroy was walking down the stairs with hubby and a cub scout troop of little clones. Various parishioners passed them by with polite nods but nobody stopped to chat with Danroy and her husband. Helen stopped one woman by thrusting her arm out suddenly. The woman smiled and escaped with a few quick comments.

Helen took her husband's arm again and he escorted her down the stairs.

"Boy, I sure had her figured wrong!" I told Marya. "At first I thought there was something a little lesbian about her, but I think I'm feeling so isolated I'm seeing company everywhere."

A violent honking split the air. A black limousine honked again, anxious for a space at the curb. Then there were bells— bells I never thought I'd hear in Montana. They rang over and over again, the same three tones, big deep notes which traveled deep into my chest from the belltower of Saint Luke's. I looked up at the church. The crowd had separated to leave a big path in the middle.

A long shadow stretched down the steps and I followed the

black shape until I came to the sparkling hem of a gown any drag queen would have died for. But this wasn't someone cut out for fun.

He was holding a long golden staff with a hook on the end. His white gloves had long golden gauntlets, reaching almost to the elbow. Brocade robes, like some boudoir wallpaper, and over it a shawl fringed with gold. His face was pinched and bitter-looking and a knot of wrinkles set between his eyes. Small, even little animal teeth showed with the unwilling smile.

He raised a hand to shoulder level, and then higher, almost as high as his big hat. That hat was covered with glittering stones and pointed at the top. His white gloved hands were poised in gesture, two fingers bent, two fingers pointing upward. His eyes were so pale they fused with the spacious whites all around, making him look like a blind statue.

He made his way slowly down the stairs, the local parish priest bowing and scraping before him. Every now and then someone was lucky enough to kiss his ring, which gave him an opportunity to show his little teeth again.

"Your Excellency, Your Grace," Helen Danroy lined up for her turn and fell on her knees so swiftly even the old patriarch appeared startled.

"Oh, no!" I read her husband's lips as he pulled away from the crowd, but it was too late.

Helen Danroy was putting her hands deliberately on the freezing pavement. She sank lower and lower, in that perfectly tailored wool suit, into the muddy slush at the bishop's feet. The crowd froze. Already her gloves were stained with black water from the sidewalk, and then the wool hairs and then the entire front of her jacket were submerged. Everyone stood transfixed.

She extended first her left and then her right arm away from her body, and then stretched her legs out, so that her entire body lay soaking up the muddy pool. Her shoes pressed together, her body formed the shape of the Cross. And then a moment too horrible for anyone to imagine . . .

Helen Danroy's mouth opened and a pink tongue found its

way into the mud, up and down and then from side to side. She was making the sign of the cross.

"Sweetheart!" Mr. Danroy stepped from the crowd and pulled her to her feet. Helen seemed to awaken suddenly; she looked down at the stain which covered the front of her suit, wet and dark, as her husband whisked her quickly into the car.

"Bless you," the Bishop said to the crowd, hurriedly making the Sign of the Cross over them.

Somehow the Catholic Church had seemed romantic in Italy. But how much had Italian culture really affected my life? No, it was all my projection—Catholicism seen through rosy love lenses supplied by Ilona Jorgensen. This particular kind of Catholicism was Helen Danroy on her knees kissing the ring of the patriarch, who told her to stay married and not use birth control.

The Bishop slid into the limousine with the help of a few altar boys. His hem never hit the slushy ground.

The crowd dispersed just as another one gathered. Down the street more screaming children drew our attention. Another church was letting out on the next block. Within one group was the plumber who had the hots for our underwear drawer. I watched him escort a pleasant looking, stocky, middle-aged woman to the passenger side of a car at the curb. Two pubescent boys, replicas of Dad, yanked open the back doors and waited sullenly for him to start the car. Normal—so amazingly normal. Queers die. Montana had a good harvest in hatred, I thought.

"That poor woman," Marya was muttering and shaking her head. "A fixation on a form of terminal torture."

"To think, Helen Danroy's just about your age, it could have been you," I murmured.

"Honey, that would have *never* been me!"

Marya was sure a lot more attractive than Helen Danroy, I thought. And yes, they were just about the same age.

And then—suddenly—I made the connection, the connection that linked Helen Danroy to the past. She was the same age as Marya and she knew the woman with the long red hair that rested in the box at the top of the cabinet. Probably an older relation—and it was odds on that it was someone who lived in Montana.

Bishops, nuns and plain white underwear with two button drawers. A particular friendship weaving a tangled tapestry sixty years later. I had been looking for lesbian liaisons in all the wrong places. Mary Poppins indeed.

I resolved to go to the library the next day. I would start looking through the microfilm of Montana. I would be looking for the obituary of a woman, 85 through 95 years old. She would have died in Montana but spent a hidden part of her life in a more southerly clime. And her name would not be Rebecca.

"Let's make today a celebration," Marya said. "Like a birth-day—" She stopped suddenly and turned to look at me. "You know I don't even know when your birthday is!"

A diesel semi-truck interrupted any answer I might have given. Blasting its horn, it demanded Marya hug the far side of her lane and I was saved from telling her.

"Rude shithead," Marya shouted, and I was glad that the windows were rolled up. Tangling with the locals wasn't going to increase our chances of survival in Montana.

"Marya, there is something that I want to do."

"What, honey, just say the word."

"I want to go to San Diego."

Marya nodded silently and then we drove home.

26

"**Y**ou're sure it's Ellen you're visiting down there?" We were lying in bed, and for a moment I saw that hard, near-violent look flash across her face.

"Yes. Of course." There was no need to worry Marya with Rebecca's past as a nun. And I didn't think it would interest her.

It had been an easy enough trip to plan. Marya's credit card had a new credit rating and it got me a rental car. A phone call to the nuns at the order assured me I could arrive in time for Mass.

"It's not that you're tired of me? You seem so distant," Marya said. I stroked her back absentmindedly.

Suitcases! I thought with happiness I would take the little box with me. How I loved to pack, get out, and move on. Ever since Italy it had been my litany. Ever since Ilona it was the only thing that made me feel better.

I awoke early to go to the library on the way to the plane. Marya had mumbled goodbye, but her face was fierce. She'd get over it. The ice-axe was already next to her on the bed. Was she protecting herself from an intruder, I wondered, or from the fear of my infidelity? I was glad to be getting out of town.

The Billings library was better than I could have imagined, considering what I had to compare it with—the memory of those lovely antique archives where Ilona used to take me, especially the one she took me to on my birthday. The day I would never speak of. To Marya or anyone else.

I shut the memory out as a helpful librarian set me up at a microfilm carrel. I started with newspapers from two years ago. I squinted in the dark carrel at the tiny type—row after row of green, lit-up lettering.

But this was just a long shot, and library searches could be time-consuming. I didn't want to miss my plane. I turned the dial faster and faster through the obituaries. She would be the same age as Rebecca, or within a few years.

And then an image flashed across the screen. A face extralarge for the obituary section. Something about it arrested my attention—the size of the picture, the pale features, barely visible eyebrows, eyes made more intense by the lack of pigment in the lashes, and long, wavy hair. With that coloring, her hair was just *bound* to be red.

"Former socialite, and founder of Montana's Catholic Charities, cherished wife of the late Fenton O'Brien, Teresa Oliphant O'Brien died today at the age of 89."

Died today. I looked up at the date. Only days before Rebecca had died. Was there some connection? I read further.

"Mrs. O'Brien was the loving mother of Georgina, Agnes, Helen and Clare, and grandmother to twenty-five grandchildren, and seventy-three great-grandchildren. She is survived by her brother, His Grace, the most Reverend Edward Oliphant, DD, Archbishop of Chicago."

That was it—the woman with the red hair, the hair that was sitting in the hatbox. She was the reason why Rebecca had come to Montana. Teresa. It was Teresa's hair.

"Born to Lucille and James Oliphant, Teresa was educated in Catholic girls' schools in Chicago and, later, Los Angeles. Originally from Chicago, the family moved to Montana in 1892 and

were major contributors toward the establishment of Saint Luke's Church in Billings. The Oliphant family maintained relationships with dioceses throughout the country. Mrs. Oliphant's brother was a bishop in Chicago, and the parents of James Oliphant had helped to establish a convent in Peoria, Illinois, where two of his sisters entered the vocation.

"Before her marriage, Teresa Oliphant O'Brien had been a novice of the Sister Adorers of the Most Precious Blood, in San Diego, California."

Bingo! My eyes raced quickly over the rest of the obituary as I started putting on my coat, feeling in my pocket for the plane ticket.

"Mrs. Fenton O'Brien will long be remembered as one of the founding Catholics in the state of Montana, by her many friends in the congregation and in the community at large which was aided by her many good works on behalf of the poor, elderly and ill.

"Friends may visit on Sunday, after 2 pm, and are invited to attend Mass on Monday at 10.30 am at Saint Luke's said by His Grace, Bishop Pascal O'Brien, grandson of the deceased.

"Simultaneous masses will be held in Peoria and Chicago, Illinois, Fond-du-Lac, Wisconsin and Helena, Montana where five of Mrs. O'Brien's grandchildren have entered the religious vocation."

I wound the microfilm back onto the spool and put it in the box.

What a clan for Christ! I thought. Teresa O'Brien swam in a sea of rich Catholics, big fish caught in Peter's net and handed over to Christ. Daughters and sons in every generation were sacrificed to the religious life.

The young nun, Teresa O'Brien, had been recycled from a bride of Christ to a bride of mortal man. It was a neat trick, and one performed with difficulty in old Catholic families. Teresa had avoided the shame of losing her vocation, but had redeemed herself with good works and huge broods of children.

I returned the microfilm to the librarian and left. The sun peered between big cumulus clouds that filled the sky and touched my skin for a moment. It looked as though a storm was on the horizon.

I stepped into the car and drove carefully along icy roads to the airport. I thought about two Catholic women—one very rich, one probably much poorer—and their dissimilar destinies. Just like mine and Ilona's. I scratched my nose, and thought about how great it would be to find sanctuary, if not answers.

27

The nun had informed me that it might be difficult to get an appointment with the Mother Superior on such short notice. She was a relative youngster, I found out. Just over forty. But the library was off limits for the laity. The order was strictly cloistered. And I knew enough about nuns and nunneries to know what that meant. I could see them and talk to them, but they would always be behind a screen.

I felt safe on the plane. The anonymous familiarity of the airport, the preened businesswoman sitting next to me and the uniformed hosts offering plastic food on plastic trays all seemed so normal after the last few days.

I thought of all those plane rides in Europe, with Ilona. Stuck in those seats, arriving stiff at airports, Ilona's hand clutching mine under the watchful gaze of stewardesses, or airport security boys with Uzi machine guns tucked under their arms.

The memories of Ilona and Italy had been recurring with startling clarity. I would close my eyes and not only see images, but smell the sweet warm breezes, and feel Ilona's hands lightly touching the back of my head. I could fight the memories, the stories—but I couldn't fight off the sensual impressions which revisited me. My past got in the way when Marya wanted to make love.

How Ilona had sulked across the continent on that vacation. Our love-making had ground to a halt. She wouldn't let me touch her any more. There were so many unsaid things between us, so many things I was afraid to say.

"I can't fuck unless we talk," she'd tell me, but I was afraid her talking meant hateful words intended to hurt me with an almost physical pain. I kept my hands to myself and Ilona stayed in a better humor.

Fuck, talk—we didn't do either. But it wasn't because we didn't want to. I would look at Ilona getting dressed; the slight swaying movements of her breasts with their little star centers would stir me between my legs and cause me incredible pain.

I was still in love with her, giving way to her moods and feelings and trying to understand all the difficult things that were happening to her—her lack of employment, her impoverished background, her depression in the face of the hopeless political situation in the world.

Oh, how I'd tried to make that vacation with Ilona work! I would lie next to her at night, my hands reaching out a hundred times in my sleep toward her, wanting to encircle that delicate ribcage, feel the long muscles which ran up her arms and along the tops of her legs, her white skin like silk, the masses of red hair I longed to bury my face in, biting her tender neck. But my hands were tied with the horrible imaginings of what she might say and I knew I couldn't risk it.

How I'd scraped those spaghetti dishes as I watched Ilona tending that sick kitten under the tree just a few dozen yards from our tent. Her hair would catch the sunlight as she bent over the diseased animal.

In between the cars and screaming children I would watch her apply the water dropper to its mouth. The perfect nurse. A portrait of compassion. The kitten was too sick even to raise its head, and she'd dribble the water between its fangs and then let go so that its head fell onto her lap.

"*You'd* let this animal *die!*" she'd said, looking at me in shock and horror. And for a moment her features would twist with the self-righteousness she was so good at expressing in the lecture hall.

That day at the campsite I watched Ilona for some time. She was reading intently. I knew she was aware of my watching her. She stretched her legs out and smoothed suntan lotion over them, put down the bottle and continued reading as her hands went to the inside, to her thigh, a patch of skin still white and untouched by the sun.

That was the spooky thing about Ilona. Sometimes she was so self-conscious I felt as though I could smell and taste her awareness of me. It usually meant she was in a bad mood. I would never tell her I knew she was watching me watch her. That could cause a tremendous fight. That feeling of the watcher and the watched was in the air again. I prepared myself for trouble when I approached her under the tree.

"Couldn't we go into town now, darling? It's nearly dusk. The kitten can lie by our tent."

Ilona agreed reluctantly. She put the kitten down on our dishtowels in front of our tent with exaggerated tenderness. Fresh fecal matter was evident under its tail. Ilona regarded that as a good sign.

Our time in town, that night, had been uneventful. Ilona seemed bored with my choice of restaurant, with my choice of conversational topic. We arrived back at the campsite, tired of looking for simple Tuscan fare and getting taken in by tourist traps. Ilona's grumpy mood and her displeasure at my suggestions made me nervous, overly cheerful, and finally worn out. She pretended not to notice. Only when we returned to the tent did she begin to talk to me again.

"The kitten looks sicker than ever. Feel it—it's cold." She put her hand on the tiny ribcage. It barely moved.

She held it up to me till I could see its pus-filled nose and runny eyes, imagining a stench that would envelop me if I came any nearer. She brought the kitten toward me, closer and closer. She demanded I pet it.

I stretched out a tentative hand and, trembling, ran it over the fur, hard and matted with diseased juices, until she seemed satisfied. It was cold. I drew my hand away quickly.

"I'm afraid it's not going to make it," I shook my head. "Why don't we cover it up in these towels, leave some water near its head in case it wakes up, and put it under the bushes where it will be out of the wind."

"Put it somewhere unsafe? Unsheltered?" Ilona spoke softly, but in a tone of outrage. "No," she went on. "The only way this kitten will survive, the only way it will remain living, is if it sleeps with us and gathers strength from the warmth of our bodies." Her pale face looked pinched, her tiny nostrils quivered.

"But sweetheart, what if it's diseased?"

"Then it's a feline disease. We'll be immune to it—"

"How do you know? I don't want to sleep with a sick animal in our—"

"Fine! If you want to *kill* this animal, if you want this animal to *die,* then you can have the whole tent to yourself. I will sleep with the kitten in the *car.*" She started to gather up her toilet bag. I had to stop her. If she slept in the car there would be hell to pay. For days.

"All right, darling," I said quietly. Maybe sleeping with the kitten wouldn't be so bad.

Ilona's face softened. She leaned forward and I felt her lips on my cheek. She smelled sweet, like flowers. Then she picked up the little feline body, limp in the dishtowels, and brought it into the tent. The kitten smelled of sickness, the sweet, cloying smell of decay. I crawled in next to Ilona and slid into the double sleeping bag.

In the beam of the flashlight she examined the kitten's dying body. Holding it aloft she slid her long legs into the sleeping bag. Then, with both hands she brought the wheezing creature toward us, raising the edge of the sleeping bag. I smelled its matted fur and glimpsed its tiny white fangs, dripping with drool. I felt the dreaded animal slide along my body. It came to rest between our hips.

"Don't turn over in the middle of the night," Ilona instructed, and I thought about how I might crush the dreadful creature, and what could be inside it.

She turned off the flashlight without looking at me.

"Goodnight," she said. Soon the regularity of her breathing told me that she'd fallen asleep.

The plane took a sudden dip and I opened my eyes to the face of the stewardess. "Something to drink?"

"Whiskey, straight up." When it came I gulped it so quickly a small drop dribbled out of the side of my mouth. I patted it with a napkin and put my seat back.

I drifted off, trying not to remember how I had slept that night in the tent, knowing a sick animal lay close to my naked legs. I stayed awake for hours trying not to realize how unhappy I was, trying not to realize that Ilona was punishing me for all the disappointments in her life.

All of a sudden, I heard a voice:

"If she behaves corruptly with another woman only by rubbing she is subject to punishment, but if she introduces some wooden or glass instrument into the belly of another she should be put to death," the voice droned over the loudspeaker, and I saw two stewardesses rubbing each other, with what the Italians called *fricatrices,* or the Greeks, *tribades.*

"Are you okay?" The businesswoman next to me was shaking my shoulder and I regained consciousness only to realize that my ears were ringing and hurting as the plane descended.

But that wasn't all. I may have fallen into a strange dream, but I recognized the voice that had spoken, and the words too. The text was one of the first written descriptions of lesbian activity in medieval Europe—the sixteenth-century *De Delictis Carnis.* The jurist Prospero Farinacci was describing the appropriate punishment. The text was sixteenth century. But the voice over the airplane loudspeakers was unmistakably contemporary. It was Ilona's.

The plane was landing and I watched my companion smooth her lined skirt. It swished over her nyloned legs as she stood. I checked to make sure I still had it with me. Yes, the little golden box was safely in my shoulder bag.

✎ 28 ✎

I was playing the rental car's radio as I maneuvered along a maze of unfamiliar freeways. A series of housing developments, miniature parks littered with picturesque fake-peasant dwellings. I would be glad to get back to an authentic past, I decided. The Sister Adorers of the Most Precious Blood of Our Lord was a holy order of religious women dating from the time of the first Crusade.

Finally I found the hill which had survived the architectural beating of the surrounding countryside. Shrouded in dark green, it looked inviting. I drove through groves of date palms, interspersed with sturdy oaks, and then a series of tall, spindly eucalyptus. At last I saw the convent itself.

Huge blocks of stone, from some far quarry, made up the enormous structure, pierced by a few dark windows. A bougainvillea clung to the large portal before the doorway, its magenta blooms looking as out of place as confetti on a coffin.

I slammed the car door getting out. The crunch of gravel under my feet served to steady me and keep me in the present.

My shoulder bag swung by my side, bouncing heavily against my hip.

I wondered how Rebecca had felt, seeing this building for the first time. Had she been saved from a bleak future, submitting to a husband, breeding a new cluster of Catholics, endless years of meals and penny-pinching and sorting socks, divorce never a possibility? This stone structure could represent more than a gateway to God.

I imagined Rebecca as a poor, silent girl, who chose the Church for its miraculous tales, where nature and history became one vast symbol.

The air was fresh and clear. I could smell the eucalyptus and hear the long skinny branches creak as they swayed over my head. I knew how Rebecca had felt. I was breathing and thinking again. The punishing images of the past were no longer haunting me.

I looked at my watch and smiled. My travel calculations had been perfect. I was just in time for Mass. I walked over to the large flagstone stairway and mounted the steps, knowing that a postulant nun, entering a cloistered order, would climb them only once. Strict obedience to the Holy Rule would ensure that the only way out was in a box. Nuns didn't travel much in those days, and cloistered nuns, never.

I put my hand on the wrought iron door handle. The nun had told me it would be open. Slowly I pushed it. The whole place would be done up in early southern Californian Robin Hood, I decided—a kind of stage set for the holy. But I was unprepared for what awaited me inside.

A massive hallway stretched to my right and left, bathed in ruby red light—sunlight transformed through thick rosette windows high above my head.

In front a large doorway beckoned and warned, topped by figures who gazed at me, pointing their fingers toward Heaven. They were sizing me up. I would have to pass under them to go within. There were patriarchs, confessors, martyrs and virgins perched above the doorway, and then the orders of angels—Seraphim, Cherubim, Thrones, Dominations, Virtues, Powers,

Principalities, Archangels and Angels—delightful and damning creatures in stone. I dipped my hand into the holy water font and crossed myself, just in case.

I entered the chapel where light and dark, mystery and revelation awaited me. More sun through more colorful windows, shining right on to the tabernacle, God's dinner table. Four apostles to the right of the tabernacle faced four evangelists on the left.

On the right side of the chapel, a large enclosure had been constructed, destroying the otherwise perfect balance of the whole. Swathed in white gauze curtains, adorned with cherubs and flowers and enclosed with bars, it looked like a giant antique birdcage. And I knew it would be full of nuns.

I walked over the inlaid marble floor to the row of pews on the right. I paused. Genuflecting and crossing myself furtively, I slid into a far pew. My shoulderbag clunked as I set it down on the hard bench.

Two ancient civilian celebrants were already kneeling, but they didn't look up. I wondered what sins stained their elderly souls that they should grip their rosaries so fervently, pray so desperately, and look up at the altar with such pleading eyes.

Along the walls breathtakingly realistic paintings formed a long storyboard of martyrdom. The Stations of the Cross. What a turning away from life it all was! No wonder Rebecca had rejected the Cross.

I looked musingly at the altar. Surely the fifties-style crucifix strung above it was a later addition? Who could have made the decision to hang that angular body on its jutting cross in this otherwise organically styled environment?

Slowly a door opened from the right and the procession emerged; an altarboy carrying a candle, a priest, another altarboy. I heard the nuns rustle in their cage. The sacrifice was about to begin.

The priest glided toward the foot of the altar, genuflected and mounted the steps. He placed the veiled chalice on the white linen *corporal* and opened his book. He made the Sign of the Cross, said a few prayers and began the *Confiteor:*

"I confess to Almighty God, to blessed Mary ever Virgin, to blessed Michael the Archangel, to blessed John the Baptist, to the holy apostles Peter and Paul, to all the saints, and to you brethren, that I have sinned exceedingly in thought, word and deed, through my fault, through my fault, through my most grievous fault. . ."

I heard the nuns, their voices mumbling the words of humility, if not humiliation, from their cloistered quarters. What was it like to say those words every single day? They were more than words—they had the power of an incantation: I tried saying them too and found the rhythm appealing: "through my fault, through my fault, through my most grievous fault." And I had faults—my soul was hardly stainless. How lovely it would be to be absolved! How lovely to think it was possible!

More prayers, and then the priest went up the steps, bowed down and kissed the altar. He pleaded for more forgiveness and understanding from the Lord; the nuns in their cage mumbled after him. *Kyrie eleison,* Lord have mercy. Slowly the old man worked his way through *Dominus Vobiscum* to the *Credo.*

"Who for us men, and for our salvation, came down from heaven." The sleeves of the nuns' habits moved in unison as they crossed themselves. I wondered if they ever felt left out of the liturgy—*"Who for us men,"* read the liturgy. Jesus did it all, and always, for men. But I found myself on my knees as the priest continued, *". . . the resurrection of the dead and the life of the world to come,"* and then the bell rang again.

"Dominus vobiscum. The Lord is with you." He was kissing that altar again. *"And with thy spirit"* replied the caged women, and I saw him reach up and slowly pull the veil off the chalice.

The chalice! It glittered at me from afar and its glow was *red.* I stood up, ignoring the ritual, as I was drawn in small, slow steps toward the altar.

". . . grant that the mystery of this water and wine . . ." The priest was pouring water and then wine into the red-gold object. I saw the liquids sparkle and as I got closer, ignoring the back of his flashy vestment, the soft rustle and muttering of the nuns next to me, the holy chalice came slowly into view. I stopped breathing.

Its detail was fine, but lively. Butterflies fluttered across its surface, unimpeded by delicate tendrils, laced with seed pearls and beetles of rubies and jade. Museum quality. An exact match of the little box I carried with me.

"We offer unto Thee, O Lord, the chalice of salvation." And suddenly I knew why Rebecca had locked herself in her house all those years, why she'd been wearing a napkin when she'd died, and what the little box contained.

It wasn't a reliquary after all. It was an *ostensorium*—the place where the holy wafers resided. And Rebecca was more than a woman who had become a nun. She had been the ultimate bad girl.

The box didn't belong to Rebecca, or to Marya, or to me. It belonged to the nunnery. Rebecca had committed the worst sin a Catholic could imagine. She had run off with the Holy consecrated body of the Lord Jesus Christ.

And I knew at that moment that I wasn't going to give it back.

❧ 29 ❧

How had Rebecca made off with the holy dinnerware? How had she come to terms with her conscience as a Catholic? But I knew the answer to that. She had created her own ceremony, her own altar. The wax-covered mantelpiece.

Rebecca had decided what she wanted to emulate—which saints and which sufferings. Out of her fervent devotion she had created a garden of statuary, a life of contemplation, even of religious ecstacy, based on the exemplary accomplishments of female saints.

The priest was consecrating the Host now, holding it aloft with both hands as he got down on one knee. How would he feel if he knew I held the matching *ostensorium* in my shoulderbag?

He elevated the Host again and replaced it on the *corporal,* kneeling once more. The bell rang three times. Had Rebecca carried out a similar ceremony, all on her own, at home?

"Hoc est enim corpus meum. For this is My body. As often as ye do these things, ye shall do them in remembrance of me."

I saw the priest take the Host and break it over the chalice, and wondered if the custom was designed so that the water-wine mixture would catch any of His crumbs. Then he rested one of the pieces on a humble tin plate, the *paten*.

After more prayers and kneeling, he turned at last to the congregation. *"Behold the Lamb of God . . ."* and the two civilian celebrants drew toward the altar rail, one with the aid of a cane. Afterwards the nuns got their turn. The priest walked to their cage and, assisted by the altarboys, offered the Host and chalice to them through an opening. I saw the robed figures shuffle forward and lean toward the proffered sacrifice as the priest fed them their share of Jesus Christ.

The main event over, he stood up. I quietly made my exit during the holy high point of the ceremony, crossing myself quickly as I left the pew and went into the hallway.

A few of the heavy trestle tables offered brochures. A door with "Cloister" written on it in gothic script barred me from the convent itself. The story of the wilful, disobedient nun who became a thief seemed beyond my reach forever.

I sighed and wandered over to the massive trestle table to pick up a brochure. This order could only have been created and supported by prominent Catholic families. And indeed, as the brochure explained, the anonymous donor of the marvelous paintings of the Stations of the Cross had been a major art collector who felt holy art should be exhibited in a church, not a museum.

I thought back on the arcane, beautiful ceremony, the two elderly civilian celebrants and the nuns inside their cages. What a contradiction of silence, beauty, guilt and superstition it all was! How could I know Rebecca's story or guess her ecstacies? My soul was so stained with sin I was practically polka-dotted. My shoulderbag hung heavy at my side, and I quickened my pace.

I took a deep breath of the cold clean air, stood a moment in the silence and then went outdoors. Even the swaying of the eucalyptus seemed too busy, the humming of bees on the bright bougainvillea too demanding. The sunlight hurt my eyes. Who came to this place any more? Surely those old nuns had no living parents? I looked back at the big chapel. All human life seemed gone from it now. The nuns were back in the cloister, safely hidden from me.

I glanced along the cyclone fence and imagined climbing over it. But I knew what I would find if I could get inside—grass and a lot of angry nuns. Not much more. I drew closer to the fence and gazed through the forbidding wires.

There it was, the enclosed garden where religious women passed their lives, day after day, year after year, immune from the outside world. A fountain gurgled somewhere within and I was reminded of the complicated symbolic imagery of medieval paintings: Mary would be seated within a garden, an angel appearing to her, the symbol of the white dove a positive pregnancy test. All would be transformed and holy for her after that moment, and depictions of the Annunciation would revel in joyous imagery. There was no more perfect setting than this garden.

Flowers crept and climbed along a series of hedges, anemones waved in the breeze. Hollyhocks stood guard over delicate delphiniums, violets popped their velvet heads up everywhere. Then I saw something move.

A shadow glided over the colorful carpet. What *was* it? It disappeared behind a hedge. I stood, holding my breath. Waiting, I watched poppies folding in the breeze. All was still.

There! Again it appeared, moving behind the shrubbery. It seemed to be circling relentlessly toward me. It moved like a hand passing over the sun. I felt suddenly cold.

Then it reappeared, a dark shape directly in my line of vision. Two points of light, like hot coals, burned into my face. My skin flushed as I stood transfixed. The dark blob came closer and closer.

The points of light became eyes and the creature emerged clearly now from the shrubbery and flowers. It made a beeline for me and I saw that its gliding movement was due to the wheels beneath the shroud.

A white flash of face was revealed beneath the scapular covering head and shoulders. The two eyes narrowed and I stood, hypnotized by her gaze.

"Come a little closer, my child," her shaky voice emanated from beneath the heavy cloth. I moved up the ridge and put my hands on the fence. Her elderly wheelchair, of light brown oak, had been fitted with dirt bike wheels and a motor on the back. New handgrips indicated modern brakes which kept her from rolling down the hillside.

The vehicle held a thin figure, encased in heavy black serge. The brown scapular covered her head, and a white semicircular bib, starched stiff as a plate, sat upon her sinking breast. I heard a slow uneven breath from her shadow-hidden face.

"Are you visiting our lovely order?" I knelt down to see the thin lips, holding back spittle, and watery, blue-rimmed eyes, almost colorless within. She must have been ninety. I hoped desperately that she wasn't too senile and that I could get her to talk to me. She was exactly what I'd prayed for.

"Come closer, I want to be *near* you," she said.

"Yes, of course." I moved along the fence, grabbing the wires, then lowered myself again, so that she could see me. She squinted, cocked her head and finally nodded.

"You have come here on a beautiful morning. Perhaps you're interested in the religious life?"

"No, no, actually the cloistered life is not for me." But as I gazed at the beautiful garden, I had a moment of doubt.

"But I can tell that something is troubling you, my child." She smiled tolerantly and leaned back. "The cloistered life can provide a sanctuary, you know. We aren't devoid of contact. The fence is merely a symbolic separation. But behind it we are safe. What is troubling you, my dear? Surely the stain of sin is not so indelible as you think—"

"I'm not looking for absolution." My shoulderbag felt heavy, like a fatal tap on my shoulder. "I couldn't see it for myself. I'm not really religious, you see—"

"Yes, well," she chuckled. "It was very different for me when I was your age. Don't think for a moment that our life was boring here." She leaned forward, a gleam of excitement shining from her eyes. "The church calendar's endless variety of liturgy and celebration, the eagerly anticipated visits by confessors, superiors and bishops, the rites of initiation and passage! There were so many of us then!" She warmed to her theme.

"Can you imagine, the soaring of Gregorian chants as the novice choir, almost a hundred of us, sang with one voice?" A bee buzzed her habit. Shopping for pollen, it tried out the taste of her black serge robes. The old nun paused, following its course, her blue eyes passively watching the insect, her breathing raspy and labored.

"It's all over now, isn't it?" she asked. I thought about the few ancient civilians I'd seen at Mass.

"Yes," I said. "It's all over now. At least probably in San Diego. Maybe not in Poland." I shrugged.

"You can't imagine, summers here at the Motherhouse, when all my friends would come back." She leaned forward and put her hand on the fence, near mine. I wondered if her skin was allowed to touch uncloistered outside air. "Years and years of friendships, holy women, wonderful women blessed by God."

"Could you tell me about one of them? One who wasn't so holy?"

"We are all striving toward perfection—"

"But someone who committed a grievous sin."

"There are many grievous sinners in God's eyes, many grievous sins."

"*Sister Roberta Claire,*" I said, repeating the name I'd seen inscribed in the small black book I'd found in Rebecca's house. The nun name that I thought had been Rebecca's.

The silence that fell was more final than the fence between us. The nun lowered her head as the bony fingers uncurled from the wires, and the hand retreated into the folds of her habit.

"Please, I'm just trying to understand. I'm a friend of her great-niece. Sister Roberta Claire died over a month ago." The old nun nodded. How many death notices had the old nun received in the last ten years, the last twenty?

"A week ago I came to her house with my friend," I explained quickly. "She's very anxious to know something of her aunt's life here. And what happened."

"That's strictly private convent business. It's old history," she said sternly. "It's over and there's nothing to be done about it." Her thin, almost invisible lips pressed together with finality.

Gulping, I made a renewed effort. "Are you sure you wouldn't like to tell me, to tell someone?"

The old nun's face softened for a moment. But she spoke firmly.

"We are not allowed to speak about any of our business to the laity. We are the servants of divinity. We are—" She sat up straighter.

"Yes, I know. I understand. But this is a personal family matter. I won't tell anyone else. My friend, well, she needs to know. To feel at peace with her aunt's dear memory." I groaned inwardly at the cliché, but I could feel the nun's sympathy with the sentiment. I looked into her face and read the history of vows, of loyalty to the community, of denial of so many things, good and bad. But there was something else. That gleam in her eye hinted at a desire to tell of former times. A secret ready to emerge. I had the perfect excuse for her.

I reached into my shoulderbag and slowly drew out the precious box. It glimmered in the sunlight, its butterflies, pearls, petals of precious metal glowing in the brightness. The old woman gasped, crossed herself, and sunk back in terror.

"Where did you find that?" she demanded.

"Will you tell me about Roberta Claire?"

"That is convent property! It's precious! Invaluable!"

"I know. And I know that something terrible must have happened to Roberta Claire to have made her take it. She was a devout, like yourself. I have to know the story."

"I can't tell you! I won't! And you have to give that back!"

"Of course! Of course I'll give it back. But first I want to know the story of Sister Roberta Claire! You tell me the story and this box goes back to the convent. You don't, and I go home with the *ostensorium*. And what's inside!"

The old nun rolled her eyes up at me, her pale blue gaze now fierce and pained. "All right, all right. I'll tell you what you want to know. And then, you will return the holy box."

"Yes," I said. "Yes, I promise."

A cagey look came over her face. "You will give it to me to return?" her voice became higher.

"Whatever you like." Convent politics. And I fingered the box, provocatively, just out of her reach.

"So tell me about Roberta Claire. Tell me how she left here."

"She left more than the convent." The voice was quiet, subdued now. She spoke as if from somewhere far away, shielded not only by the cloth, but by years of denial of a memory that must have tormented the Sister Adorers of the Precious Blood for years. *"She left God,"* the old nun whispered.

"I know. She did something terrible. But I'm just trying to understand. I come from a different world from yours or hers. This all looks very beautiful to me, but I want to understand why she made the choices she did. It's hard for me to see why someone would join an order like this, and then, having made that choice, do what she did."

"Why did she join the order? The reason we all joined. To be with God. To live this simple life." The nun's thin papery white lips curled into a smile, and I saw the ghost of a former happiness. The ghost of a young, hopeful, girlish face.

"What were the alternatives?"

"Secular life? For me it would have been marriage to some businessman. Oh yes, I could have married wealth. But what would be the wealth of the world, cooped up with a man and children, children, children? Do you understand now, you modern young woman who can do what she wants, what it is like to be denied an inner life? Sometimes," she lifted her head, "I think I wanted to join the order just so that I could read!" She slapped her brittle hand down on the armrest of the wheelchair. "Women weren't supposed to do a lot of things in those days. This may look like prison to you, but in 1915 it looked like freedom to me." She leaned back and laughed for a moment. I took the plunge.

"And Sister Roberta Claire?"

Her head fell forward and from her dark cowl I heard the deep intake of breath that I knew signaled the beginning of her painful story.

30

"Sister Roberta was a quiet one." The words came slow and tentative. "Maybe too quiet for even the Grand Silence. But we do the best we can here—striving for perfection isn't easy. And Sister Roberta was one of the most pious.

"It was so long ago, so very long ago. I can still remember the day she first arrived. She spent most of her time in the chapel, arms outstretched, bare knees to the ground. I went to her after dinner and told her that homesickness was a natural thing. That she would get used to it. That she should let herself get used to the life here before she punished herself too severely.

"I told her, 'Sister Roberta, impure thoughts are only venial sins as long as you struggle against them. They become mortal sins only when you allow yourself to *enjoy* them.' But she just continued with her rigorous self-discipline. I think she came from a family that didn't treat her right. Do you know what I mean?

"There's times," the old nun leaned toward the fence conspiratorially, "when pain just parades as piety. Anyway, I felt sorry for her. I encouraged her to come and talk to me. Sometimes she did. But then she was assigned to take care of the altar and clean the statuary. And that became everything for her.

"We couldn't get her to stop working. She was forever polishing and even restoring bits of broken plaster on the large figures of saints. She read up in books about restoration and spent hours looking at the paintings, the Stations of the Cross. She talked to Mother Superior about how they shouldn't be in such a damp environment. She was worried about their condition, you see.

"God intended art for prayer!" Mother Superior would sniff, and send Sister Roberta Claire to do penance for the pride of ownership of such items.

"One day Sister Roberta Claire got hold of some modeling clay. I was helping to clean up the store room when I saw her take it off the shelf. Moist it was, still in its packing. Well, I saw Roberta Claire open the plastic package and dig her fingers into the wet mass.

" 'Sister!' I said, worried that she would dirty her habit. But I should have been worried about a lot more than that. That was the moment of her downfall. That was the moment of pride and possession, something extremely good or horribly evil." The nun's eyes met mine and I was drawn away from the beauty of the garden, the peacefulness of the day, into the horror of that cold, dark room.

" 'Don't soil yourself!' I said, but Sister didn't seem to hear me. I watched as her fingers dug into the bag again and came out holding two lumps of the plastic gray matter.

"I shall never forget what happened." The nun shook her head slowly. "To this day I don't know if it was the Devil that guided those fingers." She raised her hands into the air, cupping some unseen form. "She put her hands up like this, with the clay in between them, and just twitched her fingers over the surface of the mud. Little movements, a push here, a long smooth stroke there," the nun's index finger worked the air in front of her.

"And then, from between the two hands of that simple farm girl something emerged, something I didn't want to see, something too sophisticated to be made that simply, that easily. Why, with just a few movements, a little massaging of mud, a perfect image of Our Lady appeared from between the palms of Roberta Claire!

"And that wasn't all. The Divine Virgin was balanced on a globe, her dresses flowing as if a fresh breeze had just caught them and a smile that was the embodiment of divine maternal love on her face." The nun crossed herself and looked up at me, her eyes glittering with the memory, her thin and trembling hands still describing that moment of miracle.

"Then what happened?"

"Sister Roberta stared at the holy image and then looked up at me. She seemed as surprised as I did. I can tell you that. She put the clay image of the Virgin down on the table, but I guess the clay was wet because the statue seemed to sort of sag backwards. Then it fell over, squashing the globe the Holy Mother stood on.

"So then Sister Roberta took another lump of clay, bigger this time, and blessed be Our Savior if another Holy Virgin wasn't formed right then and there between her palms! This one stood on a crescent moon and had those almond-shaped, Indian sort of eyes, with high cheekbones and a protruding nose. It was even more beautiful than the last."

"Our Lady of Guadalupe," I murmured.

"Well, she put that one down on the table and got more clay and kept on going. Our Lady of Lourdes, the Virgin Enthroned, Virgin Lamenting—she did them all. Those hands just kept fashioning Virgin after Virgin with perfect robed bodies and splendid faces with divine expressions. Sister Roberta looked as though she was in some kind of trance. She didn't even look as if she knew what she was doing.

"I didn't know what to do. I felt so sure I was in the presence of a heavenly spirit—or the Devil! Blasphemy! I thought. Yes, blasphemy! A terror seized me and I ran out of the room and back to my cell, where I prayed for the deliverance of Sister's soul.

"But Sister Roberta Claire stayed there in that room, all day. Missing Mass. Missing dinner.

"The next morning, Sister Roberta Claire was at the communion rail when Mother Superior seized her by her ear. Mother gripped tightly and twisted bringing Roberta to her feet and pulling her away from the rail.

"We found out what happened at breakfast. Mother Superior had found one of the statues before it had been put into the oven. Sister Roberta Claire was forced to kneel in front of Mother Superior's place at the table and crush the little statue with a hammer. And then, when she had crushed her upon the floor, Mother Superior got a spoon. And made her eat the raw clay!"

"Jesus Christ!" I whispered.

"No, the Virgin." The nun crossed herself.

" 'The Devil's temptations are legion,' " Mother told us that morning. But then, our Mother Superior at that time could have found fault with the Virgin herself.

"Sister Roberta Claire wouldn't last long after that, I thought as I looked at her lips smeared red with the clay. It would come to no good. But worse was to follow."

"What happened?" I whispered.

"Now child, you must promise to keep this a secret."

"I will."

"You must promise to return the property of the community."

"Yes, yes," I said. "Go on!"

She looked at the box with an expression of memory and pain. Then she drew her eyes away and looked into my face.

"The Lord be with you, my child," she said quietly, sadly, and for a moment I was frightened of what she saw, of what I thought I could see.

"What happened?" I whispered again.

"Well, Sister Roberta Claire was banned from making idols, as Mother called them. But I knew where that clay was. I saw it mysteriously disappear, the bag getting smaller and smaller. And Sister Roberta Claire spent more and more time at the library. We all knew it was happening. Whispers heard along the corridors. From whence came this amazing skill? It was frightening.

"I knew it would come to no good. Sister Roberta Claire had a fine and special spirit, but she needed guidance. Her confessor was useless. He couldn't distinguish between venial and mortal sins, just prescribed self-punishment that was useless in the face of the huge force that lingered in her hands. I could see the Sister drifting further and further away from the Lord as her enjoyment of sin increased."

I looked up sharply. "What else did she enjoy?" I asked. I glanced around at the profusion of flowers within the compound, but I knew. Flowers, art and silence wouldn't have been enough for the passionate young woman.

The nun leaned back in her chair. "Pride. And a particular friendship. *That's* what she enjoyed."

"I beg your pardon?"

"We must always be on guard you see. Our love is intended for Our Lord and the love we feel for our sisters must be spread equally." She smiled and tilted her head back. "But you know that's pretty hard. My child, it's hard to understand the charity we must feel, the things to which we must acquiesce. There are some (God forgive me!), some real old biddies in here, and some friendships that are, well, hard to replace, hard to say goodbye to . . ." she drifted off.

I was beginning to understand more about this community of women, bound together for their entire lives, choosing a religious life and choosing each other. How did they make the adjustment?

"It must be quite a struggle. But of course women do form friendships."

"Yes, it happens," she sighed. "And Sister Roberta Claire was unprepared. She was so naïve, so simple, you see. It wasn't really her fault. Not all the hail Mary's and humiliations in the world could have saved her from her feelings for Sister Theophane."

"Sister Theophane?"

"Yes. Sister Roberta Claire arrived almost a full year before Sister Theophane. Even after being in the convent for all that time she still seemed to prefer her own company, or the company of the clay I knew was disappearing.

"She had difficulties, you see. Sister Roberta Claire wasn't particularly scholarly, and many of the women came from well-educated families. Sister Roberta Claire had a hard time keeping up with the conversation of the confident young women from privileged homes, and had a hard time at theology classes. When Sister Theophane arrived her whole life changed.

"Sister Theophane took special notice of Sister Roberta and, I think as a charitable gesture, accompanied her to Mass, and then helped her with her studies. She was very willing to be helpful to the talented young sparrow.

"Perhaps not surprisingly, Sister Roberta seemed to bloom under the generous tutelage. Suddenly she was studying and reading all the time, finding even more meaning and, dare I say it, historical, not religious significance in the art which captured her soul. She pestered Sister Theophane with questions, and Sister Theophane always had a warm ready answer.

"At dinner she would come up with ideas—remarks that not only surprised us all, but indicated a rather delightful turn of mind. Sister Theophane, for her part, seemed proud of the young talented postulant, as if her blooming intelligence was her own doing." The nun shuddered. "Such is not the way of nuns. It is the way to false pride, and a distraction from the love of Christ for which we are intended."

"What did she look like?"

"Sister Theophane? Oh, she was beautiful. Yes, I can say that. The Lord gave her beauty of face. But Sister Roberta Claire was getting far too involved in worldly subjects, far too excited by her academic studies. And far too focused on the heavenly beauty of that earthly face.

"It seemed as though they were chattering away all the time, with an excitement that was not holy. Mother Superior began to frown on them, started placing them at different dinner tables. It was no use. Their attachment was totally disruptive.

"Sister Roberta Claire would moon at Sister Theophane from across the room. Even if their eyes didn't meet, we could all feel their attention focusing on each other. It was as if the fifty sisters sitting between them didn't exist. Roberta Claire and Theophane ate together in their own private world.

"One day that world was shattered. We watched the Mother Superior enter the dining hall with a face full of fury, clutching a piece of paper in her hand. She sat down and watched us commence our meal but the pace of our eating became slower and slower as we wondered what had so thrown Mother into a fury.

"The whispers began. Sister Dolores started telling us her story over the soup. She was the Mother's Secretary and that day she had opened a letter from the Bishop. The letter commended the talents of Roberta Claire on her fine skills as a sculptress and ordered several of the statues for the diocese in Chicago.

"It was not a commission that pleased the Mother. She had ordered Dolores to deny the request, saying the statuary was no longer available and the nun who had made such things was serving a deep and complex penance.

"The whispers about the letter floated along the air in between the clank of silverware. Heads turned to give tentative looks at Roberta and Theophane who were still locked in a gaze across the dining room. They seemed oblivious to the cold eye Mother cast across the room, to the mumblings that were all about them.

"Sister Revula approached Roberta Claire with the large pitcher which held the weak black tea. Sister Roberta barely noticed her. She held her cup aloft with a finger weak with lovesick feelings. Revula, nervous herself, must have poured too quickly and the weight of the tea made the cup fall from Roberta's hands. The hot scalding liquid poured into her lap and she jumped up, dropping the cup which smashed into a million pieces on the floor.

"We all stopped eating. Even Roberta Claire was jolted out of her reverie by the burning tea in her lap. Then we heard the footsteps of Mother Superior.

"We always froze in terror at the sound of smashing crockery. We all lived in fear of breaking anything. Those were times, my child, you cannot imagine.

"When Mother Superior strolled over to Sister Roberta Claire, Roberta lowered her eyes and crossed herself. But it wasn't enough.

" 'I'm sorry Mother!' " she cried to no avail.

" 'Do it, Sister,' " Mother Superior commanded, and we knew what she meant. Another Sister drew away Roberta's chair as Roberta gathered up her skirts. Her bare knees hit the floor, littered with broken shards of pottery. Mother picked up two of the larger pieces of the cup and put one in each of Roberta's hands. Then Roberta raised both hands over her head holding the broken crockery. At a signal from the Mother we all began eating.

"That's how it went, every night for the next week. Roberta's arms trembling with exhaustion. Knees bleeding, she would kneel at the table, and we were all forced to eat in front of her.

"Only after the others finished their meal was she allowed to eat. She ate the cold food in silence, scooping congealed soup into her mouth while blood ran from her knees. I used to sneak iodine and bandages to her at night, hoping the cuts would heal a bit before the next day's ordeal."

"And Roberta Claire? How did she take it?"

The old nun smiled and shook her head. "With grace, my dear. With the grace of God she smiled through every meal.

"We were all terrified of Mother Superior. Except Roberta. She started helping Sister Theophane with her chores. To say Sister Theophane was not used to manual labor was an understatement. She didn't even pick up her clothes at home because maids had apparently followed her around and done it for her. We often found Theophane's undergarments on the floor around the bed.

"We thought it was just a matter of time before Sister Theophane was punished, but we were wrong. Somehow Sister Theophane's transgressions slid by the Mother's eyes." The old nun started wheezing. Her eyelids fluttered.

"Sister Roberta Claire took it upon herself to save Sister

Theophane from uncomfortable punishments. She instructed Sister Theophane in darning, dishwashing and floor-scrubbing. Yes, Sister Roberta Claire made it her task to instruct Sister Theophane in the redemptive power of manual work. It was a lovely friendship, really. Particular, but still, we almost enjoyed watching the two of them, so unlikely, so giving of themselves to each other. Of course, we were all struggling with sin. Sister Theophane and Sister Roberta Claire just seemed to have found some company.

"They would see each other during recreation and take long walks together. We heard them meeting under the stairwell, giggling during the Grand Silence. I don't think Sister Roberta had ever known any real joy in her life. Perhaps Sister Theophane's jokes, silliness, charming stories and light, quick step were easier and more accessible to Sister Roberta than Jesus's more demanding love."

"Makes sense to me," I mumbled.

"What?" She frowned.

"Nothing."

The nun viewed me suspiciously for a moment. I could see that telling the story was lifting a burden from her soul. She took a labored breath. For a moment I wondered if I would be her last confessor.

"I thought Sister Roberta Claire would outgrow her infatuation with Sister Theophane," she continued. "She had been so very pious, you see. I felt sure her love of Our Lord would ease her away from this worldly attachment, from the forbidden making of pagan idolatry."

"But wasn't it your duty to report any breaking of the rules to the Mother Superior?"

"My child, you are from another world, another time, sinful as I know you to be. We avoided any contact with Mother Superior. Her life was the Holy Rule and there was nothing she liked more than a long line of nuns kissing the floor in front of her, confessing their peccadilloes. So you were careful never to seek her attention. One month, we *all* ate kneeling on the floor. We had Sisters who stopped eating altogether. We had Sisters who hallucinated, stopped their menses, started screaming suddenly in the night. The search for perfection, my child, is not such a perfect thing. We lost a lot of Sisters that year.

"But that wasn't the only reason we didn't turn Sister Theophane and Sister Roberta in. There was something else. Something that wasn't really talked out. Something we chose to be blinded to, just as you are blinded to your own sinfulness." Her eyes fell on the box again. I moved it casually between my palms.

"It was, of course, Sister Theophane's family. Those Bishops, Jesuits and Abbess aunts were a lineup to be reckoned with. Not to mention her dowry. Oh yes! Theophane came with an endowment for the community. It was a coup for the Mother Superior when Sister Theophane entered *our* order. I thought I saw Mother Superior glance at her beautiful face in a secular appreciation more than once.

"Sister Theophane's attentions to Sister Roberta Claire infuriated the Mother Superior. Praise be to Christ!" The nun crossed herself, "the Church is fallible."

"But their relationship developed unimpeded?"

"Unimpeded? The religious life appeals to many for its sense of mystery and romance, my dear child. Sometimes it's hard to believe that you're married to Jesus, that you've taken a crucified man as spouse. Our hearts yearn for completion, and when there's someone so close, so wonderful that you can't help yourself from wanting to talk to them, that you find yourself talking to them all the time in your head! When the slightest flicker of a glance can make you drop your rosary, when you can't bear not to touch them—oh! It's so hard to resist."

"And Sister Roberta Claire didn't resist?"

"At first she did. I remember one night before we went to bed I saw her struggling as I glanced behind the curtain that was pulled between our beds.

"She was holding a leather thong. It was standard issue. I wasn't surprised. I came in and stood next to her bed. We weren't allowed to sit on each other's beds, you understand. I looked down and saw that Sister Roberta was crying.

"Then she put the piece of leather in my hand and asked me to tie her hands to the bedframe. She said that she was tempted to impure manipulations. I just comforted her, as I would comfort you. I gave her back the thong, and stroked her head. She was warm, a bit feverish. I told her that we were all human, and needed divine guidance and forgiveness more than mechanical interventions. I advised her to pray. I told her I would pray with her. But apparently to no avail.

"She couldn't resist. The sins of impurity and the Devil, had her soul." The nun looked up at me and I knew she saw the Devil in my soul as well.

"Go on," I said.

"I saw all the signs, my child. Often I would be the first in the dormitory at night. I would see the little offerings Sister Roberta had placed on Sister Theophane's pillow—holy cards perhaps, or a little book that she'd made. Even, once, a perfect clay rose, unbaked of course, with a pearl-shaped dewdrop on one of the petals." The nun shivered. "Secular. So incredibly secular." She shook her head.

"And then, some months later when I was having trouble sleeping, I would see and hear it happen, praise be to Christ!

"Sister Theophane padding silently, waiting until she thought we were all asleep, to Sister Roberta's bed. Holy Mary, Mother of God! I would hear the rustle of the drawn curtains, the sound of the metal curtain rings on the rod above the bed. I would hear the bed creak as Roberta crawled under the covers with her. I wondered what it felt like to them, to be so together, so warm. I would listen in the darkness. I would watch the big white square of the curtain which separated them from the rest of us and I would wonder. And then I would listen as their breathing became slower and more even. And then I knew."

"Knew?"

"Yes. That they had fallen asleep. Glory be to the Father, Son and Holy Ghost!"

"Asleep?"

"Yes," the old nun looked up at me. "They slept," she sighed and crossed herself again. "Together."

Just sleeping? I thought. Too bad! All that for a night of cuddling!

The nun nodded her head sadly. "But still I didn't say anything, Holy Mary Mother of God!"

"Why not?"

"Why do you think, my child? I am not perfect either. Pray for us, Mary, now and in the moment of our sin. I was having my own struggle, my child, with a particular friendship."

No wonder you listened so carefully, I thought. What a hotbed of denial the old nunnery must have been!

"But then came the day when we couldn't ignore it any longer." She shuddered. "It was hot and humid. There was not the slightest breeze. The Devil must have stopped the wind, shadowed us from the sweet love of the Virgin herself. Otherwise it could never have happened.

"The whole affair came to a head that day." She glanced at my hands where the golden box was resting. "That day that was supposed to be the most glorious of days for the rest of our lives. The day Sister Roberta and Sister Theophane were meant to lay their lives on the altar for Christ."

"The wedding day?" I murmured.

"It is not a wedding like any other, my child. You are a bride, but you join your bridegroom who is crucified in a holy union without touch or sorrow. But such was not the fate of Sister Theophane and Sister Roberta.

"Pray for us!" Her voice was suddenly loud. She tilted her head back on her old spindly neck, and stared straight into the sun with her eyes wide open, her pupils becoming pinpoints. "Pray for us in the moment of our death!" she cried and her head rolled back onto her chest. She began to tremble.

"Sister Theophane and Sister Roberta Claire did not join our Savior in Holy Matrimony," she whispered. "They went to join the Devil in everlasting hell!"

❧ 31 ❧

"Chastity," the old nun mumbled. "Practice it by keeping a close watch on your every thought and feeling. The Devil will try to tempt you to impure thoughts from time to time." She looked up again at me. "I can see that the Devil has tempted you, my child, but there is still time. If you are aware of his tricks you will be able to put such thoughts out of your mind!" She looked at me intently, warningly, and I felt the box grow heavier and heavier in my hand.

"Please continue," I encouraged her softly.

"It was hot," she began. "At five a.m., even in the darkness you could feel the sun begin to exert its influence, ready to bake the earth, ready to broil us all. It was as if Christ would have us walk through the fires of hell to become His brides.

"So that morning we were all excited and drenched in sweat. We weren't thinking about the heaviness of the habits we would be wearing. This day promised the ultimate fulfillment, you see, after years of studying and praying. It was the beginning of our marriage with Christ. We would take our final vows," the old nun said, smiling slightly. "Final vows! By the ministry of Christ on His altar with an odor of sweetness." She glanced around the garden. "When is that Sister George coming with my medication?"

"That morning—" I started for her.

"That morning. Yes. I'm tired."

"Please."

"It's not easy, you know, to tell this story. I wish Sister George would come. Where is she?"

I fingered the box. Her eyes narrowed and she took a deep breath.

"That morning. That particular morning the dormitory was alive with dawning sunlight and laughter. Everyone was happy, despite the heat, and we couldn't seem to look at each other without breaking into joyous laughter. Can you imagine? All those young women, so ready to be fulfilled."

I tried to imagine it. A holy honeymoon without a warm body. It didn't seem so joyous to me.

"Go on," I said, if only to hear my own voice.

"Sister Theophane's family had bought her a beautiful wedding gown. Many of the women had new gowns on that day. Our order attracted families of a higher social order, and although we take our vows of poverty, for some it's all relative." She grinned. "No pun intended.

"Sister Roberta Claire chose *her* gown from among many hand-me-downs and rejects which were given to the convent, and kept in a closet all year long, for just this occasion.

"We all knew our families would be there. We had pinned our hair up the night before, laughing even after the bell. We couldn't control our excitement. And nobody had thought, or at least nobody had mentioned, that on the following night we would have no hair at all.

"That morning, I remember watching Sister Theophane. She brushed that long, beautiful red hair of hers, stroke after stroke. Some vanity was allowed. After all, we were preparing for our bridegroom, Jesus Christ. But it wasn't Jesus who watched her that morning. It was Sister Roberta Claire. Her hair was set in a simple bun. She stood mesmerized, watching Sister Theophane. Despite the heat, she was brushing that long red hair again and again."

Heat and long red hair. Decades later it had me swooning. Tendrils of hair reaching toward me over time.

"Sister Roberta had been up all night. I knew because I had been awake that night also, Christ forgive me. There was such an air of expectation, we were all turning in our sheets, and you could feel the sleeplessness that filled the dormitory.

"Sister Roberta didn't—" she paused, "didn't visit Sister Theophane's bed that night. She'd stayed awake, solitary, with the rest of us. I wonder now if she worried, lying awake all night in the sleeping position prescribed by Mother Superior. Had Sister Roberta Claire been a good bride of Jesus? Sleeping on her back with her hands folded against her breast? I wondered as I watched her mesmerized by the sight of Sister Theophane's hairbrush."

Hair that had somehow found its way into a hatbox on top of a metal cabinet, hair that still smelled sweet. I had smelled the hot summer odor of that day on Sister Theophane's hair, years later, in Montana.

"Sister Roberta Claire looked pale and wan, not like the others, who were full of hope and high color. Her family hadn't come. Rumor had it they were Lutherans.

"In any event, Sister Theophane's whole family was there—wealthy landowners from Montana—even the mother of the Archibishop of Chicago was there to witness Sister Theophane's wedding.

"But Sister Theophane wasn't thinking about that when she looked over her own shoulder in the mirror and saw Sister Roberta Claire staring, somewhat morosely, at her. She stopped brushing and went over to her, and I saw her put her hands on Sister Roberta Claire's waist, turn her around and fix some of the satin buttons which had come undone along her neck. Then Roberta reached for a small basket by her bedside. She scooped up violets and tiny roses and started weaving the little flowers into Theophane's hair.

"Your hands are touched by God," I heard Sister Theophane

say, and she kissed the tips of Sister Roberta Claire's fingers. The white satin of Sister Roberta's wedding gown had turned dark with sweat along her spine.

"Sister Theophane paused a moment, looking at that wet stripe, and I thought I saw her stroke Sister Roberta Claire, and fondling the nape of her neck.

"Oh, impurity!" the nun moaned. "Wouldst thou crucify the Son of God a second time, hold Him up to mockery a second time, for your own ends?" She swayed and her chair creaked. Don't pass out, I thought, desperately. Caught behind the fence there would be no way I could help her. Then the old woman relaxed and took a few more deep breaths.

"You mean they didn't hide their affection?" I asked gently.

"I don't think they thought to hide such gestures, everyone else was so excited helping each other with getting ready for the big morning. And it was—" the old nun looked at me through her watery blue eyes, "it was in some ways so innocent. I was so confused. I didn't know what to do, Lord forgive me. Perhaps if I had said something, broken into their reverie—but we were all so carried away, *waiting* to be carried away."

"Go on."

"Then church bells began to chime, and we all lined up, two by two. It felt like a dream, all these women floating in their white clouds, sailing through the stifling heat, toward the church. I remember my friend, my—" the nun squinted at me, "my *particular* friend, took my hand, dripping with sweat, and squeezed it. Then she quickly went to stand next to someone else.

"We entered the church and stood still, the two long rows of virgins, ready for the supreme sacrifice. The organ boomed, we saw our families and the other nuns standing silent and still in the stuffy, oppressive heat. Then we all turned our eyes toward the bishop. We were in awe of him and terrified. He was the male representation of God—the closest thing to a bridegroom we'd get.

"I remembered his stern words that morning as they seared our hearts." She took a deep breath.

" 'Your life will be hidden with Christ,' he boomed, his brow beaded with sweat. *'His eye only* will know your prayers, your vigils, your mortifications. *His eye only* will see your early risings, your great fidelity to a rigid rule, your patience in trial. *His eye only* has knowledge of the victory of self, of your sacrifice of all human consolation. Give,' he cried out, almost yelling over our pious, bended heads, 'give your pure heart to Him to Whom you have consecrated your love. Become as Him, a Divine Victim.' "

The nun was yelling too, her thin elderly voice carrying through the garden. I looked beyond her nervously.

"And then the bishop called out our names. One by one we approached the altar heaped with flowers, orange blossoms exuding fragrance in the heat, and flaming with candles. We heard mothers weeping, older nuns just holding back their tears, and siblings looking at us with awe, everyone wiping their foreheads in the heat of the chapel. They were all admiring us because they thought we were going to become something other, something holy, something divine. Victims. Divine Victims.

"The bishop blessed our habits and we each went silently to the altar and received the heavy bundle of clothes that would separate us from the rest of the world forever.

"Silently we filed out of the church to gather in the library. There we would don our habits and cut each other's hair. When I got there, Sister Roberta Claire was waiting. She still had her wedding dress on, large stains of sweat beneath the tight white sleeves."

I gripped the cyclone fence tightly.

"Everything was in such chaos. Our huge class of postulants, hair sticking damply to foreheads, were eagerly yet fearfully struggling with the huge amounts of heavy, dark serge. As a clumsy postulant gouged away at my scalp, I glanced around me, trying to escape the moment. Others were crying or frantically absorbed in the complexities of their new raiment. I barely noticed the quiet Sister Roberta Claire, still in her hand-me-down wedding dress, greeting Sister Theophane.

"Sister Theophane came toward Sister Roberta Claire as if in a trance. She gathered up some of her red tresses in her hands and offered them to Sister Roberta Claire. Roberta didn't look at the hair, but back at Sister Theophane. They looked at each other for what seemed a long time.

"Then, finally, Sister Roberta Claire picked up the scissors, one of many pairs that were sitting waiting on the table, and motioned for Sister Theophane to sit in front of her on the stool.

"Sister Roberta Claire put her hand on Sister Theophane's shoulder, and I saw Sister Theophane touch her hand in reassurance. Then, with the sharp shears, Sister Roberta Claire cut one long strand of hair and then another. She held the long strands out, away from Sister Theophane's head, then put the blade scissors around the hair, pressed her fingers on the handle and watched the steel blades slice through the strands. She watched each long curl drop to the floor and then picked up another strand. They were both horribly still.

"And as the last of that red hair fell on the floor, it wasn't Sister Theophane who cried, it was Sister Roberta Claire. Tears streaming down her face, she reached over onto the table for the *serre-tête,* the white frame which would set Sister Theophane's face apart forever.

"There was something too final about this action, and Sister Theophane put her hand up to Sister Roberta Claire's just as she had reached for the straight pins which would secure the linen bands at the back of her neck. It was the yoke of Christ, and I think, at that moment, neither Sister Roberta Claire, nor Sister Theophane wanted to bear it.

"Sister Theophane was crying now too, realizing they were both denying their vocation. Sister Roberta Claire's little sobs were becoming audible, they were getting hard to ignore. The room became quieter.

"Slowly we all turned to watch them—Sister Theophane, her face frozen in that *serre-tête* and without that red hair. Within that perfect black and white frame, she looked beautiful but static, dying, dead. Then Sister Roberta Claire took Sister Theophane's chin with both her hands, drew her perfect, wet mouth up to her own and kissed her.

"In that moment they were free, perhaps, but we all stood there, transfixed as much by the image as by the horror of the transgression. Sister Roberta Claire in her hand-me-down white lace gown, her feet lost in a cloud of red hair that billowed all over the floor, and Sister Theophane, her face fixed in a nun's frame, the two of them locked in an embrace that would release them from God's goodness forever.

"With Sister Theophane's chin held firmly in her hands, Sister Roberta Claire wouldn't let go. She was kissing Sister Theophane's lips again and again, kissing her all over her mouth, all over her tear-stained cheeks.

"Theophane reached up and pulled Roberta closer, the two women knowing that in this moment they were casting themselves out of the community with a fearful velocity. We all sat there, not just looking, but longing, because it is a terrifying thing to become a bride of Christ, to take the solemn vows of chastity, obedience and poverty, and there were these two beautiful women who, at the last moment, had turned their backs on that terrifying, torturous, holy path. And then the door to the sacristy opened and closed. Mother Superior walked in."

32

"Complete silence fell as she entered. It was more frightening than anything I have ever felt before or since. Mother Superior's face went dark with fury. I saw her mouth working back and forth, twitching as she witnessed the embrace.

"We all stood frozen to the spot. Wet with sweat, shears in hand, waiting habits draped on tables, wedding dresses hung up on pegs. Our eyes traveled from the furious face of Mother Superior back to Sister Roberta and Sister Theophane, who were embracing each other desperately, their faces shining with tears and perspiration.

"Mother Superior slammed the door behind her, but still the two women did not stop kissing. Slowly she made her way across the floor, like a tiger silently preparing to strike. We watched her advance, her feet crushing the hair where it lay. And then she stood before them, a towering figure of rage, and still they did not see her. Without taking her eyes off the offending pair, Mother Superior reached behind her onto the table. Someone gasped as we watched her strong, sure hands find the scissors. Mother's fingertips curled around the pivot point of the shining shears. Her hand forming a fist around the steel.

"Something in the silence of the room penetrated the two Sisters' embrace. Their faces turned, but knowing no shame, they did not let go of each other. We could all see the sparkling blades hovering behind Mother's back, but no one cried out as we watched her raise her hand.

"Suddenly, her hand fell. With a terrible certainty and a flash of metal Mother brought the handle of the shears down across Sister Roberta Claire's arm and nearly knocked her off her feet. Then Mother drew her hand up, turning the scissors around as she did so, and blade first, brought the horrible instrument deep into the flesh of Roberta's face. Wild streaks of blood appeared, rivers of red coursing down Roberta's face and soaking into her white satin bodice. Sister Theophane screamed and Sister Dolores came up behind her. Holding Theophane firmly by her half-clad waist, Dolores slapped her palm over Theophane's mouth.

"Sister Roberta Claire held her hand against the onslaught and Mother dropped the shears. Roberta sank to the floor.

"We stood, frozen. Then Mother took Sister Theophane's arm and pushed the rest of the habit on her—the knee-length cotton, the heavy black habit. And then, twisting Sister Theophane's arm behind her back, Mother Superior marched her to the entrance of the church. Sister Theophane obeyed, as if in a trance.

"Mother Superior turned and looked at us. For a moment we remained dazed, then we saw what she wanted. Slowly, we moved to form a line behind her. Leaving Sister Roberta Claire on the ground, Mother Superior marched us back into the church.

"No longer postulants, we had left as radiant brides, but returned as terrified, terrorized nuns. As the organ crashed through our procession we scanned the wondering eyes of parents, siblings, relatives and nuns. And we tried to forget the horrible scene we had just endured."

❧ 33 ❧

"'You can't have the glory without the Cross', we were told, but I was horrified, my faith shaken in that moment." The old nun shuddered and crossed herself. "Could I leave the convent? No, but could I live there knowing what had happened? I asked myself many questions on that day. I was in danger of losing my faith.

"We filed into the pews and celebrated the Mass, but for me, at least, it was just mechanical. My heart was with Sister Roberta Claire, lying on the floor, and my hands were shaking with fury at the injustice done to her. I glanced over at Sister Theophane after the Offertory. *Lavabo inter innocentes manus meas,* we heard the priest say. I will wash my hands among the innocent. I looked over at Sister Theophane. Fury was overcoming the shock on her face. I knew what she was feeling as if we had one heart. Sister Roberta Claire, an innocent, was the victim and Sister Theophane was spared because of her well-connected family in attendance that day. Theophane started crying. Another Sister handed her the plain linen nun's handkerchief we'd been issued."

"How could you bear it? How could you stay there after that?"

"Spoken like a twentieth-century child." The old woman narrowed her eyes and put her face to the fence. I saw infinite wrinkles, wrinkles lining wrinkles. Stripes of confusion, anxieties, troubles, intelligence and transcendence playing around her eyes, cheeks, mouth, and forehead.

"One didn't leave the order in those days. You had no choice. To leave would have meant returning in shame, admitting more than defeat—admitting that the Devil had got the better of you. There was no future for former nuns. Praise be to God!"

"So you didn't tell anyone, any of the visitors, none of your family what you'd just seen? I mean, a woman had been beaten—"

"Tell anyone? Ha! I should say not. For months the Mistress of Postulants had been censoring our letters. Those who complained to their families were punished and besides, our parents regarded such complaining as symptoms of our unworthiness. No, we had learned after months and years that the only way out was suppression of every thought that went against the grain of the Holy Rule.

"And there was more than the scene with Sister Roberta Claire to suppress. The doubts about our vocation, about the institution, seemed to be symbolized by the discomfort of our new habits. The layers and layers of cloth under which we sweated and itched. The headdress which seemed to pierce our chins, the heavy cloth draped over our heads, the starched linen pressing our ears flat against our scalps in an effort to control any hair that had escaped the scissors. The scene with Sister Roberta Claire? That was just one cross among many." The nun nodded her head back and forth.

"And nobody from the outside could have guessed. We were so good, we were the perfect brides of Christ looking angelic in our new habits that morning. For the sake of the laity we smiled and smiled. *And said nothing.*

"Afterwards, when we were outside, chatting with our families for the last time, I noticed Mother Superior. Her eyes were darting everywhere. I knew what she was looking for. She was making sure that no one defected from the placid scene on the lawn. That no one went to find or comfort the unfortunate Sister Roberta Claire.

"The noon bell rang and we went to take lunch. Our group started to say their goodbyes to families. There were tears, little last-minute presents. Somehow, in the confusion, I managed to slip away unnoticed, and made my way across the lawn into the library.

"It was cool and dark inside, the ground still littered with hair. I walked quickly to the end of the table and looked at the floor. Someone had taken the long strands of Sister Theophane's red hair. There was a smear of magenta blood on the floor, but Sister Roberta Claire had fled.

"I went to the refectory. I just had time to get in line to pass the Mistress of Postulants and the Mistress of Novices. We all bowed, our new gowns making black puddles on the floor. There was tension in the air, but we all kept our eyes suitably downcast. None of us wanted to risk mortification that day.

"All through the noon meal I looked for her. A flickering white shadow across the lawn? A figure in the balcony over our dining tables? I knew what we were all wondering. Had Mother Superior found her? Had Roberta fainted somewhere from loss of blood? I watched the Mother's eyes as she glared through the windows, and I was sure that Sister Roberta Claire had avoided her detection."

"And Sister Theophane?"

"At one point, after the soup, Sister Theophane's chin started trembling. She pulled her mouth back, stretching her lips across her face in an effort to hold back a sob. In the silence we heard a strangled cry escape her mouth. A few Sisters giggled and Mother Superior looked up sharply, ready to pounce. Sister Theophane composed herself with great difficulty.

"That afternoon the Mistress of Postulants, Mistress of Novices and Mother Superior decided to devise some particularly hard manual labor for us all, to quell any feelings of superiority.

We shouldn't feel privileged in any way by assuming our holy habits.

"But I knew that the added work and humiliation was intended to keep us busy and keep our minds off Sister Roberta Claire. So we scrubbed toilet bowls with our toothbrushes, and kneeled on marble floors to polish the inlaid terrazzo until we could see the reflections of our crucifixes. Meanwhile the Mistresses and Mother strode about the abbey, searching every corner of the convent for Sister Roberta Claire.

"At seven fifty-five, they rang the evening bell. Our class of postulants, now nuns, were taken to our new cells. As I entered my own personal chamber I didn't need to be told what the next ritual would be—the ritual I would practice every night for the rest of my life.

"First I put the nightgown over my head—"

"Over your habit?"

"We can never be naked. We undress beneath large nightgowns."

I remembered the large nightgown I'd found in Rebecca's cupboard. And all the elements of the habit.

"As I undressed, I realized I was now a woman. I had left the dormitory for my own room, and I was beginning a life with my new husband—the invisible, ever-present Jesus Christ. I said a prayer as I took off each part of my habit. Slowly I removed and kissed each garment, taking care never to let any part of the consecrated cloth touch the ground. I didn't want my faith, my wedding night, destroyed by what had gone before. I prepared myself mentally for prayer.

"I had expected to be alone with my crucified husband, but instead I had a flesh-and-blood visitor." The memory seemed to fill the nun's frail frame with new energy. She sat upright and grasped the armrests of her wheelchair as if she would rise up, and cast off the vehicle behind her and walk away.

"I heard a noise at the door; it opened and Sister Roberta Claire came in, still in her bloodied wedding gown. Her cheek was livid, swollen with a deep, angry gash. I looked at her in shock. Her face is ruined forever! I thought. 'Sister Roberta—' I cried, but she put her hand over my mouth. We stood still in the darkness, and we heard the swish of Mother Superior's skirts, the clinking of the large keys she wore at her waist, as she came down the hall. Sister Roberta Claire looked terrified.

"We heard Mother Superior flip each latch over as she ducked her head into every room. Brides on their wedding nights!

" 'Get under the bed!' I hissed, and Sister Roberta Claire slid noiselessly under the frame. I tucked away a part of her white lace skirt and hurriedly finished putting the elements of my habit in the correct position for the morning. I heard Mother Superior at the doorway of the cell next to mine. I went quickly down on my knees, grabbed the crucifix off my pillow and started to pray like I'd never prayed before. I heard her footsteps coming closer.

"I put the crucifix to my lips just as she put her head in the door. I pretended I didn't notice her. The holy rapture I was supposedly feeling would make my lack of response plausible. I heard the door close and the latch slid into place.

"As Mother Superior continued down the row of cells, as her footsteps became more distant, I could breathe more easily. Eventually Sister Roberta Claire rustled under the bed. I reached a hand under the frame and pulled her out.

"We didn't dare sit on the bed, we were afraid the frame might squeak. I put my face close to hers. 'Where have you been?' I asked.

" 'Never mind that. Where's Sister Theophane?' she asked.

" 'Sister Theophane must no longer be your concern.'

" 'How is she? What's happened? Did the Mother—'

" 'Enough!' I cried. 'Haven't you had enough of this? You must stop, put her out of your mind. There is no other way. It is finished for Sister Theophane and you. You will be lucky to get out of here alive! Forget Sister Theophane. You don't have to worry about her. There will be protection enough for her through her family. You must think about yourself now.' I looked at her wounded, tear-stained face, her blood-stained dress and disheveled hair.

" 'Where have you been?' I asked her.

" 'I've been down in the cellar.'

"The cellar where I had first seen her make the clay figurines. I looked down at her hands and reached out. They were covered with a thin film of dried mud.

" 'What have you been doing?'

" 'What I always do, Sister Adorata. It's all I know how to do. And somehow I have to do it.'

" 'The figurines?'

" 'Yes. Oh, Sister—' she turned toward me, her hand lightly covering her mangled cheek, but looking almost happy. 'The figures almost jump out of my hands, the beautiful women with the kind faces. How could it be wrong?'

" 'Blasphemy,' I chided her. 'You should be careful with such things; such a strange talent could come from an evil source—'

" 'But it doesn't, Sister Adorata,' Sister Roberta Claire looked up at me and her face seemed amazingly relaxed. 'I thought so too, at first. But Sister Theophane showed me how my talent was special and God-given—'

" 'God-given? What would Sister Theophane know about God-given?'

" 'But it is. And now I know it. Now I have proof.'

"I looked at Sister Roberta Claire's face and saw something I'd never seen before. For a moment I wondered if this soul was truly touched by God.

"She smiled then. A fresh, clean, radiant smile, as if there were no scar upon her face, no recent trauma in her memory, no stain of sin upon her soul. She spoke slowly but with a great and terrifying conviction.

" 'I was down in the cellar,' she began, 'and I was still bleeding—leaving a trail of blood all over the convent—but I'd managed to still the flow on the stairs down to the cellar. So I knew I would be safe for a while.'

" 'I knelt there on the floor and prayed. For understanding;

for escape. It was damp there, and I was starting to feel chilled. I didn't know how I would leave and I was so visible in this horrible dress. Oh, Sister, I was so tired and frightened, and so desperately wanting to know about Sister Theophane! My heart was aching, and I think that was even more terrible to me than the wound Mother Superior had inflicted upon me.'

" 'I started to cry and then I started to pray. Finally I just lay on the floor and listened to the noises around me and slept.'

" 'When I awoke my hands reached out for the comforting bags of clay. I sat up and pushed my hands once again into the mud. Figures started to form, but these were new ones. A fat woman in a fancy, old-fashioned gown, a woman gardening with horrible skin on her face . . .'

" 'As my fingers formed these figures a presence started to fill the room.'

" 'I looked up in the corner by the ceiling and I knew that someone was there.'

" 'And then there were words. Not sounds in the air, but clear in my head, little bells that made a melody, that formed a sentence.'

" 'The voice said that I would be safe, and something in the quality of that voice made me know it was true. It had a plan for me—instructions! Like a beautiful prophecy pictures unfolded inside my head—how I would leave the convent, take certain things, leave others behind. How I would bear in front of me a holy object—' and then she stopped herself. I was frightened.

" 'The voice said that the way will become clear. That she would lead me to some northern area. To live on the banks of a river, between three ranges of mountains. There I will do penance and self-mortification in the name of the Virgin for thirty days to purify myself for the deed ahead.' "

"Self-mortification?"

"Yes, the flagellant's whip and more." The old nun looked embarrassed, as if she'd been talking about something as forbidden as sex. "Taking only water and wild grasses."

I remembered the rotting whip in the basement and the Madonna with the nails.

"After the mortification she was to bury the implements and begin a second pilgrimage to visit a certain shrine in Northern Italy." The old nun shook her head. "Italy! Roberta was a deluded fool—a young uneducated woman, disturbed, infected with evil. And then I knew it had been the Devil who had spoken to her that day.

"After visiting this shrine, the voice promised her, gold would be transmuted to land. Roberta was to return to the place where she had carried out her penance and there build a house and begin her life's work."

"And that work?" I asked.

"Statues! To build statues of saints based on the ones she had modeled in the cellar that day." The old nun scoffed.

"Saint Rose of Lima?"

"Yes, yes—she was one of them."

"Saint Rose of Lima lived as a recluse in a hut in a garden. She made herself ugly by rubbing pepper and lime on her face," I mused.

The nun breathed out, looking at me with new respect.

"And Catherine of Siena, who baked bread and worked ceaselessly at her writing, keeping scribes awake—"

"Yes! How do you know the Saints Rebecca had sculpted?"

"And Saint Hildegarde, who celebrated the healing and holy powers of music and art—"

"Yes! Yes! But tell me, how do you know?"

"Because I've seen it! The statuary in the garden! Roberta did make her way to her final destination! Saint Hildegarde exists—in the garden! Saint Rose, the scarred face, like Sister Roberta herself. The skills endowed by heavenly—"

"Heavenly? You don't know what you're talking about! Sculpting! The voice would have her continue with her blasphemous work. Oh, how that demon must have tasted his meal, converting the lovely piety of this woman to foul excrement! He promised her wealth, travels and finally the most heinous reward of all—reunification with Theophane."

I looked around at the birds and flowers fluttering on the wind. Why couldn't the two women have just stayed here together,

Theophane's instruction informing Rebecca's talented hands? This could have been Rebecca's garden instead, I thought.

"She didn't reunite with Theophane," I said sadly. "She came close, but I think Theophane died a few days too soon."

The old woman shook her head as if to cast off any interest in the matter.

"And Theophane, how did she leave the order?" I asked.

"Like the rest whose faith was not great enough. Her faith had been polluted. I could see it at every Mass. She could not enjoy the sacrifice. She drew away from humiliation. In the end she could not even pray." The old woman clicked her tongue with disapproval. "There was a visit from the Abbess, even a call from the Archbishop of Chicago. But it was no use. Theophane was no longer suited to religious life. She disappeared like the rest of them. One day she was just gone from Mass. Gone from the dinner table. An empty chair. She joined the laity. And we never saw her again."

"You never thought to ask?"

"We do not speak of Sisters who have left the order. It is as if they are dead. Their souls have died. And Theophane's was dead long before she left this place. And Roberta Claire's. I remember how I felt later when I heard what Roberta had done after she left my cell." The nun pounded a bony fist on her armrest. "How could she? How *could* she? Only the Devil could have thought of such a deed!" She fixed me with a glance full of hatred.

"That is what you now hold so brazenly in your hands! The result of the Devil's work!" The old nun's chin was trembling. "The Devil who takes so many forms, who slithers on his belly, laughing like a loon in the night, feeding on blood like a coyote! The Devil who, on that bitter day, took the most sacrilegious shape of all for the most sacrilegious of deeds. The form of the Holy Virgin Mary."

The Virgin Mary. The voice that had instructed Rebecca, bequeathed her property and a trip to Italy, and financed her enormous talent so that she could leave a landmark legacy of amazing artistry. The Virgin Mary.

And then, even I crossed myself.

34

"What happened next? How did she get out of your cell?"

"Yes, how *did* she get out of my cell? The door was locked but the window was big enough to crawl out of. I gave Sister Roberta Claire my habit and my cloak—"

"You gave her your habit? But—"

"I had to! There was no way she could make her escape across the big lawn in that white wedding dress. So I gave her my habit."

"You're a hero, you know!"

"Ha! I'm just a fool. Giving her my habit to help her commit crime.

"She waited till everyone was asleep. Then, in *my* habit," the old woman crossed herself, "she went into the chapel and approached the altar. There she reached into the tabernacle itself, where the Blessed Sacrament resided.

"She must have put her hands—her blood- and sin-stained hands—inside the silk-lined chamber and removed the solid gold paten—the plate which holds the Host."

"Solid gold? Probably weighed two pounds. On a depression market, she could have got—"

"Silence!" The old woman cried out in outrage, but it was important to me. Roberta Claire—Rebecca—would have raised a sizeable sum hocking *that* in a depression. Easily enough for the down-payment on a house.

"Did she take anything else?"

"She took the *ostensorium*—the receptacle which holds the Heavenly Food, the body of Jesus Himself." The nun sat back, shakily. "That is what you are now holding in your hands."

"Is there more?"

"Yes. Yes, there is more. And if you know where it is you must tell me now."

"But I *don't* know! What else was there?"

"Not content with her plunder, she then climbed upon the altar itself, to steal the altarpiece, our most precious possession. The beloved image of Our Lady. The Veronese Madonna of the Sacred Heart by Alessandro Bronzino."

"Alessandro Bronzino?" Was it possible? I was absolutely amazed. Bronzino was the founder of one of the major schools of painters in Verona. The late medieval master!

But then I knew it *could* be. I had seen the artistry of the little gold box and I knew that the donor who had given these pieces to the abbey was no secondhand dealer. No collector of curiosities.

Alessandro Bronzino! How I would have loved to tell Ilona that I was hot on the trail of an unknown, uncatalogued Alessandro Bronzino!

"The exaltation of female holiness as seen through female beauty," the nun confirmed. "It was a piece of profound inner equilibrium. Sister Roberta Claire told me so. She loved to pray to that painting and used to pray to that Madonna, gazing for hours into her violet eyes, meditating on the perfect gestures of her fingertips, pointing to the flaming of her Sacred Heart, made visible by our Lord Jesus Christ." The nun crossed herself and mumbled a Latin phrase. "The Mistress of Novices cried when it was discovered that the painting had been stolen."

A Bronzino, I thought. What would Rebecca have done with it? Surely she wouldn't have hocked that too?

How I would have loved to lay it at Ilona's feet! It could have resurrected her career, giving her a reason to love me again. But it was too late.

Thoughts of Ilona fled as someone joined the old nun in the garden.

"May I help you?" came the question from beneath the veil.

"I—I—" I stammered. But it wasn't just the fear of being caught out, it was the strange familiarity of the tall, dark shape. As she approached the fence I saw a beautiful face of about forty years, floating within the white linen frame. She had dark eyes, lively black eyebrows, brown skin made darker by the contrast of the hard bleached surface surrounding it. Her smile was simple and direct; there was no way I could match it.

"I'm Sister Redempta," said the nun, her long frame balanced evenly on both feet. A most attractive posture. A posture just like Ilona, I thought. Suddenly I felt dangerously off-balance, dangerously close to losing my grip on reality.

"The Mother Superior?" I asked, remembering her name from the phone conversation.

"Yes, I'm the Mother Superior here." She bent over the old nun, putting her hand on the woman's back and peering into her face. "Have you been wasting our visitor's time, Sister Adorata?"

"Oh, no!" I protested. "Sister Adorata has been telling me about how much more the garden has bloomed this year than last."

"Don't be silly!" Mother Superior said, looking at me, a bemused frown on her face. "Sister Adorata talks about only one thing to anyone, don't you, Sister Adorata?"

"One thing?" I swallowed.

Suddenly another Sister appeared from behind Redempta. "Sister George, would you wheel Sister Adorata back to the fountain where she can talk to the birds?"

"But I haven't finished telling her," the old Adorata whined theatrically.

"You can tell her all about the Sacred Heart next time."

"She won't come back. I didn't really have time to tell about how Jesus appeared, and the five rays that came from His halo, and how He took my heart out of my body—"

"Just like Saint Catherine," Sister Redempta smiled at the elderly nun and winked at me.

"Yes, like Catherine, and then I lived for seven days without a heart and when He came back He gave me His own—"

"Yes, Sister, we know—His own Sacred Heart—"

"It beats inside me still," Sister Adorata proclaimed.

"The beat of a different drummer," Redempta nodded at Sister George, who put her hands on the handles of the old woman's chair and slowly turned her away from me, but not before Adorata had raised her palms toward me. "Wait! She has something for us!" the old nun cried out. "Wait! The *ostensorium!* Thief!" she cried, but shadows enveloped her face.

"I'm sorry, she's a little senile—" Redempta apologized smilingly.

"Stop her, Mother Superior! Stop—no! The Devil, Sister! He appears before you in the guise of a young woman!" Sister George put her hands firmly on the elderly woman's chair and pushed her hard over a lump in the grass. "The Devil! Killer of conscience!" Sister Adorata kept crying out.

"I'm so sorry, this is really quite embarrassing."

"No, please, it's I who should be embarrassed," I protested, feeling the heavy lump of the *ostensorium* now in my shoulder-bag by my hip. I could feel the sweat running down my sides. My hands were trembling.

"I hope she didn't trouble you too much," Redempta said, arranging her long, slender hands within the folds of her sleeves. "She's getting old, you see, and senile. She loves to talk to visitors and ever since we put the dirt bike tires on her wheel-chair she sort of traps people here at the fence."

"Sinner, mortal sinner, damned to hell!" I heard Adorata's voice float over the flowers.

"My apologies."

"Oh, don't apologize—she's probably right," I laughed uncertainly, but my chin was trembling.

"What is troubling you, my child? Perhaps I can help."

"No, everything's fine, really," I said. But I wished she could have helped. I was a thief and worse. And Redempta, and even Adorata, could see that.

"Yes, there is redemption and peace in a spiritual life. Are you—" she raised the delicate eyebrows and I caught a Hispanic lilt to her voice, "interested in the religious life?"

"No. More in the history. Women who chose the religious life."

"It is a very deep, a very rewarding history," Redempta assured me. The clarity of her speech, her confidence, her very demeanor assured me that she was no kin of the former scissor-wielding Mother Superior. "The religious life represented a great opportunity for women, and attracted some of the best minds, and best hearts, in female history." She grinned. "Or *herstory* as some like to call it. But I find the spelling too distracting, don't you?"

"Yes. I did my dissertation on Wilhelmina of Breught."

"You did? I did my dissertation on the collaboration of Sister Cecilia and Madre Maria. It was published by a small university press. I called it *Leyendo Yo y Escribiendo Ella*. 'I reading, she writing'. The communication with Northern European orders in the seventeenth century, such as the one that Wilhelmina—" She stopped suddenly, hearing a sound unnoticed by me. "Oh, I must stop. Any minute now the bell will ring for Profound silence. It comes, sometimes, at the most regrettable moments, but that is our discipline." She nodded at me. There was a lot to regret, not only silence, but that there was no way through that fence, if only to shake hands with Sister Redempta, the latest in a long line of Mother Superiors of the Sister Adorers of the Most Precious Blood of Jesus Christ.

"Will I see you again?" I asked, blushing immediately at the incongruity of the remark.

"I hope so. Please come back. We do our work in the morning before Mass, so this is really the only time—"

"What sort of work do you do?" I thought about toilet-scrubbing, imagining Sister Adorata in earlier years mopping the terrazzo floor.

"The work we took over from the Jesuit Brothers in the Valley when their mission closed. Ever since 1983 we have spent every morning at the bakery."

"You make bread?"

"Bread?" she laughed, and I saw the convent had taken good care of Sister Redempta's dental work. "Heavens, no! We make the wafer, you see. The wafers that become part of the Sacrifice. We have to support ourselves. Why, they're shipped all over the country, our wafers." She paused, looking at me, but she must have seen the confusion in my face.

"We create the stuff of the Sacrament here. The Host." She continued, amused at my puzzled expression. "Jesus Christ. In whole wheat."

Through the garden a bell tinkled. It seemed to dance along the flowers and even the bees stilled their humming. Without a further word, Sister Redempta folded her hands back into her sleeves and bowed her head.

"All the way to heaven is heaven," I heard her say as she hid her glorious, lively face from my view. The words of Saint Teresa of Avila, I thought. "All the way to heaven is heaven." Where had I heard that before? And then I knew. Ilona. Ilona had whispered those words the first time her fingers found their way inside me.

Redempta turned. Her black serge shoulders merged into anonymity, and I watched her glide away among the tall grass and hollyhocks, leaving me with my fingers clutching the cyclone fence. Looking after her, I saw my chance of redemption fade.

35

Alessandro Bronzino. The painter who helped tear the veil of symbolism in the late Middle Ages. The expressions on his subjects' faces held the beginnings of individuation. Tenderness, charity and mystery found expression on his two-dimensional canvases. Pure emotion expressed in paint. There were only seventeen Bronzinos extant, carefully guarded in major museums.

How amazed Ilóna would have been! It would have been the discovery of a lifetime. Suddenly I was filled with excitement, but an excitement tinged with sadness. There was only one person who could have understood this feeling—that could exalt with me in this discovery—Ilona. And she was gone.

Alessandro Bronzino. The master who began to articulate the humanist ideal, to represent nature in its real relationship, and who had depicted this flowering of thought and culture in the face of a woman. Soon, I hoped, it would be in *my* hands.

Now I knew how Rebecca had made her way, and that her destination, as prescribed by the Virgin, had been Montana. Skills—perhaps natural, perhaps spiritually endowed—such as sewing, nursing and accounting had supported her through her journey. Guided, she believed, by the Virgin, Rebecca had bought the land, drawn up the plans and overseen the building of her home in Montana.

Rebecca had left this convent a blessed woman, with a small painting tucked under her habit. Would she have sold it? I thought not. Even in 1930 it would be hard to sell the most minor of masterpieces, especially for a young, inexperienced woman. The gold paten, perhaps, but probably not the painting. Besides, she had loved that image too much.

How museum curators would shudder to think about the young woman wrenching the masterpiece from the wall, scraping its gilt edges, the acid of her sweat absorbing into the painted oil canvas as she hugged it to her chest! How top-security guards would fume at the thought of such valuable property, worth millions, being hauled over fences and the abbey wall as Rebecca made her escape!

But those days were different, and I knew that this church, like many others, had never insured such works. The general public wasn't even aware of their existence. And the Sisters would have been too ashamed to tell anyone about the events leading up to the theft.

The solid gold paten. Solid gold. What was gold going for, by the ounce, in 1930 when Rebecca visited Italy? It was upon her return from Italy that she converted hard cash into mineral rights. I smiled.

The Virgin Mary took care of her and Rebecca took care of herself, all right. She took care of herself better than I had. And things would take a turn for the better for me if I could find that painting. That Italian painting could create a future for me that could wipe away the unfortunate Italian past.

I took one look back at the abbey. Vatican II might have brought more liberal nuns to the forefront, and the Host might be made of whole wheat, but the basic tenet was still repression and guilt.

I got into the rental car and drove away. Alessandro Bronzino. I drove through the maze of suburban housing, traveling through architectural time, from stone abbey to light industry. I saw the green freeway sign and pulled onto the big cement ribbon. Alessandro Bronzino.

The little box was still in my shoulderbag, and the voice of Sister Adorata was still in my ears, along with other voices, more urgent, more damning voices that told me to find that painting.

Again my thoughts turned to Ilona. No matter how much I tried to escape it I was still in love with her. Being in love didn't take two. I could be in love with Ilona all by myself.

Freeway deadlock ahead. I squeezed on the brakes behind somebody's bumper. *Lab animals never have a nice day,* I read. I was stuck in the creeping rush hour traffic. The sun was setting behind me.

It was late, nearly eight o'clock, and I'd been awake for almost twenty hours. My nose was itching as the jet fumes were recycled through the cabin. Alessandro Bronzino. Could Ilona ever have guessed what would be in my future? Why was I always the lucky one? Why was Ilona always so short-changed? So jealous? It didn't matter anymore, I told myself. But it did. It did.

After take-off I put the seat rest back and tried to take a nap. I closed my eyes. Happiness. Holiness. Sin. Damnation. And a life without love.

I wanted to be at home. I wanted to lay my eyes and hands on the Virgin Mary of Alessandro Bronzino. I wanted the Virgin who had inspired and guided Rebecca to wipe away my past. I wanted to be able to sob out loud in this plane, because what I really wanted was Ilona.

❧ 36 ❧

Ilona, airplanes. I remembered the time she had wept. The only time I had seen her cry. I closed my eyes. The air in the plane was heavy, still laden with fumes. I tried not to take in deep breaths. The jet engines hummed.

Just as they had hummed when we had flown to Stockholm to meet her parents. Ilona was nervous, a bit testy, but occasionally squeezing my hand, even nuzzling my neck a few times. I knew why she felt that way.

Ilona's childhood stories had been grim; her salesman father, who left frequently, ignoring family responsibilities; her mother, a cross, tight-lipped perfectionist; a simple, stupid sister who married a mousey accountant. She was unaccountably happy—a fact that irritated Ilona no end. Ilona's description of her family was derisive, tinged with shame. As that plane landed in Stockholm, she had been quiet. She was worried about what I would think of them.

We took a taxi to their house. I hoped she wouldn't get depressed. I wanted to be supportive.

But Ilona's shamed description hadn't prepared me for her

falsely charming manner when we were all together. Her nervous parents met us at the door. Ilona was all laughter and kisses.

Ilona didn't look at me much that day. She smiled and chattered, glowing at them as she opened her briefcase. Tentatively she showed them her latest publications in academic journals. I couldn't understand her sing-song Swedish, but I recognized a hopefulness in her tone. The articles were in languages they couldn't understand. Ilona, I thought with surprise, wasn't interested in my approval—she was interested in theirs.

Then she introduced me properly to them. I understood words like "America, Boston, exchange student", Ilona's parents nodded politely, and she didn't bother to translate.

The before-dinner drink was made longer by translations of safe subjects: recipes, the weather, the arthritis problems of their aging dog. The ticking of the clock during frequent pauses was the only language we all understood.

Finally, it was time for dinner. Ilona went to help her mother in the kitchen. I was left nodding mutely at her father, noticing his huge fingers and broad palms. He nodded back at me, looking me up and down a few times before grunting an apology and picking up a local paper to hide his face between the pages. I remembered what Ilona had told me. When he had found out she was a lesbian he had hit her so hard she fell down a flight of stairs. But that had been years ago.

I went into the kitchen where Ilona was helping her mother. Her mother, about whom she'd complained so bitterly, who had assumed near-monster proportions in her descriptions, seemed to be perfectly normal. She fussed about with the soup, stirring and tasting it nervously.

Dinner was quiet. Several bottles of wine were offered, and consumed. But it was after dinner that the drinking became more earnest. Ilona and her father sat in the living room watching a news program in Swedish. They were sipping cognac.

I went to help Ilona's mother dry the dishes, but soon tired of trying to guess where all the dinnerware was kept. I eyed the dog which looked restlessly at the door. I picked up the leash just as Ilona's father came into the kitchen. He helped me on with my coat and I was given to understand that he would show me something outside.

In the darkening dusk Ilona's father walked me along the fence toward a back gate. The dog strained at the leash. He eyed a field separated by a big bush from the back of the house. We freed the dog, who ran into the distance, a small dancing creature on the horizon. We smiled.

Ilona's father pointed out a hidden wildflower which had survived the summer, at our feet. He leaned closely over me as I bent down to get a better look at the delicate blue shape between my fingertips. His leg was close, pressing against my shoulder. It was dark. He wanted to see too. I moved forward to bring the bluebell between my fingertips. I didn't know if it would be rude to pick the blossom, and I knew wildflowers didn't last when picked. I felt something warm on my neck, the smell of cognac, the feel of his heavy leg against me. Then his legs were on either side of my arm. But the hard thing I felt on my shoulder wasn't his leg. Ilona's father was humping me.

This isn't happening! I told myself.

When I stood up quickly he didn't draw back. I looked in his face, but his eyes were glazed, expressionless. His hand was moving, his big palm covered my breast. I pushed him away. I had no words in any language for this, so I turned and ran. I rushed through the gate, up the walk, and into the warm kitchen where Ilona's mother was putting away the remains of the soup. Ilona was sorting out the silverware, and drying tiny water spots off the dessert spoons.

Nothing Ilona had said had prepared me for her father. And neither she nor her mother looked up when I came in, panting, from the garden. Nor did they look up when her father came in five minutes later, petting the dog, hanging up his leash. I had kept silent for him, for myself, for Ilona.

After two nights at Ilona's parents' house, we returned home. Some time later she had an uncontrollable sobbing fit which lasted for hours. She cried with her head on my lap, and I stroked that fine red hair over and over again as her tears soaked my jeans. Afterwards she didn't attempt to explain. And I didn't ask her to. I never told her what had happened to me, what her father had done. I guessed that some time in the past he must have done it to her. But maybe she just didn't remember, and I wasn't going to burst that precious bubble of defense against the monster of the past.

The plane was aiming at the chilly Montana horizon. A rising sun tried to warm the icy landscape. The clouds overhead meant it would fail.

But I would not. I would find that painting, I thought grimly. My mouth felt dry and sour.

Where would we have all been, I wondered—Marya, Ilona, myself—forty, fifty, a hundred years ago? Where would we have fulfilled our love of scholarship, our organizational skills, our need for clarity, safety, challenge, pleasure in the company of other women? My mind seemed crowded with talented, hardworking women. Writers, critics, sculptors, historians, social workers, mothers. All in collusion. Or in competition. Or in love.

I hoped Marya wouldn't be at home when I got there. I needed to be alone. I wanted to look for the painting without having to give explanations. I was tired of defending aesthetic desire to Marya.

And I needed time to regain the present. The past was leaking in so quickly. The past was a flood that threatened to carry me off. I went quickly to the rental car desk.

I would find the altar that Rebecca, Sister Roberta Claire, had created. I would find the Alessandro Bronzino, the Veronese Virgin. And then I could concentrate on the present.

I rented another American sedan with snow tires and made my way along the frozen prairie, a hermit's terrain of choice, a landscape which I now thought of as Rebecca's.

I pulled up to the house, the shabby asbestos shingled box. The sun shone wanly on the horizon. The shingles reflected the muddy light but the forlorn house cast no shadow. Who could guess that this place was a treasure chest? Rebecca and I alone, alone with a treasure, bereft of the women we loved. The shoulderbag bumped against my side.

With what feelings had Rebecca built that altar? What feelings of anger, guilt, smarting of injustice? Were the bruises still on her back? And how much did she suffer with her continuing love of Theophane, a woman she would never see again?

I opened the door. There were no signs of further break-ins. I breathed a sigh of relief but within moments I felt dizzy. The air was warm and still. It was hard to think and I stood in the doorway unwilling to enter. The place stank of fear and loss and lack of air. Marya must have left the heater on. She had also left a note. I recognized her handwriting on a big piece of white paper on the dining room table. I reached for my reading glasses.

She was on a long free-climb and wouldn't be home until dawn. I smiled at the thought of her driving off with her ice-axe, excited at the challenge of testing her limits. Then I stopped smiling.

Marya had left another message. A telephone message. From Western Union. Someone was trying to reach me. Someone with an urgent request from the Italian consulate. Someone from Interpol.

I grasped my stomach and my bag fell off my arm. I heard the thump of the little box as it hit the floor.

I stumbled into the living room, looking for the mantelpiece, ripping off my glasses. I needed a ritual, a sanctuary, a painting. But I was losing the strength to find it.

Little brown dots danced in front of my eyes even as my stomach turned over. I gasped, then saw the layout of the room more clearly through the little brown dots. I saw the recliner and aimed my body into it. I was weak and losing consciousness—a loss which was aided by a sharp blow with a heavy object to the back of my head.

From far away I heard the squeak of the reclining chair as it leaned back with the force of my falling weight, and then I was lost in darkness.

37

"*Introibo ad altare Dei*. I will go unto the altar of God." Latin words lingered at the edges of a deep darkness. I opened my eyes but the darkness remained.

Blind! I thought. Forever in darkness! Was this a stroke? A hysterical symptom? But then a small hole pricked the dark canvas in front of me.

Then another. One by one little pricks of candlelight illuminated Rebecca's living room. I could just see my toes at the end of the recliner chair.

"Dominus vobiscum." A voice.

Who was it? I couldn't move. My legs were bound. I tried to twist my arms but heavy bands cut into my wrists as I turned them on the armrests.

"Et cum spiritu tuo." The words issued from invisible lips behind a black cowl. I could see the vague dark outline of a nun's habit. But her voice was crystal clear as she glided in front of the candlelit mantelpiece, then bowed down and kissed the wax-coated surface.

My eyes were finally focusing. Candles were ablaze everywhere in the house! Across the mantel, dripping and set on windowsills, with only the darkness of the kitchen and dining room beyond.

"Deus, tu conversus vivicabis nos. Et clamor meus ad te veniat. Thou shall turn again, O God, and quicken us, and let my cry come unto Thee."

I craned my head upward to try to get a better look at the black, floating figure, but I was paralyzed on the recliner. I could only move my eyes. Over the horizon of my cheeks I could see the figure which floated back and forth. My hands were strapped firmly to the arms of the chair with leather belts. Tight bonds pressed my legs together, cutting off my circulation and making my toes numb.

"Awaken, thou that sleepest! Arise from the dead! Christ shall give to thee light!" I heard the figure sing, the melody drifting out from her cowl as she extended her hands, flesh-covered hands, strong female hands. She twisted them together, palms and fingers knotting and unknotting. It reminded me of something. A woman who knew her knots.

"Thou who takest away the sins of the world, receive our prayer. Thou who sittest at the right hand of the Father, have mercy on us." Her habit made a black puddle on the floor as she bowed deeply before the altar, a parody of the Mass I'd just witnessed at the Sister Adorers' convent.

"Mmmph!" I tried to make a sound but realized that I was gagged. A piece of fabric had been stretched across my open mouth. My lips and teeth were spread apart as the cruel cloth dug deep, drying my tongue and tickling my throat. My head hurt, pain emanating from a small, deeply pierced place at the back of my skull. I started to choke but the nun didn't notice. She was reciting the Nicene Creed. That would take awhile. I started working my fingertips around the buckle of the belt that held my right wrist.

"Et in Spiritum sanctum Dominum et vivificantem, qui ex Patre Filioque procedit. Et Expecto resurrectionem mortuorum, et vitam venturi saeculi. Amen. The Holy Ghost, the Lord and giver of life, who proceedeth from the Father and the Son. I await

the resurrection of the dead, and the life of the world to come."

"Not me!" I tried yelling through the cloth gag, hoping my sound would distract her, but she went on regardless.

I squirmed against my bonds; the chair squeaked and rattled on the floor, but the nun took no notice. She was floating out of the room, into the kitchen. Something was wrong with this picture. I tried to move my head, hoping for a glimpse of her face, but my forehead was strapped down with a heavy leather belt, the buckle pressed into my brow. I continued to work the other belt around my wrists so I could get my fingertips nearer the clasp.

Was it a nun from the Sister Adorers, come to retrieve their rightful possessions? I wouldn't mind Sister Redempta putting me in this position, I thought, as I tugged at the leather thongs. But this situation did not promise pleasure.

"Sic fiat sacrificium nostrum in conspectu tuo hodie, ut placeat tibi, Domine Deus. Grant that the sacrifice we offer this day in Thy sight may be pleasing to Thee, O Lord God," the nun whispered, returning from the kitchen, her habit dragging along the floor. In her hands she carried an object, covered with a tattered dishtowel. She put it on the mantel and slowly unwrapped the golden box. My box. She had found it in my shoulderbag.

The candlelight bounced off its finely wrought surface, shimmering with organic life. I saw the nun's thin, tapered fingertips push on a butterfly wing.

She knew the secret of opening the box! Between her two fingers she pressed on its jewelled head and pulled at a golden antennae. An opening in the box, a little door, slid open. She knew what she was doing. But what did she want to do with me? My fingers continued their frantic search around the heavy leather strap. Closer, the buckle must be getting closer.

The nun bowed at the mantelpiece and struck a little bell three times. She turned her back and I knew the way she was ignoring me bode ill. It was the way you ignored a piece of furniture, a thing, an offering. A sacrifice.

She returned to the kitchen and I continued to work feverishly at the metal edge of the buckle. I tried pushing the gag out of my mouth with my tongue, but to no avail. It was too tight. There was a heavy rope across my chest, my breasts were flattened against the twisted twine, and another rope across my waist. The nun was returning, head bowed, with a wine glass in her hands. As she glided past me I saw that her delicate hand also held a long, thin spoon, with which she stirred the wine.

Since when did Jesus Christ come in powder? I thought. But then the realization hit me and nearly stilled my heart with fear. I struggled more violently against my bonds. The chair rattled and squeaked, its legs bumping on the vinyl floor.

The nun continued her sacred, horrific duty, as if I were the ghost, not she. Finished with stirring the red liquid inside the chalice, she froze for a moment, took the spoon out, wiped it carefully on a piece of linen, put it down on the mantelpiece and genuflected again.

She reached into the box and pulled out a thin wafer. The Host. With both hands she held it aloft. I could see it rising over her cowl, her head leaning back so far I could almost make out the white band that held her hair off her forehead. She stood as still as a statue, her long black body intersecting the mantelpiece, the Host held aloft, the chalice in her hand. I trembled at the tableau of terror.

She rested both hands for a moment on the mantel, as if gathering strength for the coming consecration. But I was wrong. My lousy Latin had left me behind. The transubstantiation was finished. It was the sacrifice that was about to begin. And the sacrifice was me.

38

Slowly, she turned around. I watched every fold in her habit twist as I tried to drag my eyes up along her figure, up to the face that was still in deep shadow. The figure glided toward me. I heard the sound of the habit sweeping along the floor. That was what was wrong. The holy habit was never supposed to touch the ground. This nun wasn't wearing a habit made for her. She was an impostor.

Closer and closer she came. The candlelight behind her gave her figure a halo but didn't illuminate her face. Then a pale hand extended from the folds of her habit and I felt her cool palm over my eyes. A rustle, and I could smell fresh soap, and perhaps some perfume, then her hands reached into her habit and pulled out the flagellant's whip from the cellar. It was old and moldy, but not entirely rotten. As she grasped the handle and brought it high above her head, two knotted thongs split the air with a vicious crack, snapping somewhere just in front of my nose.

"We have a lot to talk about," the voice said. And then I recognized her. I looked up at the twisted features. It was Helen Danroy, the would-be nurse.

"I can't talk with this gag on," I protested, my words nearly unintelligible. But she understood. Slowly she drifted over to the mantel and brought the chalice into my view. She raised it with one hand and with the other she raised the Host.

"Not exactly consecrated," she smiled, nodding at the wafer, "but then, you're not all that religious, are you?"

I stared at the chalice.

"Yes, it's not just wine," she confirmed. "It's wine with the punch of cyanide." She smiled and I suddenly remembered the wet wool of her winter suit as she prostrated herself on the pavement; how she had made the Sign of the Cross in the mud with her tongue.

"Now the Host, here, is just a simple flour wafer. I would really much rather offer this to you. But perhaps, if you cooperate, you can save yourself."

"What do you fucking want?" The words came garbled through my gag, which was getting wetter, looser.

"Want? You know what I want. You must, or you wouldn't have gone to the convent. I want exactly the same thing you want. The difference is, I'm going to get it. The difference is, I'm not a thief."

"I don't know what you're talking about."

"Don't you now? Then why are you carrying around this box, this sacred, holy vessel, in your bag?"

I said nothing.

"Answer me!" She picked up the whip again. "How do you think I know how to open this box?"

I looked at her and at the whip again, but I guessed her question was rhetorical.

"I knew how to open it because it used to belong to my grandmother."

"Your grandmother?"

"Yes, my grandmother, a Sister Adorer of the Most Precious Blood. A most holy and pious woman. She redeemed her life with many good deeds. She redeemed her former sin."

"Former sin?"

"Don't play stupid with me! Joe at the 7-Eleven had you two spotted right away. The whole neighborhood knows."

"Your grandmother, Theophane—"

"Shut up! My grandmother wasn't one of you. She told me, on her dying day. She received Extreme Unction and she was cleansed, *cleansed!"*

"How do you know?"

"Before the priest came she told me everything—"

"Everything? About Sister Roberta Claire?"

"My grandmother wasn't the instigator, she wasn't the lesbian. She was *normal*—it was the other one, Sister Roberta Claire—"

"Normal?" I pushed aside the gag with my tongue. "Theophane was spared punishment because of her money. She was in love with Roberta Claire. It was she who came to Roberta's bed, who got in between those convent sheets every night. And when the kiss of Christ came, it wasn't Jesus she found sweet—"

"Shut up!" Helen Danroy slugged me hard across the face, her fist crashing into my jaw.

"But it was Theophane who got into *her* bed—"

"Quiet! Blasphemer! I know the truth. I heard her final confession. I heard how she had been influenced by the Devil himself! Roberta Claire wasn't a woman—she was a man, and that was how she seduced my grandmother. She was the Devil. My grandmother didn't know. Her heart was too pure. Only the Devil could have stolen the holy Host in the *ostensorium*. A most valuable piece of property. My grandmother told me the secret of opening it, so clever, so fitting to protect Our Lord—a secret shared only by the Sister Adorers of the Precious Blood. Only they and the priest knew, and now I know too."

"How did you find—"

"Rebecca wrote to her. Rebecca never left her alone. Not even as my grandmother was dying. I remember her last night, the night I visited her.

"The room was dim, but not frightening. It was filled with her sweet being and loving scent. Her white hair, which had been so red in youth, was spread out over the pillowcase, like the rays of a star. Her voice was strong and clear and she reached out a hand to me. I came closer; her face was like a glowing ember of light in a dark corner of the world.

" 'Sister,' she said, and I thought she mistook me for her daughter, my aunt, the one who is Abbess at Saint Joseph's. I drew my dark scarf over my head. Perhaps I wanted to play the part, perhaps I thought that at last Grandmother would bestow on me a holy habit in her imagination. 'Yes?' I said to her.

" 'Sister, what has passed between us was holy,' she began quietly. I rushed closer, feeling her amazing faith, her piety, her fear of the end. I took her hand and she grasped mine. I felt that finally my special faith had been recognized.

" 'You must return the body of our Lord,' she said. I realized then that she wasn't addressing me but my aunt, the Abbess.

" 'What, Grandmother?' I asked, confused.

" 'Darling,' she continued, 'you must return the Holy Sacrament. No harm will come to you now. And then you will join me, in a garden called Heaven, where we can have the whole day for chatting and reading, you can make your figurines and I'll sing songs to Her, just as before. We'll do everything together and no one will be in our way this time.'

" 'What?' I felt a terrible fear. My grandmother seemed sweeter to me at that moment than any other, she looked at me with softer eyes and even more perfect sympathy.

" 'The painting is very valuable,' she said. 'It shows the beginning of a new sense of perspective, an atmosphere of subtle vibration—' and then she closed her eyes and took a deep breath. She told me just about the painting. Or shall I say, the Masterpiece?

"She explained about the theft of the Holy Sacrament. About how important the little box was, its secret mechanism, its sacred contents. That's when I started to understand that she was relieving the burden of a mortal sin, one that involved a theft, a theft of something more valuable than I could conceive of.

"She made me promise to return these things, and even

though I was not who she thought, I made that promise to her.

"And then, my Grandmother pulled at my hand. I hung back, but some final force was driving her. Like steel those muscles pulled at my arm and brought me forward so that my face nearly touched hers.

"She put her fingertips to her lips, then reached up and touched mine. 'Goodbye, my darling. Kisses will never get us in trouble again.' And then she died." Helen's chin was wobbling and soon covered with wet tears. She fell on her knees on the floor, buried her head in her lap and sobbed.

I started fiddling with my bonds again, and, as if suspicious, Helen looked up, her tears vanishing with righteousness.

"I only found out later what it all meant," she said, cocking her head to one side, puzzled, as if she still couldn't believe it. "I discovered the letters of Roberta Claire, bundles of them, tied together with bits of blue ribbon. I railed and screamed as I read every word. Roberta—Rebecca's letters of perverted love and loathing were a devil's legacy which infected my granny even on her deathbed. And it made me *sick,*" Helen's voice rose.

"Those letters had been arriving for months of the last year of my grandmother's life. Rebecca had wanted Theophane to give up her married, consecrated life under Jesus Christ. The Devil wrote my grandmother every year for sixty years. And my grandmother read and kept every letter. Her confession showed me how she was tempted to leave her family, the holy charge of her matrimonial duty and enter the garden of evil!" Helen was waving her hands about, as if to indicate the enormous scope of this evil. Then with her arms above her head, she let them fall one last time. They hung limply by her sides as she concluded her story.

"My grandmother's sin is cleansed by her mortal issue, those souls she has engendered and offered up to the example of Christ. I am that one. Oh Lord," she hurled a final sob, "how I wish to be taken to you!"

She caught the look of amusement that flickered across my face.

"Shut up!" she cried, and the whip lashed across my cheek.

"You laugh, just like all the others! She was good, she was holy, she sacrificed for the Lord. How I longed to be like her. My brother was a Jesuit. My sisters both novices at seventeen, and my aunts Abbesses at convents that tended the sick in Africa. But for me, piety was suspect. I slept on the hard floor in my bedroom for fifteen months but no one seemed to notice. I tried, like Saint Catherine, to live only on the Eucharist! I prayed for visions, for Christ's holy ring to land upon my finger as I became fed only by His body. But they laughed, told me I was overdoing it. Said my passions were too vehement to be pure!

"How I hated them then! Couldn't they see that I had heard the calling? That I was the one, not the others? How I longed for the holy habit! My pleas, my applications, my letters were rejected from all over the country. Then they married me off. They all had a hand in it. My great-uncle the Archbishop saw to it. He didn't like me, he never liked me. I was neglected. My piety, my humiliations laughed at! I was ignored. I, who was truly the most devout, the most perfect Catholic of them all. Only my grandmother cared."

"I'm sure you're right," I said, and I wasn't lying.

"Stop laughing at me!"

"I'm not laughing at you."

"No," she said, eyeing me carefully. "You're not, and you won't laugh. Because you know, and I know, what's at stake." Helen smiled complacently. "When I return the *ostensorium*, missing for all these years, with its holy Host, and when I return the beautiful face of the Virgin Mary to her rightful place above the altar, I will receive the blessing of the Archbishop himself. And nobody will ever laugh at me again." She paused and then went on quietly, "And that's where you come in.

"When Grandmother died I got Rebecca's address from the letters. But by the time I got here, she was dead. And what was here when I got here?" She laughed. "The two of you!"

A car drove by on the road outside. Marya! I thought, but my hopes faded as the sound of the engine disappeared into the distance. Helen Danroy was smiling.

"I found a way in, a window that was left open. I found an extra key and copied it. I was ready to begin my search, but you were at home all the time. Home, while your friend, your *man* was out every day."

"My man!" I protested. "Marya isn't a man. She wears pantyhose. And if you think I'm a housewife—"

"I know what you are. Sick! And I couldn't wait to make you sicker. Every time you went out of the house, I came in. I turned up the gas pressure, hoping the water heater would explode. I stuffed rags into the exhaust of the furnace, knowing the place would fill with carbon monoxide. I even found a chemical sprayer in Grandpa's storeroom and sprayed the place with enough solvent to dissolve your ceiling." She looked up. "Or some of it, anyway. Chemicals are so useful. Or harmful. But who cares about the chromosomes of queers!" She leaned over me, leering.

I could see the whites all the way around her eyeballs. She seemed to be staring at me, but she wasn't seeing anything. "Yes, your eyes. It would be a pity to see the light go out in them." She loosened the gag and before I could say a word, she leaned back and spat on my lips. She tasted sweet and terrifying, and I wondered about the taste of cyanide.

"So let's get on with it," she said.

"Roberta Claire never spent any of the money," she mumbled. "How could a young girl know what to do with such priceless antiquities? So that's where you come in. I knew you'd discovered something that first time I came over. I knew from the way you ran into the kitchen that you were hiding something. And I knew from the art books scattered about that if you'd found something, you'd know what its value was."

"The little box." I tried to nod my head toward the mantelpiece.

"The little box." She walked over toward it and held it in her hands. "It could be worth a lot. But I know there's more. My grandmother mentioned a masterpiece, something so precious, so sacred that even the Mother Superior wept when it was gone.

The abbey didn't report the theft to the authorities, so officially, whatever it is, it hardly even exists. What a find it will be! And you're going to tell me where it is."

"Why should I?"

Helen went over to the mantelpiece and held the Host up again. "A simple white flour wafer, blessed in Latin. I could offer this to you, should you confess all your sins. Tell me what the work of art was. You know. I know you know. Where is it? Give it to me. Give it to me now!"

"And if I don't know where it is?"

"The blood of Christ will taste much worse than the body, my dear." She walked over with the chalice. "You see how the little grains have fallen to the bottom? I'll have to stir it again before I pour it into your mouth."

"Maybe the painting isn't here," I said. I had to keep talking. I had to keep *her* talking.

"Oh, no—you came back because you know that it's here. You came back to get it. I could tell from the way you came in," she said matter of factly, walking back over to the mantel. She held the chalice in front of her, as if it might explode. She brought it closer to my face.

"Tell me!"

"I don't know where it is. I've never seen it!"

"You lie! It's here in this house and you've hidden it."

"Don't be foolish. If you kill me, you'll be caught. No one's going to believe I tied myself up to a chair and poisoned myself. That's ridiculous. You won't be able to get away with it."

"Oh no? Well, you're wrong there." Helen smiled, clasped her hands together and raised her eyes to the ceiling. "After you've swallowed this poison, after your body finishes its final convulsions and your tongue has turned black, I'll untie you. Everyone will think you did it. You see, your past has got the better of you."

"What do you mean?"

"Your past." She strode over and picked up the note by the telephone. "Your friend left this handy little piece of evidence, which fits perfectly into my plans. It's a telephone message from

Interpol. The Italian Consulate and I have caught up with you at precisely the same time."

"So?"

"Don't think I haven't checked you out. I lifted your wallet that night at the bar. You actually thought I was making a pass at you! Oh, it took me a while to check things out. But your old student card led me to the German university and they put Interpol on to me. They've been looking for you for quite some time. I told them I was an old friend trying to track you down, but they must have decided to check out this area, after they'd heard from me. They want you badly. Whatever you did must have been pretty serious." She smiled delightedly. "Pretty soon everyone will know your secret. It will look quite logical. You came home, you discovered this note, and you knew your sin was catching up with you. They'll find your body, they'll find the cyanide, they'll find the telephone message in your hand. They'll think *suicide*."

Helen bent forward, her freckled face shining with the sweat and excitement of what she was about to do. But she wasn't the only one with a plan.

I reached beside the recliner with the hand I'd finally worked free. I picked up the heavy statue plaster replica of Saint Jude, patron of lost causes, which had lain for days against the base of the chair. I brought it down hard on Helen Danroy's head.

❧ 39 ❧

"And I thought my life of crime was over," I said out loud, just to hear the sound of my voice after the unsettling thump of Helen's body hitting the floor. The black cloth of the habit was stained with the blood of her hatred—the cyanide and grape juice flowing swiftly from the chalice. The little box stood open, gaping next to the deadly mixture.

Frightened, I tugged at the wrist restraint, the taut thong which kept me bolted to the chair, and unwrapped my legs from the leather belts which bound them together. I leapt out of the chair, leaned over and picked up Helen Danroy's wrist. Her pulse was still strong. I put my hand under her head and lifted gently. She moaned. I sighed with relief. It would be a while before she came to.

I put the piece of cloth that had been my own gag around her mouth. I used her leather thongs to tie her legs together, and the wrist bonds she had chosen for me now became her own. Her body stirred in the black habit. What the hell was I going to do with her? I looked at the crumpled telegram on the floor. What the hell was I going to do anyway?

Run! was all I could think. Don't pack. Just leave. But it would be a bad farewell note, leaving a dead cyanide-stained homophobe to break the news to Marya. Run! I thought. The woman on the floor moaned and I reached down to check her wrist bonds. I couldn't kill her. I couldn't even throw her in a frozen snowbank.

But I had to dump her somewhere and run. I would explain to Marya later. From a pay phone. From another state. I still had Marya's credit card.

"Mrph!" Helen moaned. I ran to the hall and got my coat. I bounded up the stairs, taking two at a time, and threw my toilet bag into a suitcase.

"Idiot!" I cursed myself. Why should I care about a tooth-brush at a time like this, when my whole future was in the balance? I thought I heard Helen moving on the floor, and ran back downstairs. I saw her bag by the fireplace and started riffling through it. I stuffed her wallet and address book into my purse and looked over at her.

She was still quiet, a black puddle with a face. Her eyelids flickered. I grabbed a dishtowel and put it around her eyes. Then I leaned over and started to put my arms under her, ready to scoop her up and dump her somewhere convenient. I noticed the little box glimmering at me from the floor where she'd dropped it. I stuffed it quickly into my bag, and began to struggle with her body.

She was heavy. I leaned back, nearly losing my balance. My shoulderbag swung off my shoulder, the weight of the box giving it a pendular motion. Thief! Thief! I was thinking.

I got as far as the door when I started losing my grip on her. I dropped her body to the floor and started dragging her. The door open, I started pulling at her torso. Her head bobbed forward, her feet went bump, bump, bump down the stairs. Her heels scraped two lines through the snow as I dragged her to the car. I had to rest her on the frozen ground as I opened the car door. One heave and I got her into the back seat.

I turned the key and waited. Letting the engine warm up, I glanced over my shoulder into the back seat. Marya's gay guide was still there on the floor, along with some prurient lesbian publications. Maybe that was why we'd had "QUEERS DIE" scraped onto our car, I thought, looking at the cover lying publicly on the back seat.

I heard a rustle from Helen, and quickly scooped up the magazines and stuffed them into my shoulderbag. Then she moaned. She was definitely stirring. I gunned the engine and tore out of the driveway. In no time we were on the open road.

"Myhph grbb!" I heard from the back seat. She was coming to.

"I like you too, honey, and your costume really turns me on." I pushed down on the accelerator and took the turn which led to the airport. "But your party refreshments are too Hallowe'en for me."

I saw it up ahead. The Bed 'N' Rest Airport Motel would be host to a scene they hadn't expected. I pulled in and parked down at the far end, Room 17. The carpark was nearly empty.

"Be quiet now. Don't say a word. Profound silence or pro-found punishment—take your pick," I warned her as I got out of the car. I ran the short distance to the office, checked in under the name "Helen Danroy," and ran back to the car. With a quick glance in either direction, I dragged her out of the car and hauled her up the cement path in front of our unit. I kept an arm around her torso as I fumbled with the keys and opened the door. Inside the room I threw the big body of black cloth onto the bed.

The rest was easy. I tied her wrists above her head to the bedframe. Each leg was spread out and similarly tied to either end of the bedpost. Bed 'N' Rest had just the right furniture for such a scene. I checked Helen's gag and made sure all the knots were good and tight, if not downright painful.

I rested a moment, looking at my handiwork: the splayed would-be murderer in nun drag. It was hard to choose a torture that was appropriate. Helen's eyes looked panicked. I smiled. She started struggling with her bonds, but I was better at knots than she had been.

"The ultimate femininity test, Helen—macrame. And you

lose." I grinned. Her hands flapped helplessly above her head, knots pressing hard into the skin at her pulse.

I took her address book out and perused the names. "Kitty Calendress," I read. "Women's Historical Association." That would do, I thought. I called Kitty's number and heard an answering machine. I put my palm over the receiver to change the sound of my voice.

"Kitty, this is Helen. I've been trying to reach you for days now. Actually, I've made an important discovery that could be of great interest to the Historical Association. But I want to keep it quiet. Please come and see me. I'm at the Bed 'N' Rest Motel, the one near the airport. Room 17. The door's unlocked. Hurry—this is something that's really going to excite the membership!"

Helen's eyes were quiet now, and full of a steely hatred. I knew she was thinking "You'll never get away with it!" And worse, I knew that she was right.

I pulled the button out on the doorknob so that it would be open for Kitty Calendress when she arrived. I reached into my bag and took out the copy of *Bad Attitude*—Marya's lesbian sex magazine. I found a suitable pictorial featuring bondage. I laid it on the bed next to Helen, and left.

40

But my delight at non-consensual bondage with a homophobe wore off quickly. At the airport, looking at the entrance, watching jets take off and land. Jets. Tickets to faraway places. Places that would never be far enough.

I reached into my pocket and found the telegram from the Italian consulate. So, the whole thing was up.

I looked into my bag and brought out the little box. A jeweled butterfly was swinging off the lid. Inside, a few more Hosts were revealed. But they were the wrong color.

Those turn-of-the-century Hosts would have been made out of white flour, and these were purple. Stained purple. I put my finger on one. It was soft. The blood of Christ. Helen's drink of death had spilled into the sacred area of the box, and had melted the Hosts into a poisonous paste.

Perhaps as deep as a thimble, the purplish mush seemed to foam and move before my very eyes. I looked around the airport carpark. There had been so many airport carparks. I was so tired. I had hoped that Marya would have been right for me, would have given me a nice, trouble-free marriage. Perhaps passionless, but quiet. If I could get away, if I could find the right collector for this artifact, if I could get far enough fast enough— what would happen to me then? Would I be safe?

And now Marya would be after me too. I looked down at the box she'd given me, thinking about the trust she'd placed in me, the future I'd wanted to make with her. The future I was afraid wouldn't be enough for me. I was so eternally dissatisfied. As Ilona had never hesitated to point out.

I'd even thought that I would get on with my work, get on with something without Ilona! Fucking Ilona! The horrible truth was that I was still in love with her. That I wouldn't have any future until I came to terms with that. Until I stopped living the charades that masked me from myself.

I started crying, the telegram undoing my future in one hand, the little box offering its oblivion in the other. The airport entrance was just a few hundred yards in front of me.

I thought about how I got here, a nice white middle-class girl from Boston, Graduate *Cum Laude*. I was a different person then.

I was innocent, fresh. I didn't seem to have a single sin on my soul. I had no past—all my hopes lay in the future, the future that became Ilona. The future that had ended on a day in Italy. On my birthday to be exact. To be very exact.

41

It could have been last week, last month. If I closed my eyes I could be there if I wanted. I lay in our vacation tent in Italy and thought, "So now it's my birthday."

I didn't like thinking about my birthday. I didn't want it to have to be a big deal, but the more I thought about it the bigger it became. And I really didn't want any squabbling with Ilona on that day. But more than that, I wanted to think that Ilona and I were happy enough together, and that this day at least would be a positive one. That we would be happy to celebrate each other's birthdays.

Ilona had apparently woken up early. I opened my eyes and saw the colors of crinkled flowers and rainbows of paper streamers weaving their way over the ceiling of the nylon tent. She had decorated our little chamber with every kind of Italian party papercraft known to the Mediterranean. There was a little almond cake that she'd bought in the village, a thermos of coffee, a melon and a bottle of champagne.

And a small present. A handmade book, endpapers in feathered faux marbre linen stock, a watermark on every page. It lay in my hand like a treasure.

"Thank you," I said. The book was unique and our reunion was the more precious because we'd had a fight the night before. It was about that cat.

Ilona had wanted to put the cat in the tent again. When I said no, there was a scene, but eventually we compromised. Ilona found a shoebox and put the cat in it. I had let it sleep in the box at the foot of our bed.

"It's lovely! Thank you, darling," I said as I looked at the book. Ilona smiled. She knew how perfect it was. I looked around the tent, through the streamers. She'd apparently put the cat outside before I'd woken up.

"Darling, it's a beautiful book. And my favorite cake." I hugged her.

"Blow out the candle," she said.

I hugged her again afterwards, and my hands found their way automatically to her firm little breasts. She didn't respond, but I hugged her a bit harder, flattening my breasts against hers. My fingers found her nipples anyway.

"No, don't," she said, squirming out of my grasp. "I haven't had my coffee yet." Bad feelings about the sick cat lingered, dampening her desire. Ilona had had her way as usual. But she couldn't have her way with everything, could she? If only I could kiss her, make love to her, everything would be all right, I thought.

I looked up hastily, with a smile, but the damage had been done. Ilona was busily cutting the cake and a scowl had taken hold of her lips. She was angry. I tried to chat lightly over coffee and eventually managed to engage her in conversation. After all, it was my birthday. She became more cheerful and with a salutory make-up kiss we went outdoors. I opened the tent to the sun. The campsite was already hot and dusty. Ilona was unfolding a campstool. I looked over at the side of the tent and saw the open shoebox. Flies buzzed around it.

"It died in the night," Ilona said simply, opening up the

morning paper. The cat lay stretched out and stiff, its bright yellow eyes wide open, its claws extended into the air, as if it were trying to climb out of the box.

"Oh!" I made sympathetic noises. After a moment, I said, "I'll take it away." I picked up the box. Ilona snapped the newspaper shut.

"You're not going to throw it in the *dump?*" she said. I thought about the campsite dump filled with pizza wrappers, disposable diapers and aluminum Coke cans.

"OK—I'll pick some flowers, put them in and make a lid for the shoebox," I said. *"Then* I'll throw it in the dumpster."

"You can't do that!" Ilona's face clouded and I steeled myself. I really didn't want to have a fight with her on my birthday. Why couldn't she just let me put the kitten in the dump? I looked over at her, but saw only the newspaper that she'd opened. It was hiding her face.

"I want to bury it," she said slowly, from behind the pages.

"Ilona!" My voice was rising quickly. "I don't, I absolutely *don't* want to put this thing in the car and drive around looking for some field, then scratch away at the dirt to make a hole for its body. Another animal would just dig it up anyway. It's more sanitary to dispose of it here." I tried not to look down at the festering orifices among its matted fur.

"It is *not* more sanitary," Ilona protested. "This animal has a soul. And I'm not going to just throw her body away."

"Her? The cat has a gender now?" My voice was rising and the glances of nearby campers drifted our way. "Listen. It doesn't have a gender. It's dead. It's a *dead cat.* And I don't want to drive around with a dead cat or a dead anything in a shoebox on my birthday."

"We won't have to drive around all day. We'll get in the car and find a place right away. I just don't want to throw it in some garbage." Ilona's patience was wearing thin. She threw the newspaper down by the side of her campstool, stood up and came closer. "Listen, if you don't like this idea I'll go right now and bury this cat." She jerked the box out of my hands. The stiff body of the cat shifted and its outstretched paws pointed at Ilona's face. "I don't know when I'll be back. So have fun."

"Ilona—" I spoke to her retreating back. "Ilona, okay. Okay." Ilona stopped, but she didn't turn around.

"We can take the cat with us and bury it," I said to her back. "But first, let's go into town. Can't we do something nice today as well?"

Ilona turned around and smiled. "What do you want us to do?" she asked. But it was a rhetorical question.

A truce was in the air. I rushed off to the shower rooms, hurrying because it was already getting hot, while Ilona dawdled with the paper. When we went to the car I carried the shoebox with the cat inside and put it in the trunk.

We started the engine and in no time we were soaring through the fabulous countryside, dotted with vineyards; winding through medieval villages and cooling our hands in fountains. There was a cordial truce between us, an uneven joviality.

Ilona *wouldn't* ruin my birthday, I thought. Although she always managed to blame our arguments on me. "You're so anxious, you always turn everything into a conflict," she'd complain. But that, of course, was what I thought *she* did. Eventually I always conceded. But it was the constant concessions that caused me so much anxiety in the first place.

"Here we are," Ilona said, pulling up in front of a beautiful villa. A library built by the Medici in the fourteenth century.

"Great documents for your delight!" she cried, and I looked over at her face, wondering how her expression could change from scowl to smile so quickly. She really had prepared a wonderful birthday surprise for me. I realized she'd been saving this outing, this fantastic archive, for my birthday. This smile was an offering and an apology. I was immediately ashamed at my fuss about the cat, which lay blissfully forgotten in the trunk of the car.

I loved Ilona so much at that moment. I followed her with so much appreciation for her curiosity, her surprises, as her slender body fairly flew up to the entrance.

A gracious concierge showed us inside. Ilona, of course, had written for permission to see the rarest of collections, and permission had been granted.

Inside the cold womb of the palace she showed me letters and illuminated manuscripts by scribes telling tales of saints. Their miracles were told in tiny jeweled paintings which adorned the beginning initial of every paragraph. When we'd had our fill we went back outside into the beating sun.

"We've forgotten the kitten," Ilona said when we were in the carpark outside. I stood silent, afraid to say anything. It was too hot to fight.

"Let's take it out of the trunk and put it on the back seat so we don't forget it," she said to my still, stiff expression. "Don't worry, honey—we've got the whole day ahead of us," she added kindly. She opened the trunk and put the box in the back seat. I wondered when the cat would begin to smell. She was right. We should bury it soon.

But first we went shopping at the local market, and laughed at odd, inventive and inexplicable Italian kitchen devices: tomato blanchers, olive-oil extractors and self-cleaning garlic presses—just about anything caught our attention, just about anything was interesting. We were amused and amusing. I felt as if I was discovering Ilona again, in all her lively imagination and sweetness. We found a family-owned trattoria, the perfect restaurant in a small medieval *villaggio*. We pulled up under the sign, still smiling at each other.

We got out of the car. Each positive event swelled us with the relief that things between us would be okay. It also meant that Ilona suddenly grabbed me, and kissed me hard and long on the mouth under the swinging sign of the restaurant.

Her tongue was playing across my lips but all I could think about were the local villagers, the strolling groups of young men, who might discover two figures in dresses, kissing.

"Not here, honey," I pushed her away.

"What are you so uptight about?" she demanded, but held her anger back. Maybe it was the fact that it was my birthday. Or maybe she was just saving the big guns for later. "Let's go in and check the place out." She grinned and led me down the red-tiled path and into the dining room. It was lit by candles, with primitive paintings, harvest symbols hung on the walls. A huge counter was spread with local cheeses and fresh fruit. But the dining room was empty. A maître d' came over and showed us outside, to the terrace.

The large flagstone plateau was covered with tables, where families and jovial groups were drinking, talking and enjoying the late-night meal of fruits and cold meats. The tinkling laughter of women, Italian women with those dignified profiles, mingled with the confident humming tones of their husbands and brothers. The terrace was strung with colorful lanterns, swaying in the small breeze which refreshed us all.

The maître d' showed us to a table and we told him to bring us the best of the evening menu. We ate, and drank a bottle of wine, and afterwards leaned back and took a good look at each other.

What would I do without Ilona? I thought. Life would be so dull. So empty. I thought about those illuminated manuscripts, the careful planning she'd taken for this vacation. I took her hand on the tablecloth, in front of the whole restaurant, and told her with the bravery of an entire bottle of wine that I would make love to her tonight, all night. Ilona leaned forward, and for one moment I was afraid. The maître d' came over.

"These gentlemen are offering you a drink. Do you accept?" he asked. But instead of waiting for an answer, he put the small triangular glasses down on the table. I slid my fingers tentatively around the heavy glass base, as I heard Ilona say *"Grazie, es mia favorita, questa grappa."* Thank you, it's my favorite grappa, she was saying, and I could tell, even though her head was turned, that she was smiling.

42

I looked up over the grappa to Ilona and followed her gaze. Two men were sitting on the far side of the room, watching us none too discreetly. Ilona raised her glass at them, and they replied, raising theirs. I knew it would be mere moments before they came over.

But they waited awhile, turning their eyes back to each other. I thought I detected a pseudo-enthusiasm in their renewed conversation, but perhaps that was because there was a pseudo-enthusiasm in ours.

"How will we ever live without fresh prosciutto and fine grappa?" Ilona lamented. "Finally, here, I'm happy!" she crowed, but her enthusiasm made me wary. "Italy! 'Thou art the garden of the world'," she quoted. She leaned forward across the table, my passivity intensifying her need for confirmation. "Aren't you sad to think about leaving?"

I assented carefully. I suspected that she wanted to preserve a romantic notion about herself, rather than about Italy. There was a kind of danger in Ilona's monologues on beauty. Sometimes they were instructive, sometimes their content was transformational, but sometimes, like tonight, they were not to be messed with, only to be agreed with, to be matched. But not surpassed or modified.

"Yes, darling, it's wonderful to see and experience all this—"

"*Buona sera,*" a deep voice slid between our strained words. I looked up and saw two middle-aged Italian men, one short, one tall, hovering behind the halo of Ilona's red hair—the hair which seemed to send a hormonal signal to Latin men. Try me! it said with every strand. Go for it!

A thin moustache outlined the upper lip of the taller man. He sat down quickly next to Ilona, not waiting to be asked. The shorter one, with a cockscomb of curly black hair that extended from his forehead back to his neck, reluctantly joined us. I knew they had made a silent deal over her. I knew that Ilona was the biggest prize. Or the only prize. I pulled my skirt down over my knees.

"*Questa grappa es per mi villaggio,*" I heard him begin, looking first at Ilona and for a moment at me, to see if I understood.

"*Lei non capisce Italiano,*" Ilona apologized for me, and I couldn't formulate a sentence fast enough to protest. I understood that he was explaining about the grappa, I understood he was putting the moves on Ilona.

On and on he went, the word *grappa* punctuating his sentence regularly, with Ilona's enthusiastic agreement keeping him going. It was all too specific for my tourist Italian. Ilona listened, nodding and interjecting the odd comment, sipping occasionally as if to taste the validity of his description. The cockscomb man sat beside me in silence.

"*Un altro!*" called the man with the moustache to the waiter, and before we could say anything another round had arrived. "*Sono un architetto, en questo villaggio sono molti interessanti edifici. In Quattrocento . . .*" he began, and I knew the evening was over. So he was an architect? Big deal! His friend piped up from the sidelines. Apparently there was an "*edificio antico*" of great interest to them, and before we knew it melon had also arrived at the table.

I watched the men carefully slice small pieces of the green juicy fruit. Their table manners were impeccable, their knives slicing cleanly through the succulent flesh, perfect pieces arriving at their mouths. And all the time the man with the moustache talked, his hands making architectural models in the air over our table. All the attention was fixed on him.

"Un altro!" he called again—our glasses were somehow empty. I'd been drinking quickly. The glasses were small, the grappa smooth and easy to get down. My bloodstream was slowly saturated and the terrace seemed so warm and inviting with its swaying lanterns. I wanted to be alone with Ilona, and in love with her again. I wanted everything to be all right. But after a half bottle of wine and two grappas, anything would seem rosy. Almost anything.

"Un altro!" he called again. The waiter hadn't heard him and there was a slight tone of urgency to his voice that I didn't like. The prey would get away, I thought, far back in the recesses of my mind. Words came forward, heavy and slurred.

"Ilona!" I hissed, hoping the architect wouldn't understand English. "Let's go easy on this stuff—"

But moustache interpreted my tone correctly. *"Senoras, es l'estate, una sera dolce,"* but I knew he thought more than the evening was sweet.

"Ilona—" I said.

"Lei es difficule," she apologized to him for me, for my reticence, my non-Italianate sense of pleasure. I withdrew into a stony silence, holding my latest grappa and turning my back slightly to the disappointed Cockscomb. I was not going to make a particularly exciting escort.

"In questa villaggio," Moustache was saying, and Ilona's excited reply told me that we were in for a new chapter. "Drink up!" Moustache managed in English, pushing my glass to my lips, and following Ilona's cue I downed the last of my third grappa. It tasted like water.

We were standing up now. We were leaving, apparently off to see the *edificio antico*. Moustache pushed back Ilona's chair.

When I stood up, I towered over Cockscomb by more than a head.

The maître d' arrived with the bill. Glancing at his face I knew, even as my head was swimming, that we were no longer the lovely touristas he had thought we were. I threw some money down on the bill, but Moustache threw down more. The maître d' gave him a hearty thanks and a conspiratorial look passed between them.

Moustache let Ilona out of the door, and I followed them, noticing the cut of his linen shirt, the way his broad hands swung by his sides, his fingers twitching. Cockscomb was somewhere behind me.

The evening was full of the fragrance of night flowers. It was so glorious here, a timeless summer night in Italy. I was walking through a painting again, and I was getting so drunk, I hardly noticed that Moustache and Ilona were several hundred yards in front of me, on their way to the *edificio antico*. I could see their figures standing close together as Moustache pointed out something on the façade of a building.

"Ilona!" I called, but the words caught in my throat. I looked over at Cockscomb, who was watching his feet as he strolled next to me. I guessed this wasn't so great for him either.

"Ilona!" I held on to a stone wall for support. I was drunk. The stones felt so uneven beneath my feet that every step was a surprise, requiring a quick balancing act.

"I'm having a good time!" Ilona shouted back at me. "Finally!" Her voice bounced off an ornate façade which still held the day's endless heat.

But by the time I reached the façade, they had gone. I heard Ilona's laugh around the corner and turned to see her farther up a small street which wound its way through to another square. Moustache was gesturing excitedly and Ilona seemed to be listening closely, concentrating hard on his words, as if she were having trouble comprehending them. Maybe her Italian wasn't that good after all.

I hurried, focusing on keeping a straight path toward the two figures. The distance between us was narrowing. I put one foot determinedly in front of the other. A narrow alley, lined with antique structures, a picturesque promenade for tourists, lay before me. A niche for the Virgin had been carved out on one wall. Flowers were heaped against it just underneath her feet.

"Ilona!" I called, but I didn't want to scare her off. Her back was turned. When I finally arrived by her side she twisted around, the smile which was meant for Moustache fading quickly from her lips.

"What?" she said.

I took her arm and pulled her over to the side of the street, near the alcove where the Virgin Mary radiated benevolence.

"Ilona, watch out for these guys. I mean, do you know what you're doing?"

"What's the big problem here?" She threw up her arms in frustration. "I'm having some fun, okay? Do you *mind?*" she was joined by her ever-present Italian escort.

"Is very beautiful, this Madonna," he said. "Many have their picture taken with her." Ilona smiled at this and took out her camera, handing it to him and bobbing her head at me. They grinned conspiratorially.

"Ilona, I don't want my picture taken."

They laughed and took a few steps backwards, collaborating over the composition. Me and the Madonna.

"Ilona, no. Please—"

Click! The photo was taken and the Italian gallantly swung Ilona's camera over his shoulder. He gave me a triumphant smile and turned his back. Pointing to a building further up, he took Ilona's arm again and they meandered further up the street. I heard his Italian words and even I knew what they meant.

Medieval building techniques, the hammer-beam roof, pendant post, collar brace—Ilona knew all this crap anyway, I thought. She was massaging his ego with batting eyelashes and nodding head. For a moment I hated her. He went on and on with his lecture.

I hung back with the Virgin Mary and let my eyes roam over her pretty porcelain face, her fingers pointing to her Sacred

Heart. Her heart had a little flame coming out of it, and tiny rosebuds encircled it, entwined with thorns. I knew just how she felt.

"Ilona, we've got to get back to the campsite. The grounds close and they lock the gate," I called after her, but she and Moustache were already lounging on the rim of a fountain in the square. I looked at their two figures. He hasn't really touched her yet, I thought.

I struggled for an awareness of my body, to make my legs obey, to give myself a purposeful stride which would get us out of this. Ilona's glance found me and I started to see some possibility of getting her attention. I approached them.

"I think we need to go back now," I said to the uncomprehending Italian. I took Ilona's arm and brought her to her feet; feeling her wobbliness reminded me that she was probably as drunk as I was. I gripped her arm tightly.

"We're going back to the car," I said between gritted teeth. *"Arrivederci!"* I called as I started marching up the street.

"We've got to get back to the car—where the hell is it?" I said to the stumbling Ilona, pulling her down the street.

"Senore!" I heard Moustache cry, and he was soon by our side. Ilona threw my arm off her, but kept on walking, keeping my pace. We were at the end of the alley. One more right turn, I thought, and through another tiny square, past the church, and we'd be back at the restaurant and the car.

Moustache and friend glided along with us. A big man, he could clearly hold his liquor, but I was aware that I was practically holding Ilona up as we sped along the streets. Where was the restaurant? Where was the car?

I kept my concentration on walking, Moustache striding alongside us. Ilona kept him going, taking in his Italian words, formulating sentences of her own, her language getting more tentative, her grammar slipping along with her feet on the stone pavement of the square. The car would be just past the church, I thought.

Cockscomb was lurking behind us, his feet shuffling along the cobblestones. And finally, yes, there it was. The restaurant.

The swinging sign where Ilona had wanted to kiss me. The car.

Moustache was making no polite leave-taking gestures; he didn't want to leave, he was stalling for time, and Ilona let him. Then, just as I turned to say something polite to Cockscomb, my manners getting the better of my common sense, I heard a cry. Moustache had draped Ilona's long body across the side of the car and was sticking his tongue down her throat.

"Hey!" I grabbed his linen shirt in my hands, but his tongue was still slithering between her teeth. He pulled her body closer to his.

"Fuck off!" I said, pulling harder on his shirt, noticing how the thin synthetic material of Ilona's rayon dress was soaked underneath the armpits, a dark circle which matched the half-moon stain under the sleeves of his linen shirt.

He pulled her tighter and I saw, suddenly, how fragile and slender her body looked behind his barrel ribcage. His big hands, ravenous, worked their way over the front of her body. His palm covered her breast.

Ilona's small white moon of a breast. A wave seemed to catch my brain, and my insides rolled with it. I let go, stumbling backward, struggling to keep my vision through a layer of little brown dots. I thought I saw Ilona's hand, those fine-boned fingers, try to pry his palm away, but his hand was stuck to her dress, determined to find her nipple, to capture it.

"No!" I fell on them, pushing the big man off Ilona and barely registering his surprise. He wouldn't have seen many girlfriends rescue each other on double dates, and nothing could have prepared him for the right hook I landed on his chin.

I grabbed the car door, pushed the chrome button and took Ilona's arm. Her body lay listlessly against the sheet metal of the car, her mouth agape, her chin and cheeks grazed by the man's stubbled beard.

"Get inside!" I yelled, pushing at the back of her dress, at those silly, flaming poppies, and shoving her over the gearshift until her body reached the passenger seat.

"Stronza!" I heard him yell behind us. Cockscomb's feet

were shuffling through the dust in the street, coming to the aid of his friend who was massaging his bruised jaw in disbelief.

"Pazza!" he yelled. I shoved the key into the ignition and turned it, revving up the engine. Ilona was still swooning on the seat, sliding off the edge of the upholstery onto the floor.

I shoved the gearshift into reverse and, turning on the headlights, barely avoided a tree that marked the edge of the carpark.

I cranked the wheel and shot forward, the headlights illuminating the two Italian men in front of us. I saw the glint of their eyes, their furious expressions. I careened around them and headed through the village.

Gripping the wheel I avoided fountains, couples strolling through the streets, Italian children still out of bed, as I concentrated on how to get out, trying to outrun the alcohol-saturated condition of my brain. The car was stuffy and smelled bad. I opened the window and was taking deep gulps of air when I saw Ilona coming to. She was grabbing the edge of the seat and pulling herself into an upright position.

"Where are we?" she demanded, and I saw that she didn't remember anything of the enforced kiss and the ensuing struggle and flight. She was still back at the dinner table enjoying a revengeful flirt with a man. She was still angry with me.

"Why the hell would you even care, just so long as we're out of there?"

"What's the big deal? So we had a little kiss—"

She couldn't feel the red beard burn on her chin. She didn't look so fragile or helpless as I saw her bruised mouth form the words, "I suppose this is your idea of a good time."

I grasped the steering wheel. "Listen!" I yelled. I was pushing the words out, but they kept getting slurred around the middle of my tongue. "I didn't lure those guys over to the table."

"Lure! Lure!" she spat the words. She wasn't having as much trouble with articulation as I was. "If you didn't walk like Marilyn Monroe we wouldn't have men hitting us up day and night in Italy—"

"That's right," I drawled. "Blame it on me." Every word

came out thick and syrupy from between my lips. Suddenly I saw a turn in the road; the tires squealed as I took it, trying to hold on tight to the wheel and my temper.

"I'm sick of this vacation!" I yelled into the windshield and into the night. "And it's my goddam fucking birthday!"

But before I could continue, two bright lights seared my vision through the rear-view mirror and distracted me. I tried to concentrate on the road ahead. This stretch was familiar. One more turn and I'd find the road, the straight ribbon that would lead us to our campsite. The lights again, the car behind us was moving faster. Closer it came, tailing us. I glanced into the side mirror just in time to see the moustachioed man leaning out of his car window. Smiling in the red glow of our taillights, he waved.

"Ti do un bacio!" he yelled, laughing. "I geeve you a keeees!" They honked the horn again and again. Ilona and I were two animals being hunted, a quarry and a kill they barely took seriously.

"Fuck! They're following us!" I muttered and was pleased to see a moment of panic on Ilona's face.

"He's got my camera!" she cried.

"Well, we're not stopping now," I said, determinedly. I stepped harder on the gas, hoping my motoring skills would keep control of the vehicle, in spite of the alcohol in my body.

I clamped my teeth down on my tongue as I coordinated gear lever, accelerator and steering wheel through the blanket of alcohol that threatened to suffocate my senses. The headlights faded, retreating into the darkness behind us. Maybe they were just tired of the chase. Ilona was quiet, sullen, beside me.

Then I saw the narrow road leading to our campsite. I cut the headlights and took the turn, hoping that if the Italians were behind us, they wouldn't see us around the bend. Speeding through the darkness I made my way down the road. I was crazy to be driving drunk, without headlights, but the darkness felt like a friend.

I aimed the car between tall poplar trees which lined the pavement, glancing out over the ridge which edged the road and the moon above it. The icy moonlight shone through the leaves and lacy shadows whipped across the hood of the car. There was no sign of a vehicle behind us. I turned the headlights back on and began to breathe.

"And I'm sick of this vacation too!" Ilona's thick voice came out of the darkness, a dangerous warning tone in each word. I slowed down the car. I didn't want to have a showdown at sixty miles an hour. I didn't want to have a showdown at all. I was still drunk, and still angry at having had to save us. And she wasn't making me feel like Galahad either. All right, I thought. Let's have it out. But not in the car.

I saw a graveled area off the road. I slowed the car down, aiming the headlights into the valley. I switched off the engine, pulled the hand brake up sharply, and for extra measure put the car in gear against the slope of the hillside.

The night was so beautiful. I could see over the edge of the precipice toward a perfect valley, twinkling lights far below, the moon hanging in the sky like a birthday present. Ilona and I should be parking and necking. I didn't want to fight. I struggled to find some source of affection, some way of approaching her, but my head was swimming, the alcohol winning as I pondered the valley below.

Ilona and I should be loving and not about to tear each other's guts out, I thought. But the car was so stuffy, the air so cloying and thick. Then my stomach sent me an urgent message and I grabbed the door handle and stumbled into the darkness.

Moving away from the edge of the precipice, I found a tree and leaned on it. I started to retch, my body ready to expel the poisons of the evening, of the month, of the vacation with Ilona.

I remembered that my shoulderbag was somehow still attached to my arm and I concentrated on trying to keep it out of the stream of vomit I hoped would emerge from my system. But I wasn't that lucky. Instead I had to hear a stream of invective from Ilona, her voice issuing from the blackness behind me.

"You think *you're* sick of this vacation! Well, let me tell you, I've *had* it with your uptight anxieties! I'm tired of tiptoeing, walking on eggshells to keep you happy."

I tried to shut out the words and concentrate on the beautiful valley below, the large sky shimmering with stars.

But Ilona knew, she knew I was trying to shut her words out. It only made her want to say more.

"You know," she continued, "when I met you I thought you were kind, that you had something special. But you're just a spoiled wimp, a phony, without one new thought, one creative opinion; you're just a shell parading along with your eager social skills."

I turned around and looked at her face. Ilona was smiling, standing next to me, her hands on her hips, her silly dress blowing in the nighttime breeze.

"Go on!" She pointed to her chin and drew closer. "Hit me!"

And so I did. I lunged at her, but she stepped aside neatly and my blow grazed her shoulder. She laughed. The alcohol had apparently evaporated in the heat of her bad humor and she was standing before me, cold sober. Mocking and invincible.

"So," she said, "I'm going." She turned, went to the driver's seat and gave me a pleased look through the open door.

"No you don't, fuck you! You—" I yelled, running at the car. "You're just jealous!" I screamed. "Jealous of my dissertation, of all the attention, of the reviews!"

I saw Ilona's body stiffen, go hard inside that dress, but I couldn't stop.

"You're a has-been, that's what you are! You've had your day and now it's over and now I'm having mine and you can't stand it!" I screamed. She sat quietly, deadly still in the front seat of the car. Somehow my words were keeping her here in the parking lot. They'd been stored up too long and I couldn't stop.

"I've got two job offers and a publishing contract," I hissed at her, "and you don't even know how you're going to pay your rent."

"That's right, just worry about employment. You'll always be okay, you pedestrian pedant!" she sneered. "You've never had an original thought in your life. You'll find a job all right, *and* the life of mediocrity you were intended for. You're just a researcher with nothing to say. A career-track troll."

"I'd rather be mediocre than a troublemaker, Ilona," I lashed back. "You think you're so smart, but everybody's tired of you. Nobody even wants you on their committee. They'd give Godzilla a post before they'd give you—" My own words were frightening me but I couldn't stop them.

"You don't have a theory!" I screeched, my throat burning raw with hatred. "You just have a string of aphorisms!"

I saw Ilona's fury gather. Tighter and tighter she drew into herself and suddenly I regretted all the words I'd said.

I could see anger in her face, her body; even that long red hair looked like furious fire. Then I saw her slowly, carefully reach into the back seat and take something in her hands.

From out of the opening of the car, a large black shape flew at me. It was long, it had legs and a head. I knew what it was. It was the dead cat. I saw the yellow orbs of its eyes with the ink-black bullseyes in the middle, its white fangs curving out of the mouth around its bluish tongue. Then it hit me with all the force and bad intentions of Ilona's frenzied hatred.

I put my hands up but not fast enough. I felt the matted fur, the brittle bones which seemed to break across my nose. Its stiff shell cracked, the matted, pus-covered fur brushed my cheek, leaving a trace of foul-smelling slime, the claws—extended in rigor mortis—sliced through the fabric of my dress. The carcass clinging to me even in death.

I screamed as it hung on me, imagining strange twisted sounds coming from its mouth. Desperately I pulled at it, but the claws seemed to sink in deeper as with a final scream I yanked at it, tearing open the top of my dress. My skin underneath, hooked by the claws, had split open. I was bleeding, and my hands were covered with pus and oil from the cat's ravaged coat.

I looked down at my hands, my tattered dress, my chest where the cat's claws had raked over me and I screamed again, but the sound was drowned out by the grinding of the engine. Ilona was starting the car. She was leaving me.

I saw her hand on the gear lever, finding neutral, and I went toward the car slowly. I thought I heard her start to speak, but

I put my dirty, trembling hands on my ears because I knew I couldn't take any more.

I was full of hatred, of disappointment, of despair over what had become of us. Over what Ilona had done. And full of the stench of the dead cat. The only thing Ilona had shown any tenderness for on this trip. The putrid smell crawled along my flesh as I told myself this wasn't happening.

"And do you know what?" I heard her continue, sneering at me from inside the car while it idled there in neutral.

"No," I whispered, with no strength left to fend off her accusations, with no way to garner any affection, to make any peace, with no defense against what she was about to say.

"No!" I cried louder, looking at the entrails hanging off my fingers, smelling the fumes of death saturating my breath. "No," I sobbed, hoping she would hear me, hoping Ilona would know enough to stop.

But she didn't, and as the car idled I saw that Ilona really was going to drive away. Leaving me there stranded and bleeding. I stumbled toward the taillights.

"Don't leave me, Ilona!" I whispered, but I knew she couldn't hear me as she pushed in the clutch. "Don't leave me, Ilona!" I cried more loudly, holding up the front of my dress. But then I heard the engine and saw the headlights illuminating the valley ahead. At any moment she would release the brake, put the car into reverse and back up the hill, out of the parking spot and on to the road.

"You can't leave me, Ilona!" I sobbed. "You can't do this—"

"Do you know what?" she jeered. "The only way your dissertation was accepted was because I was fucking your advisor. Five months we fucked and you didn't even guess! We couldn't believe it!"

I was at the trunk of the car now. If Ilona put it into reverse she would run me over, I thought, but before she got the car into reverse, before she could shift out of neutral, leaving me in the dust and entrails, I would have my moment. She released the hand brake. I went for the trunk.

I put my hands, hard, on the back of our car. Hard, with all the sorrow and fury of the affair with Ilona, with the anger borne of the many cruel things she'd done to me. She couldn't do this to me. She couldn't leave me soiled and stranded on the road, and she had to, she absolutely *had to* shut up.

With my hands firmly on the trunk, I dug my feet into the ground, tensed, and gave the car a hard shove. Instantly, it was moving on the gravel. The sheet metal left my hands and I saw Ilona push the clutch in and try, desperately, to get the gear lever into reverse. But the gear shift had stuck.

The car moved quickly on the slope. It rolled easily over the gravel, through a few feet of weeds, toward the precipice where a hundred-foot drop waited. I stood and watched.

The car was picking up speed now and I saw Ilona struggle with the door, but she was too drunk and the front wheels hung for a moment on the edge. The car was at a forty-five-degree angle, ready for flight, and as Ilona finally got the door open I heard the grating of the car's body on the precipice and I knew that the door wouldn't open any further and the car slid into the air. The back wheels made their way slowly and inexorably over the cliff. A final flash of the red taillights, and it was gone.

A crunch of sheet metal and a cloud of dust followed, and then another groaning of metal, and another crash—and I knew the car was falling again and again, battering Ilona to bits. Finally a boom filled the quiet Italian valley and the hillside was illuminated with flame. The gas tank had exploded, silencing Ilona forever.

❦ 43 ❦

It was a different season, winter. In a different country, in a different carpark. An airport in Montana. And my finger was coated with a purple cyanide paste. Hadn't I better eat it, get it over with, push myself off the cliff the way I'd pushed Ilona?

The wind outside the car was picking up. Hurry up now, it won't be so long. It'll be over before you know it. And you'll never know anything again. How did people, called *suicides,* ever make this decision? Go on! It'll be over with so soon. The car was cold, my fingers were already numb.

But I didn't. I put my finger down on the seat and smeared the purple glob onto the upholstery, and then I stared at it, thinking about death, about murder.

It had been so easy, getting away with it. On that hot night, the night my future ended, I had stood listening to the burning in the valley below. I had even walked over to the cliff and stared down into the abyss, filled with the flaming remnants of our car, our vacation vehicle, with Ilona inside it.

"Machina," I remembered thinking, the Italian word for car. The end of our tragedy, Ilona's and mine. But no deus ex ma-

china would get me out of Italy. I remembered stumbling back to the road, leaving behind me the reflected lights of the burning car, and the dead cat lying on the ground.

I had walked swiftly down the dark road, the tall poplar trees bending over me, forming a long aisle which would lead me to the campsite. Think, plan, and get away. I wasn't drunk anymore. But stark sober. And cold. Shivering on a hot summer's night. Think. Plan. I had pushed my mind into a linear mode. The facts were simple.

The car was rented in Ilona's name, I had told myself. There was nothing to link me to the vehicle, to the unfortunate "accident."

We were registered at the campsite under Ilona's name too. I would go there and pack up the tent in the night. No, I would just leave it, taking only my belongings. They would find the car, the body, the tent, as if Ilona had been a solitary traveler, as if I'd only been a shadow by her side. Those had been my thoughts. That had been my plan.

My shoulderbag had flapped against my hip as I walked down the road that evening. My passport and credit card were still inside it. I would buy a train ticket that would take me out, back to Germany. I would move far and fast. Back to the US. A big city that would swallow me up. Somewhere I could hide. Only my transcripts would follow me, I had thought. But I'd forgotten that one fact. The fact that had come back to me in Rebecca's kitchen. The Italian architect had the picture of me with the Sienese Madonna, undeveloped in Ilona's camera.

On that night I had told myself over and over again that everything was going to be okay. I had told myself I hadn't really meant to do it. I had told myself a lot of things, a lot of things which didn't matter. Because I had murdered Ilona.

I'd found a teaching position in a San Francisco university and a new lover. I'd almost found a way to keep that evening at bay, but I couldn't cure the disease that infected my every thought. It wasn't that I'd murdered Ilona. It was that I was still in love with her.

And now I was still running, and it was just as useless. Even in Montana a homophobe, a detective, an international police agency, a new lover had, or would, find me out. Unlike Roberta Claire I didn't rate a Virgin Mary. There wasn't even a road map or a nudge in the right direction, much less holy guidance. There was just me and my fucking ass and I wondered how I was going to save it.

Cyanide was another kind of exit from another kind of love affair, during another kind of vacation. But I couldn't do it. I took a last look around the carpark and started the engine.

The fact was, I couldn't do it to Marya. I couldn't create a past for her that would poison *her* future. If and when I left the world, I wouldn't leave it with more destruction.

Perhaps it wouldn't be so bad—to give up and turn myself in. There was the distinct possibility of prison, of course. But with good lawyers, minimum security could be better than Hell. Even if Marya never forgave me, at least I could forgive myself. And the running, if nothing else, would be over.

Sister Adorers of the Precious Blood, would there have been a sanctuary for me there? A continued life of scholarship if I took the veil? Redemption in mortification? I wondered about the antique artifact, the box. It wasn't so special, not compared with the painting.

Yes, that was it! The Virgin Mary would save me after all. My mind started working. Who would it belong to? Perhaps the abbey, but a case could be made for the Italians. A national cultural treasure.

Could its discovery, its validation at the hands of an up-and-coming art historian, its generous donation, redeem me in the eyes of an Italian judge? The press alone could generate a positive image, erasing the memory of Ilona in our car, burning at the bottom of the cliff. I had had amnesia! But upon seeing the Virgin Mary, it had all come back to me! The Italians were nothing if not Catholic.

I quickly pulled out of the carpark, the white trees whizzed past the car as I careened down the gray, icy ribbon of road.

I made the last turn and saw a garbage truck. It was Thursday, the day we took out the garbage. I might never do that again, I thought, my mind dwelling on prison. I veered around to the left of the big truck, passing it recklessly. Perhaps another car was coming toward me. Perhaps we'd all die in a head-on collision. The Virgin Mary, I thought, was going to save my ass. *She* was going to save my life.

That's why I was going back.

I heard every piece of gravel crunch beneath the wheels as I pulled into the drive. I saw Marya's car outside. She was at home. I cut the engine. I had to find that painting. It had to be there.

The car door was heavy, like a coffin lid. I heaved it open. *"Never was it known that any one who fled to thy protection, implored thy aid, or sought thy intercession, was left unaided. I fly unto thee O Virgin of virgins—"* I mumbled the *Memorare* as I sped up the walk. I heard Marya's skipping step inside, as she came to greet me. Her brown curls lifted in the wind, her face fresh with the happiness of seeing me. She had no idea who I really was.

"Hello, darling!" Her red cheeks rose on a smile. Another day at the ice fields, I thought. I put my arm around her and we went up the walk. The line of her bra was visible beneath the popcorn weave of long underwear. "Let me tell you about the cross-country skiing possibilities," she said.

I wanted to cry, but I didn't want to ruin this moment. I didn't want to say goodbye to that look on her face. I knew she would never look at me like that again.

"How was your trip?" she asked, hugging me. But she didn't wait for an answer. I ran my hands along the woven nylon of her expedition-quality pants.

"Yeah, I'd better get out of these clothes. And what a bummer! I think someone's broken into the house again." She shivered. I stopped her talk by kissing her, saying goodbye to those generous lips and, after our kiss, to those admiring eyes. They wouldn't be admiring for long.

"I've got to go inside." I tugged at her arm, dragging her through the door.

"The house was open when I came back," she explained, squeezing my hand.

"Did they take anything?" I asked, looking for a moment at her hair, admiring each curl. But I knew no one had taken anything. Helen hadn't found the painting. My eyes started searching the walls, the woodwork, for clues.

"They burned a lot of candles, and—oh yes, they apparently went upstairs to your study. All that expensive computer equipment and you know what they stole?"

"No," I said. They didn't steal anything, I thought. Just my future, without even a precious painting to pay for it.

"That old nun's habit you found upstairs."

"Not much good for anything, a nun's habit," I murmured. I'd have to be leaving soon, I thought distractedly, eyes roving carpeting, the thickness of the dining room table. Think, think! Where would Rebecca have hidden her beloved Virgin? I would have to tell Marya. "Sweetheart, let me explain something—" I began.

"Oh, yes—about your trip. I'm sorry if I was suspicious and jealous. I just don't want anyone else to have you, especially if I'm stuck up here in Montana. What's wrong, honey? You seem so nervous—"

I was running my fingers along a crack in the floorboard. Only hours ago Helen Danroy had lain there. And it would be only hours before she, or someone, came back to get me.

"Shit!" Marya said. "There's a glass of red wine spilled here on the carpet. Someone's had a party here. How horrible! But listen, I talked to the lawyer and he thinks we can get out of the condition of the bequest due to the break-ins. It's a health hazard too with all that glitter everywhere, and the insulation poking out." Her voice faded as I ran up the stairs.

"Honey, what *is* it?" I heard Marya call, but I was busy rummaging through Rebecca's cupboard. There was nothing, no false bottom. A false trap in the floor? No.

I went down to Marya and we sat down on the couch.

"I think your argument that the intention of the bequest is to save Rebecca's handiwork is a great one," she continued. "I went outside again and took a look at those statues. Some of those faces really are incredible—that beautiful stone inlay—"

She started stroking my face. "I've missed you so much, I'm glad you're home. I think I'm in a bad, morbid mood. Suddenly I'm frightened, and so ready to start a life with you, darling. Exorcise the past and start being normal."

"Yes," I said wearily, "Yes." I didn't know how to begin. We sat in silence and I stroked Marya's back, her strong arms. I looked at her fingers flexing in my palm, thinking about how I'd made fun of her pantyhose. I would never complain about her outfits again. If only I could find the Bronzino.

I heard the rumble of the garbage truck outside. I would be lucky if Marya didn't desert me completely, I thought. I took a deep breath. I was going to tell her my story, but she got there first.

"Sweetheart, guess what?" She was so chirpy, I didn't know how to break through her good humor to tell her.

"What?"

"When I got home I actually found a candle still burning on the mantelpiece." She looked into my eyes for effect. "That means whoever was here had just left."

"Just left," I echoed. Damn candle! Didn't matter anymore. I would tell her everything.

"I could have walked in here and surprised them! With my ice-axe!" She massaged my shoulders. "You're so tight, baby. Do you want to take a bath? I'll give you a massage afterwards."

"Yes," I said, my eyes darting once again about the rooms. In a kitchen cabinet? A secret panel in the dining room bookcase?

"This place was such a mess," Marya was chatting on. "I came in and it smelled bad, sort of stuffy and sour. I went to put the candle out. It was scorching the bottom of that Russian print—you know, that creepy Madonna and Child. The one over the mantel."

"Hmm," I mumbled. Maybe in the cellar.

"It was burning. That cheap plastic frame probably would have made quite a smoky stinky mess in here. I turned it around and there was another painting. One of the many Madonnas this place is famous for."

I stopped looking around and finally focused on Marya. The Bronzino! She had found it!

"The Madonna!" I breathed.

"Yes, with Elizabeth Taylor violet eyes and an aquiline nose. Totally Aryan. Catholic imagery has no racial integrity, and—"

"What did you do with it?" I asked, my hands on her shoulders, shaking her.

"Do with it? Hell, I threw it away! I—"

"Where? Where is it? Where did you throw it?"

"Why, out with the garbage. You don't think—" I heard her voice fade behind me as I raced out of the door. I heard the hiss of hydraulic brakes and a deep masculine voice singing, a song that spelled my doom.

At the end of a snowdrift a burly man was replacing our empty garbage can. I flew out of the door.

The Bronzino! No, a priceless artifact from the past could not receive such a fate! The icy path stretched out in front of me, the garbageman seemed miles away. I put a foot on the path and propelled my body toward him with all the force I had.

But my foot gave way on the glacial path and I saw the sky spinning before me as my chest pounded the pavement with a thud, the wind knocked out of me. I saw blood staining the ice as I pressed my palms against the path and hoisted myself up again.

I scrambled forward, slipping and sliding, arms flailing, my body a desperate windmill racing to where the truck stood, ready to digest its new contents.

"Stop!" I screamed, but it was too late. In the back of the truck, huge metal claws descended on our week's garbage.

I slid forward, my hands grabbing the back rim of the truck. I peered into a heap of refuse just in time to see the arm fall, metal teeth ripping into something colorful. An ancient piece of Italian canvas.

Quattrocento! I caught a glimpse of violet eyes, and an upraised hand, delicately rendered, a finger pointing to a heart alive with flames and circled by rosebuds.

"No, wait!" I cried, but the garbageman was already in the cab, ready to pull away.

The claw descended again, gouging the center of her serene face. I cried out, stretching my arm into the back of the truck. Metal fingers threatened my own and found the canvas again. The claw continued shredding, a heap of kitchen scraps fell from above, and the divine masterpiece descended into the belly of the machine, accompanied by half a dozen eggshells and a shower of cat litter. Then it pulled away.

The truck continued down the road and I watched as it reached its next stop. I watched because I couldn't move, I couldn't breathe.

Finally I whimpered. It was the end of Rebecca's story. It was the end of mine, too.

"Sweetheart," I heard Marya's voice from the doorway of the house. I walked back up the path, not thinking about its iciness anymore. Inside, the house was warm. I touched Marya briefly as I walked past her into the living room. I heard her voice behind me.

"I meant to remind you, there's a message for you lying on the table. It must be important. It came all the way from Italy. From the Italian consulate. And it's a telegram."

"I know," I said. "I read it."

I walked into the living room and sat on the couch. Marya followed me, chattering on about cross-country skiing, ice fields and softball barbecues. She had a life ahead of her. I could hear it already—skis parting endless paths of snow, laughter over sizzling hot dogs, the crack of a softball bat.

Marya sat down next to me on the couch. Only for one moment did I think about the cyanide paste. And then I told her.